Going Home with Phoebe

by

Yvonne Beverly Blake

(Cover illustrated by Jann Richardson)

Copyright © 2015 Yvonne Beverly Blake

All rights reserved.

ISBN-10: 1495907635
ISBN-13: 978-1495907630

Dedicated to Nancy Ouellette,
my Missus Thomas, who mentored me in my teen years,
She exemplified dedication, compassion, and elegance.

CONTENTS

1	Butterball	11
2	Facing Feona Reynolds	18
3	The Wild Girl	27
4	Meeting the Kittles	33
5	Maseppa's Guest	39
6	A Job for Phoebe	44
7	The Town Meeting	53
8	Gimpy	60
9	The Parson's Wife	67
10	French Classes	73
11	Needlework	77
12	Skating	83
13	Maseppa's Calf	91
14	Lucky the Chick	100
15	Punchinello	107
16	Delly	117
17	Coals of Kindness	123
18	The Cave	127
19	Phoebe's Critters	136
20	The Camp Meetings	142

21	The Baptism	150
22	Bucky	155
23	Building Trust	165
24	Fiddling Around	173
25	The Tree Fort	182
26	Rising Prices	193
27	The Cougar	201
28	Mixed Feelings	208
29	Zeke's Duty	214
30	The Paw Print	223
31	Tessa	230
32	Hiding	238
33	Keeping Quiet	243
34	The Plan	253
35	Found Out	261
36	The Erie Canal	267
37	The Weigh Lock	275
38	Baby Moses	284
39	Going Home	294
40	Christmas Blessings	299
	Algonkin Glossary	304

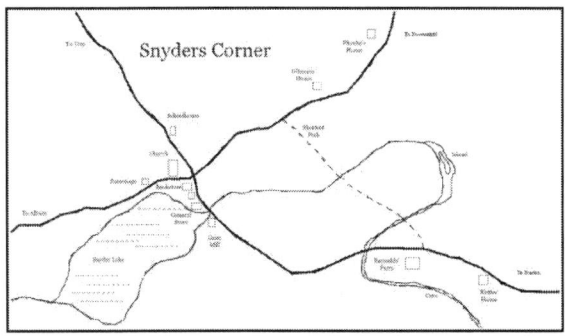

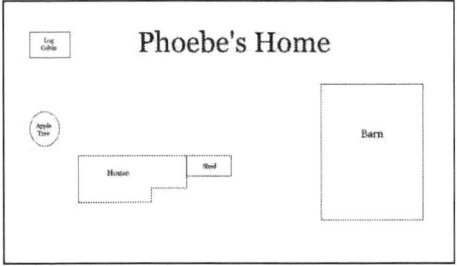

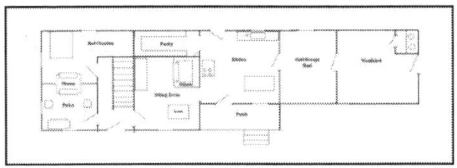

1
BUTTERBALL

Phoebe didn't mind waiting for Maseppa, especially if there were kittens involved. She sat on the hay-strewn barn floor and let the kittens crawl all over her shoulders, and back. Their little sharp claws pricked her skin. One little yellow kitten slept in her skirt.

Phoebe could see Missus Reynolds standing on the door step with her hands on her hips. Her sleeves were rolled up to her bony elbows, and her apron was stained with whatever she had been cooking that day. Like most women, she wore her hair in a bun, but strands of gray dangled down her neck, as if they were tired of being proper.

When anyone stopped by for some eggs, Feona Reynolds took advantage of having someone listen to her woes or the latest gossip about her new neighbors. "I don't like the looks of that new family . . . shifty sort of lot, if you ask me. The man's a drunk and the mother's lazy, if you ask me. Their cow gets loose and their kids steal my stuff . . . into my garden . . ."

"Ondàs," called Maseppa.

"I'm coming." Phoebe put the kittens with their mother one by one, except for the yellow one sleeping on her lap. He had a crooked foot. Missus Reynolds said that a cow stepped on him at milking time when all the cats gathered for a squirt. She said that it was too bad he didn't die. With a lame leg, he wouldn't be any good for catching mice.

Neither Maseppa nor Missus Reynolds was paying any attention to Phoebe. She tucked the sleeping kitten under her apron and walked nonchalantly to the buckboard, climbed up onto the seat, and waited for Maseppa.

"Now, you come back soon, you hear?" invited Missus Reynolds. "If you ask me, the day seems brighter when company stops by."

Maseppa sneaked in a quick farewell before Missus Reynolds could think of something else to talk about. "Thank you for the eggs, Ma'am. We will come back next week."

"Yes, you do that! I'll be right here. Good day, now."

Maseppa shook the reins, and Ginger trotted out of the farm and along the winding dirt road. "That woman talks too much."

Phoebe smiled. She knew Maseppa would say that. Maseppa never liked it when people chattered on and on.

The sun shone on the fresh green fields. The snows of winter had melted and the world was alive again. A few lambs bounced around in the pasture. A young colt snuggled close to his mother. Its mane stood up in stiff tufts and its tail looked like a fuzzy brush. The mare gave a nicker to Ginger, who greeted her back, as if to say, "Yes, I see your new son. He's a handsome fellow!"

Phoebe carefully felt the warm lump beneath her apron. Yes, the kitten was still there, but it wasn't sleeping anymore. It started to squirm and stretch. She gave a quick glance toward Maseppa.

"Phoebe, what is in your pocket?"

"My pocket? Only my hanky."

"There is something moving under your apron."

Phoebe knew she couldn't hide the kitten anymore and pulled it out. She snuggled it under her chin, and it began to mew.

"That is not yours. You need to give it back to Missus Reynolds."

"Oh, Maseppa! You heard her say that it would be better dead. She doesn't want him. She won't even know he's gone! Please?"

Maseppa's face showed no emotion – not anger, not amusement, not even annoyance. She just looked at the kitten. "It is not right to take things that are not yours. You hear me, Phoebe? When we get eggs next week, you take it back." She flicked the reins, and Ginger trotted on. "When we get our own chickens, I will not need to buy eggs from Feona Reynolds anymore."

Phoebe smiled and snuggled her nose in the kitten's fur. "Yes, Maseppa. I know it's not mine, but I wish I had my own kitten. I think I'll give him a name – just for now. I think his fur looks like those butterball toffees at the general store. Butterball – Isn't that a good name?"

Maseppa just looked at her.

Phoebe was used to Maseppa's silence. She had her own ways.

"I can't wait to show Butterball to Zeke."

"It is not your kitten. You need to ask Missus Reynolds."

Phoebe sighed, but she had a feeling that Butterball would be hers.

They rattled through the village of Snyders Corner. The village was only being settled when Phoebe was born. Now, twelve years later, the town was growing and growing. There was the grist mill and the tall church. They passed Jarvis Cooper's general store. Phoebe politely nodded to him, but he scowled in return.

There was a new bank and cobbler shop in town, plus a bookstore. Phoebe had been in there only once. She had hungrily read the titles on the backs of the books, wishing she could read them all.

As they rumbled over the wooden bridge, Phoebe saw Matthew

and his father fishing over the railing. The boy looked up and smiled as he displayed a string of trout.

They turned right at the crossroads and followed the dirt road around the hill. Maseppa told her that at one time, their house was the only one on that road, but now there were at least three farms with barns and fields and new families.

As they rounded a bend in the road, contentment washed over Phoebe. A white house with red shutters sat at the top of a tree-lined drive. It had a carved sunrise over the front door, a big red barn, and an apple tree with a rope swing – her home.

There was also a box-shaped wagon in the dooryard. "Zeke's home!" Phoebe jumped up, and Maseppa grabbed her arm.

"You should not stand in the wagon. You will fall."

Zeke emerged from the barn. His dark hair was pulled back and tied at his neck. The sleeves of his jacket showed an inch or two of his skinny wrists. His smile stretched from ear to ear. Phoebe started to jump from the wagon, but then she remembered Butterball. She climbed down with one hand, cradling the little kitten with the other.

"Zeke, look here!"

"Oh, 'tis adorable. Where'd you find the little mite?"

"Missus Reynolds said he wouldn't be able to catch mice with his crooked foot, so I brought him home with me."

"That was nice of her to give it to you."

"Well, she . . . uh . . . she doesn't know. I sneaked it home under my apron."

Zeke's face clouded, and Phoebe hung her head.

"When you take things without permission, that's stealing."

Phoebe lifted her face defensively. "But she said it would be better if it died!"

"No matter, 'tis still wrong."

"But, Maseppa –"

Zeke looked up at Maseppa for an explanation.

"I told Phoebe that we will ask Feona Reynolds next week when we go back. I am not able to hear any more of her talk today."

His eyes twinkled with amusement.

"It is good that you are home," Maseppa said. "I will make you some food."

"I'm working on a wobbly wheel in the barn. I'll be in soon."

Phoebe put the kitten on the ground, and it hopped a few steps, holding up its broken paw. It mewed pitifully and looked at her. She picked it up again and carried it into the kitchen. "Maseppa, do you have some herbs that we can wrap around his foot?"

Maseppa cocked her head. "I do not think a kitten will keep it on his leg, but I can rub this salve on him." She massaged a brown paste on his paw and set him down. Butterball immediately began licking it. "That is good. Maybe he will heal, maybe not." She put the salve back in the pantry. He should stay outside or in the barn."

"Oh, Maseppa, he's so small and can't walk very well and Butch might bother him. Please, may I keep him in here, with us?"

"Only until he gets better."

"Thank you, thank you!" Phoebe found an old saucer with a chip on its edge and poured a little cream in it. She set it on the floor behind the cook stove. Butterball licked it tentatively and got

15

some in his nose. He sneezed four times before trying again. Phoebe found a wool rag and put it near him. He kneaded it a couple of times and curled up in a ball.

"Phoebe, you need to get clothes from the line."

"Yes, Maseppa."

She went through the wood shed door to the clothesline, grabbing a basket on the way. The garden plot behind the barn was newly plowed, and soon they would plant it with beans and corn and squash. The apple tree wore a coat of pink and white blossoms that fluttered like snow each time the wind blew. The wind was blowing now, and their aprons and shirts snapped in the breeze. Phoebe loved the smell of freshly dried clothes. They smelled like sunshine. She buried her nose in their folds and dreamed of warm summer days.

As she entered the kitchen with a loaded basket, she smelled something else.

"Phoebe, I tell you that I do not want that kitten to make a mess. Look over near the table. It made a stinky mess!"

Sure enough, there was a brown circle of goo under the table. Phoebe curled her nose at the thought of cleaning it up, but she knew she better not complain.

"Bad Butterball, you need to learn to go outside to make your mess." Phoebe carried the naughty animal outside the back kitchen door and put him in the grass.

He mewed again.

"I'm sorry, but if you're going to make your stinks under the table, you'll be out here all the time."

Holding her nose with one hand, she wiped up the worst of it with a wad of grass and threw it out behind the shed. Butterball investigated it. She then used an old rag to scrub the spot with hot water and lye soap.

Butterball mewed at the back door. Butch was barking. She had had belonged to Phoebe since she was six years old, and didn't he like this fluffy intruder. Phoebe ran outside to rescue the little kitten cowering under the steps.

"Butch, leave him alone! He's hurt and can't run away." She picked up Butterball, and Butch followed her, his tail hanging down between his legs. Taking care of this kitten wasn't as easy as she thought, but he was so cute and pitiful with his crooked foot. Maybe he'd learn to be good and sweet like the butterball candy.

2
FACING FEONA REYNOLDS

Phoebe loved summer evenings when they all sat on the porch and listened to the world go to sleep. It was nice having the sun linger in the sky and the tree frogs peeping to each other.

Zeke rocked back and forth on the porch swing. He smiled at the kitten swatting at a moth. "Y'know, Li'l Angel, instead of waiting a whole week, why don't I take you back to the Reynolds' farm tomorrow morning so you can ask about keeping that kitten?"

Phoebe sighed, and tears filled her blue eyes. "She doesn't want him, Zeke."

"Well, that may be so, but you've got to be sure. It's stealing to take something that ain't yours."

Uncle Pete, who bunked in the old log cabin behind the house, lounged on the steps and watched Phoebe playing with Butterball. He took off his floppy hat and scratched his tangled hair. His scruffy yellow beard and mustache covered almost all of his face. "You can't stand to see nothin' hurtin', can you, Phoebe?"

"No, Sir. It sets my heart to aching when something is in need of loving."

Maseppa joined Zeke on the porch swing with a bowl of seeds to be sorted. Zeke put his arm around her shoulders. Phoebe caught his eye, and he winked at her. Everything was perfect. She wished it would stay like this forever.

The kitten crawled on her lap and mewed. She sighed again. It wouldn't be perfect if she had to give Butterball back. Just thinking about it made her stomach hurt. *Missus Reynolds scares me.*

It was getting darker, although there was still a bit of a glow left in the sky. The peepers sang in the pond, and bats swished through the air, chasing mosquitoes. The air was rich with damp earthiness.

"Phoebe, it is time that you go to bed."

"Yes, Maseppa." She slipped the kitten in her pocket. "Good night, Uncle Pete. Good night, Zeke."

"G' night, Li'l Angel. Don't fret none about that li'l tyke. I'm sure Missus Reynolds will let you keep him."

"I hope so."

Uncle Pete pulled his pipe out of his yellowed teeth. "Come wake me, in the mornin' and I'll go with ya. I need to ask Morris Reynolds about hirin' me on his farm this summer. If I had my druthers, I'd be out trampin' my trap lines instead of fixin' fences, but a man can't sit aroun' doin' nothin' all day long."

~ # ~

The next morning, the sky warned of rain. The clouds hung low and hid the sun. Phoebe fed Butterball some cream and made sure he did his duty outside. She carried him up a little path, past the apple tree to the small log cabin backed against the tree line.

Phoebe knocked at the heavy oak door. "Uncle Pete, are you awake? We're going soon."

The door swung open. Uncle Pete was snapping his suspenders over his shoulders. "I'm almost ready, child. Hold your horses!"

Phoebe wandered around the room. This was once her father's

workshop, but she could hardly remember it. His tools were still hanging in rows on racks — mallets, chisels, saws, planes, and drills. Phoebe found a curly piece of shaving under the workbench. She fiddled with it between her fingers, and gave it a sniff.

There was a bunk in one corner. Uncle Pete's bearskin blanket was tossed back and half lying on the floor. His traps and skins lay here and there around the room. Phoebe rubbed the furs. They were soft, but it gave her the shivers to think of the poor animals caught in the traps. She was glad that Uncle Pete couldn't walk his trap lines anymore.

As she was about to turn to go back outside, Phoebe noticed some little objects on a shelf. She set Butterball on the floor and crossed the room. She pulled a wooden box close to the wall and climbed up on it. There was a collection of miniature animals parading across the shelf in the crevice below the eaves. There was a horse with a flowing mane and tail, a sitting dog, a crowing rooster, and a dozen others – all carved of wood.

"Uncle Pete, did you make these? They look real, only smaller."

"No, child, your papa made those. He was always whittlin' away at somethin'. Yeah, he could make most anything out o' wood."

Phoebe picked up a carved cat, all curled up into a ball. "Do you think I could take these up to my bedroom?"

"They're not mine. I'd say your room would be the best place for them. Here, let me help you." He filled her apron as she gathered it into a big pouch.

As they left the cabin, he pulled the heavy door closed and latched the big iron padlock. He hung the key on a nail under the eaves on the back side of the building while Phoebe waited. "Why do you lock it up? "

"I can't have anyone poking around my traps and stuff. B'sides there's all your papa's tools. They're worth a bit, but I don't know who could use them right now. Maybe we'll save them for when you fetch yerself a husband."

"Oh, Uncle Pete! I'm only twelve years old. I'm not getting married for a long time."

"It's not as far away as you think. Before you turn around, you'll be a beautiful lady, and some handsome young man will come, wantin' to court you." He pulled her braid and gave her a wink.

Phoebe blushed. "Oh, stop it! I don't want to be a lady. I'd rather be fishing or climbing trees."

"I don't blame you there, but most girls your age are learnin' to sew and cook and housekeep and things such as that."

Phoebe wrinkled her nose at the thought of being cooped up in the house all the time.

Zeke strode around the corner of the barn. "Are you two going to stand there jawing all morning? Let's get rolling. I've got Ol' Sam all hitched up, ready to go."

"We're coming!" Uncle Pete punched the ground with his hickory cane as he limped down the path. "I can only move so fast with this bum foot. "

Phoebe scuttled toward the house. "I'll be right there, Zeke. I have to put these upstairs in my room." She burst through the back door and clattered upstairs to dump all the little carved animals on her bed. A minute later, she was back, even before Uncle Pete had hobbled all the way to the wagon.

As she clambered up into the back, Zeke asked, "Where's the kitten?"

Phoebe's eyes suddenly grew big. She had forgotten where they were going. "Oh, no! He's still in Uncle Pete's cabin! I'll run and get him."

Uncle Pete paused in his attempt to climb into the wagon. "You can't reach the key. I'll have to get it"

Zeke threw his hands up. "You two will be the death of me! I'll get the kitten!" He strode back to the cabin and soon returned with a ball of yellow fur. "Here, now don't let it loose again."

Zeke and Uncle Pete discussed the weather and the price of crops and the way things were changing with new factories and stores being built everywhere. Phoebe bumped this way and that in the back of the wagon. She stared at the fields and trees receding behind them, but her mind was picturing Missus Reynolds. Every bump in the road brought her closer. *Missus Reynolds scares me.*

Soon they pulled into the dooryard of the Reynolds' farm. Morris waved from the open door of the barn. "'Mornin', Pete. Mornin', Zeke."

Zeke pulled the brake lever against the wheel. "Good day, Morris. Is your wife around? Phoebe has something to ask her."

"She should be right there in the kitchen. Today's baking day."

Phoebe didn't move. She looked up into Zeke's face. "Do I have to? When I talk to Missus Reynolds, my words get stuck in my throat, and by the time I get a chance to squeeze them in between all her talking, I forget what I was going to say."

Zeke frowned. "Yes, go do it and have it done with. 'Tis the right thing to do."

Phoebe sighed. She cradled Butterball in her arms and slowly approached the house. She tip-toed up to the open door and peered inside. Sure enough, there was Feona Reynolds' wide figure leaning over her kitchen table, where she was kneading dough. Phoebe's mouth got dry. She swallowed hard and coughed.

Just then, the woman looked up. "Come in, child. Don't stand there gawking at me. I'd open the door and welcome you, but I'm up to my elbows in flour. Do you need more eggs already? Maseppa must be doing some baking, too."

Phoebe stepped into the room. Even though the door and the window were open, the heat from the stove made it hard to breathe.

"What brings you here, child? Speak up!"

"Ummm . . . Yesterday, when I was here with Maseppa . . ." Phoebe's throat felt tight, and her eyes watered. Her heart pounded so loudly she was sure Missus Reynolds could hear it.

"Yes, you were here. What's the matter, child?"

"Well, this kitten." She held up Butterball. "This one with the crooked foot . . ." All her reasons and thoughts came pouring out like water flowing over the dam at the grist mill. "I took him home. You said he might as well have died since he wouldn't be able to catch mice. He needed me. He needed someone to love him. I'm sorry I took him, and Zeke and Maseppa said I couldn't keep him, because that was stealing." She felt that if she stopped talking long enough for Missus Reynolds to answer, she might never get a chance to say all of it. "I didn't think I was stealing, since you didn't want him anyway. So, will you let me take him and make him better and love him?"

Out of breath, Phoebe stopped talking. She was barely breathing waiting for an answer.

Feona Reynolds stood there with her mouth open. Her forehead puckered and her eyes narrowed as if she was going to give Phoebe a piece of her mind . . . but she didn't. She looked at the mewing kitten and Phoebe's innocent blue eyes. "I reckon you'd give him a good home. If you ask me, it ain't right for you to steal from a person, but seeing it's something that would be more work than it's worth around here, I'll let it go."

Phoebe let out the air in her lungs with a happy sigh. She wrapped her free arm around Missus Reynolds' middle. "Oh, thank you, Ma'am!"

"My goodness, child! You don't have to get all mushy about it. If you wait a few minutes, you could take back a mincemeat pie to Maseppa. People say that my mincemeat . . ." She filled the next fifteen minutes with her recipes of mincemeat pie and rhubarb pie and whatever other pies she liked to bake. Phoebe agreed with Maseppa. *Missus Reynolds does talk too much.*

Phoebe didn't want to be rude, but Missus Reynolds made it so hard for a person to leave. She put Butterball into her pocket, hoping Missus Reynolds wouldn't change her mind. She edged her way toward the open door and tried to squeeze in a "good day" between the directions for apple fritters and apple dumplings.

"Thank you, Ma'am. I can't stay, I have to get right back home. Thank you for letting me keep Butterball." Phoebe slipped out the door before Missus Reynolds started a new one-sided conversation.

Phoebe climbed up into the back of the wagon and rubbed Butterball's fur. It wasn't long before Zeke came out of the barn. "You look happier. I assume things went well?"

"Yes, she said that I could keep Butterball since he'd be more work than he was worth. She wasn't angry at all." Phoebe glanced back toward the barn. "Where's Uncle Pete?"

"He's going to work for a few hours. He'll be along when he's done. You can sit up here with me, if you want."

Phoebe scrambled over the back of the seat and plopped next to him. She settled Butterball on her lap and waved at Feona Reynolds watching from the kitchen door.

Phoebe liked sitting up front with Zeke. Sometimes he let her hold the reins and guide Ol' Sam through the familiar roads, but today Phoebe was satisfied to lean against the back of the seat and cuddle Butterball. Zeke whistled as they rode along. He wasn't one to talk much, but he didn't mind Phoebe's questions. "Zeke, Uncle Pete's not really my uncle, is he?"

"No, he's your papa's cousin. That's why you look like him.

"I don't look like Uncle Pete!"

"You both have curly yellow hair and those bright blue eyes. Yeah, you look a lot like him. He's also Maseppa's father. That's why she has blue eyes, too."

"Maseppa's papa? I guess I knew that, but she doesn't look like him."

"No, that's because her mama was Algonkin."

"What happened to her mama?"

"Hmmmm . . . it's a long story, but as best I can tell, Uncle Pete was married to a woman in the Algonkin village. He went trapping and when he got back, she was gone. A white man's disease had spread through the tribe, and Maseppa's mother thought she was to blame, so she took young Maseppa and lived alone in the woods. When Pete finally found them, her mother was badly hurt. He stayed with them until she died and then brought Maseppa to stay with your papa and mama."

Phoebe squirmed and rubbed Butterball's ears. "I know Papa and Mama died, but Maseppa doesn't like to talk about it."

"A tree fell on your papa, and your mama tried to get him out. It made her baby come too soon, and she died too. That's when Maseppa took you away—to protect you."

"Protect me from what?"

"From people who wanted to take you away. She was determined to keep her promise to care of you. That's about the time I met you two, camping under the trees with a broken wheel."

"I remember that. You played your fiddle, and I danced."

"Yeah, that seems so long ago."

They bumped along for a while without speaking. "Zeke, since you and Maseppa got married, it's like you're my papa and she's my mama now . . . not exactly, but like that."

Zeke gave her a half-cocked smile. "I suppose, but I reckon I'd never be as good a papa as your real one. Maseppa's been good to you, but I reckon she's not as good as a real mama either."

"I'd rather you and Maseppa be my papa and mama than living with anyone else, but it would be nice to have some brothers or sisters. I'd like to have lots and lots."

Zeke chuckled. "We'll see."

3
THE WILD GIRL

Later that week, Phoebe was arranging the little carved animals on her window sills. She picked them up one by one. Each figure was perfect. There were feathers on the ducks and scales on the fish. The horse was galloping, and the pig had a curly tail. She lined them up on her window sill. She liked the funny raccoon with little hands. There were even whiskers on the cat.

Zeke hollered up the stairs, "Phoebe, I'm going into town to pick up Uncle Pete at the Reynolds farm. Do you want to come along?"

She set down the wooden cat. "Yes, I'll be right there."

When they pulled into the yard, Missus Reynolds was fetching water at the well. "Morris and Pete are still fixing the back fence if you want to go meet them." She hefted the pail onto the edge of the well. "Would you like to sit a spell in my kitchen, Phoebe, while you wait?"

"Thank you, Ma'am, but I think I'll go with Zeke."

As they walked past the barn, Phoebe asked Zeke, "May I go down to the creek for a few minutes? I'd like to see how high the water is right now."

Zeke smiled. He knew she'd rather be wandering the woods any day, rather than sit in a hot kitchen, listening to a lot of gossip. "Don't wander too far, and don't fall in."

Phoebe bounded over the hillocks down to the edge of the ravine. The winter's melted snows and the weeks of rain sent torrents of muddy water swishing past her. She tossed a piece of bark into the water and watched it bob and twirl until she couldn't see it anymore, but she did see something on a log down a ways.

Running along the top of the ravine, she saw that it was a girl about her age. The girl dangled her legs over the side, and splashed her feet in the water once in a while. Her dark hair hung loose and wild. Phoebe hollered, "Hello!" but the girl didn't even look up.

Phoebe slid down the steep bank, grabbing small bushes and trees along the way, but one twig broke and she tumbled the last few feet. Still the girl didn't seem to hear her. Phoebe rubbed her scraped hands on her skirt, walked along the log, and sat down.

The girl jumped up in surprise and glared at Phoebe. "You don't belong here! Get off our land!"

"I'm sorry. I didn't know whose land it was."

"Well, it's not yours!"

"Are you new in our town? I haven't seen you around."

"Get out of here!" The girl held up a clenched fist.

Phoebe's eye grew wide, and she retreated up the muddy side of the ravine. When she looked back, the girl held up her fist again in warning. Phoebe took a few steps backwards, out of sight. She started to walk across the pasture and then decided to see if the girl would still be there or if she might be following her. She crawled on her hands and knees closer to the edge. The girl was gone.

Phoebe sighed and stood up. She rubbed the dirt from her hands. *That certainly was strange. I wonder if she's one of those children that Missus Reynolds was talking about.*

She walked around the edge of the pasture, following the

sounds of men's voices. She passed a brown cow that looked up from eating some grass. It stared at her and moved its jaw back and forth and up and down as it chewed. A young calf lay under a nearby tree. Phoebe knew better than to get any closer, even though it looked cute. You never know what a mother animal might do if it thought someone was going to hurt its baby.

Soon she found Mister Reynolds and Uncle Pete and Zeke. They were stringing wire with twisted barbs from one pole to another and had only three more posts to do before the whole pasture would be enclosed. This new way of fencing saved many hours of splitting logs and replacing damaged rails. The wires were hard to see from a distance, and Phoebe wondered if you might run into them if you were walking at night. It would certainly hurt.

Uncle Pete's face was all red. He kept taking off his hat and wiping his forehead with his sleeve. He cringed with each step on his bad leg. Phoebe knew he would need one of Maseppa's poultice wraps on his foot tonight.

"All done!" Mister Reynolds picked up his tools. "Thanks, fellers. I couldn't have done it alone!"

As they walked back to the farm, Uncle Pete had to stop every once in a while to rest on his cane.

"Are you all right?" asked Phoebe.

"Don't you fret none 'bout me. I'm grateful that I still have the energy to walk the boundary of a man's land and earn a day's wages."

Zeke slapped his shoulder and smiled in agreement.

As they rode home. Ol' Sam clopped along in a lazy rhythm while Zeke whistled a sad tune. The sun painted the clouds with pinks and oranges. The steeple silhouette stood against the evening colors. Lamplights shone from windows. As they passed the old pine woods, a breeze whispered in the needles, and its darkness blocked the twilight. They turned up their drive toward home, and

Phoebe could see that Maseppa had a lamp in the window. It was good to be home.

After supper, Phoebe played with Butterball. She wiggled a string and let the kitten pounce on it. Uncle Pete had already retired to bed in his cabin, moaning about being too old to be a farmer. Zeke was reading the newspaper. Phoebe could see the headline, TERRITORIES BEING SETTLED – Guides Wanted.

Maseppa worked the plunger of the butter churn. The swish, splash, swish, splash had a rhythm like the ticking of Granny's old cuckoo clock. The wood in the stove hissed and hummed. The lamplight flickered on the kitchen walls. Phoebe leaned back in the rocking chair. She noticed a scrape on her left hand and thought about the girl down by the ravine. "I saw a girl today."

"What was that?" Zeke looked up. "You saw a girl? What girl?"

"She was down by the stream near the Reynolds' farm."

"She must be of the new family that's just moved in – Kittle's the name."

"She didn't like me. She told me to go away."

"I reckon she wanted to be alone. Maybe she's scared of meeting new folks."

Phoebe pushed her foot against the edge of the woodstove to set the rocking chair moving again. Butterball purred in her lap, and Butch nudged his wet nose under her elbow, trying to get some attention.

Zeke said, "I reckon it would be neighborly to take over a pie to them. Don't you think so, Maseppa?"

She looked up from churning the butter and nodded. "I will make some tomorrow. Phoebe and I will go see this new family."

"Do I have to go with you?"

"Of course, you'll go with Maseppa," scolded Zeke. "Don't you want to meet their children? Maybe this girl needs a friend."

I don't think she wants me to be her friend.

The swishing of the milk changed sound, and Maseppa lifted the lid. Little blobs of yellow stuck to the dasher. She scooped a larger lump from the churn and dropped it into a wooden bowl. Then Maseppa squeezed and pushed the butter to separate it from the watery whey. Next, she salted it, and rolled it into a ball. Finally, she pressed it into a mold with an oak leaf design on the top.

Zeke jumped up to help her pour the buttermilk into a pitcher, then washed the churn with hot water from the kettle. Finally, he rinsed it at the kitchen pump. Maseppa stored the butter and buttermilk in the pantry.

"It would be right nice to get us an ice box," said Zeke. "In fact, I've been thinking I might be able to peddle ice from house to house. We could have cold lemonade in the middle of July. Now, wouldn't that just be living high on the hog?"

Phoebe laughed. "Where would you get ice in July?"

"We'd build an ice house, and in the dead o' winter, we could cut it from the mill pond in big blocks. Then we'd pack the blocks in sawdust, so that come summer, we'd have ourselves some ice!" He pumped some clean water into the empty churn and swished it around. Just think – meat and milk wouldn't spoil in June. I reckon it's a great idea! Don't you think so, Maseppa?"

Maseppa's deep blue eyes twinkled and her lips curved slightly at the corners when she looked at Zeke, but she didn't answer. She looked at Phoebe, and her eyes softened. "You need to go in your bed. It is a long time after the sun has gone down."

"Ah, Maseppa. I want to hear about Zeke's ice house."

"Phoebe," Zeke's low voice stopped her whine. "You shouldn't speak to Maseppa like that. You obey."

"Yes, Zeke." She put Butterball on the floor, and he stretched his back. She noticed that he put his crooked foot on the floor. "Good night, Zeke. Good night, Maseppa." She gave them each a hug and took a candlestick with her upstairs.

As Phoebe lay in bed, she thought of the girl. *What was it that made her seem like a wild animal? Maybe it was her hair, all loose and tangled. Maybe it was the way she jumped up and almost attacked her. No, there was something else . . . her eyes. Yes, it was her eyes. She looked frightened and sad at the same time. Whatever it is, I don't think she wants a friend.*

4
MEETING THE KITTLES

The next morning, Maseppa had Phoebe fetch a string of dried apple slices from the attic to make into a pie. In fact, they made two pies. They didn't know how many children the Kittles might have.

While Maseppa rolled out the flour-and-lard mixture, Phoebe broke up lumps of maple sugar. She got out the grater, a stick of cinnamon, a nutmeg, and the butter. "Don't forget the salt cellar," reminded Maseppa. Phoebe reached high on the shelf in the pantry to get the box of salt.

They added some smaller sticks in the stove and pushed the damper that sent the heat around the oven part. Within a half hour the kitchen was so hot that they had to open the porch door to let a breeze through the room. Maseppa cut a star design on the top crusts and slid the pies into the oven.

After Phoebe washed up and buttoned her high-topped shoes, Maseppa braided her long curls. "Are we taking the buckboard?"

Maseppa wrapped the golden brown pies in linen towels and placed them in a basket. "I think it would be good to walk. It has been a long time since we walked in the woods."

"Do you know the way?"

Maseppa turned sharply and faced her. "I know."

33

Phoebe hung her head. Of course – how could she even question her? Maseppa never got lost. She knew these woods as well as she knew this kitchen. She seemed to have a compass in her head and always came out where she planned.

Phoebe walked behind Maseppa. There wasn't any trail, except for what the deer made through the trees. Maseppa's leather slippers didn't make a sound as she passed through the low bushes. Every once in a while, she'd stop and inspect a young shoot pushing up through the mud. She'd grunt and look about to mark the spot in her mind.

They crossed a trickling stream on a fallen log. The water wasn't very deep. Phoebe thought it would have been much easier if she were barefoot and waded across.

In the tall pine woods, the ground was soft and springy and covered with a golden layer of old needles. The trees were so thick that Phoebe could hardly see the sun through the branches overhead. A blue jay screeched and flew away to warn of humans in the forest.

Soon they emerged into the bright, glaring sunlight. Phoebe knew where they were. *The road must go around into almost a circle.* It was a lot shorter to walk this way than to go through the town. They were down a ways from the Reynolds' house, and they walked until they came to a tumble-down shack. Two boys burst from the door, one chasing the other with a stick. They didn't even notice Maseppa and Phoebe.

Going up to the door, which hung crookedly on one hinge, Maseppa gave two little taps. They could hear a man yelling and cursing inside. Maseppa frowned and backed up a step. The gruff cursing drew closer with each thud of footsteps. Phoebe stepped close to Maseppa, who backed up more and half turned to leave when the door swung open.

A man held a jug in one hand and his tattered pants with the other. His watery eyes gleamed from between his shaggy hair and unshaven whiskers. "Whadda you wan'?" He swayed and caught his balance against the door. "Liza, you 'spectin' comp'ny? There's some ladies here."

A small woman peered around him. Her eyes looked red, as if she had been crying. She rubbed her cheeks and smoothed her hair, which was tied back with a string. "Good day, Ma'am."

The man pushed past them and swaggered to the barn. The odor he left behind made Phoebe cough.

"Come in, but don't mind the mess." The woman picked up something from the floor. "The chilluns have been raising a ruckus today."

The whole house seemed to be one room. Phoebe could see a bed behind a tattered blanket that curtained off a corner, and a ladder leaned against a square hole in the ceiling. A few cracked dishes were stacked next to a pail of water on a table against the back wall. All of the furniture seemed to be constructed of rough board tacked together. Flies buzzed about a bucket near the back door, and a dog slept near the fireplace. A toddler crawled about on the floor and sat up to chew on a bone he found.

"Good day, my name is Maseppa. This is Phoebe. We live on the other side of Snyders Corner, but we are not far away through the woods. Feona Reynolds told us that there are new people living here, so I brought you some apple pies."

"I thank you very much. I am Liza and my husband is Roster Kittle. This little one is Sammy, and I have two other boys, Stafford and Roster Junior, but we call him Ross. I have a girl, too, named Adeline, but she likes to be called Delly.

Just then Phoebe saw the girl peek in the back door. Her mother saw her, too. "Delly, come say 'hi' to the neighbors."

Delly locked eyes with Phoebe as if daring her to say anything about their previous meeting. Her mother introduced Phoebe. "They brought us some nice pies. They will taste right good for supper tonight."

Delly said, "Would you like to see our new calf?"

Phoebe turned to Maseppa, and she nodded her permission.

Outside, Delly turned and faced Phoebe. "I thought I told you to stay off our land."

Phoebe halted in shock. "I didn't ask to come here! Maseppa made me come with her to bring the pies."

"Well, you needn't come back, you hear? We don't take to having visitors or charity."

Phoebe looked down at Delly's grubby bare toes and her own black shoes. She scowled and wished she hadn't worn them. Nobody cared if she was dressed up or not.

Neither spoke for a few minutes as they walked to a weathered barn. A scrawny cow and calf lay in the corner of a stall. Suddenly Delly asked, "Do you like poppers?"

"Poppers? What are poppers?"

"They're good. I'll get us some." Delly shinnied up the ladder to a string of dried red fruit. She broke off a couple of them and dropped one in her mouth, chewing it with loud smacks. "Here's a good one for you."

Phoebe started to break it in half when Delly stopped her.

"No, it tastes best if you put the whole thing in your mouth."

Hesitantly, Phoebe put it in her mouth.

"Chew it up," urged Delly.

Suddenly, Phoebe's mouth burst with burning pain. Her eyes watered and she coughed and spit out the dried food. Delly bent over in peals of laughter.

"ARRRRGGH! What is it? It's hot! I need some water."

"Ha, ha, ha! I'll get some." She disappeared into a ramshackle shed and brought out a dipper with a some liquid in the bottom.

Phoebe tipped it up and swallowed a big mouthful. She spit it out with a spray. Her mouth felt like she was eating fire. "This is vinegar! You are a horrible girl. I'm going home!"

"I never wanted you to come in the first place!"

Phoebe ran to the house. "Maseppa, I want to go home now."

"You should not be rude, Phoebe."

"I want to go now."

Liza asked, "Are you sick?"

"No, Delly gave me something to eat that burns my mouth, a popper, and then gave me some vinegar."

The back door slammed.

Her mother shouted outside, "Adeline Kittle, get in here!" She tugged Delly inside. "This girl says you gave her a popper and vinegar. Is that true?"

Delly stiffened her back and looked straight into her mother's face. "Of course not, Ma! That would burn something fierce. Would I do that to our guest? She was running and fell down. Something must have gotten in her mouth."

Liza turned around and crossed her arms. "You shouldn't get in the habit of making up lies to cover for your clumsiness, Phoebe. I'm sure it will feel better soon."

Phoebe stared at her with shock, and she clamped her mouth

shut to keep from saying some not so nice words. Tugging on Maseppa's arm she repeated, "I want to go home now." She fled out the sagging front door and into the shadowy cool woods. *I didn't want to go make friends anyway. I told Zeke that wild girl didn't want any friends. She's wilder and sneakier than a rattlesnake!*

"Phoebe! Phoebe, stop and wait for me."

"Maseppa, she lied! She tricked me and laughed at me."

"I know. I am sorry." She bent close to the ground looking for something. "Here is a leaf of wintergreen. Chew slowly, and I will find some water. When we are home, I will give you milk. That is good for a burning in the mouth, too."

The mint soothed the burning in her mouth, but her heart still stung with shock and anger.

5
MASEPPA'S GUESTS

It hadn't taken long for the people in Snyders Corner to learn that Maseppa had knowledge of healing herbs. They often stopped in for advice and for teas to cure coughs, sores, headaches, and other assorted ailments.

This day, Deborah Gilmore was here with her child, Sally, who had been irritable while cutting teeth. Maseppa poured some pine needle tea for Deborah and sat in the other chair. Deborah chatted about the weather and her garden and her baby.

It was hard for Maseppa to keep her mind on the conversation. *I know I should be polite, but having visitors is so hard. I want to take a walk, but it would be rude to leave my guest in my kitchen.*

Deborah perched little Sally over her shoulder and patted her back. The baby put her thumb in her mouth and gazed around the room. Sally's hair was as yellow and fuzzy as the baby chicks that Deborah had brought to them. *Deborah and Stanley Gilmore are good neighbors. I will be patient and polite.*

Matthew, Deborah's six year old son, squatted beside the crate, picking up one chick after another. He lifted one close to his face and looked it in the eye. "I like this one."

His mother put it back in the box. "These are for Maseppa. We have plenty at our house."

Matthew put one in Maseppa's lap. She patted the fuzzy chick.

"Thank you much. I was hoping to get some chickens soon. I do not like to always be buying eggs from people."

Deborah smiled. "Well, I'm glad to help you. That's what neighbors are for." Sally had fallen asleep. "Well, I ought to be heading back home."

Matthew stood up and wiped his sleeve over his nose. "Ma, could Phoebe come see my other chicks?"

"It would be fine with me." Deborah turned to Phoebe. "Would you like to walk back with us? Matthew gets anxious for someone to play with. I'm usually too busy with the baby."

Phoebe nodded and looked at Maseppa for permission.

"It is fine with me. Come home when the sky gets dark. Yes?"

"Yes, Maseppa."

Deborah gathered the baby's blanket and sack of chamomile that Maseppa had given her in exchange for the chicks. "You come over and visit someday, you hear? I get lonesome for another woman's talk when I'm home so much with the baby. I'll have you look at the weaving loom, to see if you want it."

Maseppa nodded.

After Deborah left, Maseppa carried the crate of chicks out to the back yard, where Zeke was finishing harrowing the garden plot. He stopped and stretched his back when he saw her.

"I'm almost done, 'Zeppa. There were a lot of weeds grown in here over the years."

Maseppa looked at him with a puzzled gaze.

"What?" He was beginning to read her quiet expressions.

"You gave me a new name . . . Zeppa."

"Does it bother you? I'd like a special name for you from me. It sounds right nice together . . . Zeke and Zeppa." He chuckled and she blushed.

She picked up a hoe and began dragging it in the soft soil to form a row. Back and forth she went until she had drawn four rows. Then she found the sack of spinach seeds. Leaning over, she walked backwards as she planted them in the damp soil – letting the dark grains sift through her fingers and using her other hand to cover the seeds.

"Where's Phoebe?" asked Zeke.

"I let her go with Deborah to play with Matthew." Maseppa started down another row. "It is hard for Deborah to watch him and the baby. He is getting bigger and wants to be outside. Phoebe will take good care of him."

"Butch must have gone, too," he added. "Usually he's helping me dig holes."

Maseppa stood up when she finished planting the spinach. "If you could make some hills for the corn and pumpkins, that would help me."

"Corn and pumpkins together?"

"And beans," added Maseppa. "My mother called them the Three Sisters – beans, corn, pumpkins. Each one helps the others to grow."

"Interesting." He grabbed the hoe. "How many do you need?"

"I think that it will be good to have eight or ten places."

By the time they finished, they were sweaty and dirty and tired, but it was done. Zeke took off his hat and wiped the sweat from his forehead. He smiled at Maseppa's smudged cheek and wisps of loose hair. He put his arm around her waist.

Maseppa froze at his touch. Her old fears and distrust still rose to the surface when triggered by surprise. *It is not good to fear Zeke.* Her heart raced, but she didn't pull away. The warmth of his arm seeped past her skin and calmed her heart. *Zeke feels like a wool blanket on a windy day.*

After a gentle squeeze, he said, "Well, Zeppa, when I was a peddler, I never thought I'd have my own garden and family and house. It's a mighty good feeling."

~ # ~

Maseppa was interested in Deborah's weaving loom, so one day, the Gilmores brought over a collection of wooden beams and frames. Stanley and Zeke pounded and thumped the boards for over an hour, until they had assembled the loom. It took up most of the sitting room, but it was the only warm room in the house, besides the kitchen.

Maseppa had mentioned to Deborah about wanting to learn how to make cloth. She thought it would be like weaving baskets, only with threads. Deborah showed her how to string some white threads up and down for the warp. Between them she had strung yellow and green and brown threads horizontally, called the weft. When she pushed on certain treadles, half of the threads lifted higher than the others, making a hollow spot, called a tunnel. A shuttle, which looked like a canoe, was tossed through the tunnel to the other side, pulling the thread along. Deborah then pulled on the beater bar to tighten the new thread close to the already woven cloth. She shifted the treadles and tossed the shuttle through again..

Maseppa tried a few rows. Deborah gave advice on how tightly to work the weft, but it wasn't long before Maseppa was clacking away quite well. Back and forth, thread by thread the cloth grew.

After the Gilmores left, Zeke watched Maseppa weave a few more rows. "You know, not many people spin their cloth in their homes anymore. It's done in big factories where machines make the cloth and women sew clothing. In fact, many people are moving to the cities to work in the factories."

Maseppa threw the shuttle between the threads again. "I would not like to live in the city. I like to make my own things."

Zeke smiled and planted a kiss on the top of her head. "I know, and that's one thing I like about you."

That evening, at the supper table, Phoebe told of all the funny things that Matthew said. "He's so silly. I wish I had a little brother like him."

Zeke put down his fork and muttered while counting on his fingers. He turned to Maseppa. "Wouldn't Matthew be about the same age as the child Martha lost?"

A cloud of sad memories passed over Maseppa's face. "Yes, Deborah and Martha were happy to expect their babies at the same time." *That seems many years ago.* Maseppa cleared the dishes from the table. *Phoebe would have been a good big sister.*

"So, Phoebe, Matthew is about the age your brother would have been, if he lived. You can pretend that he is your little brother."

Phoebe cocked her head. "Matthew can be rather bossy. I'm not so sure he'd want me as a big sister."

6
A JOB FOR PHOEBE

Phoebe wandered along shops at the crossroads of Snyders Corner. Zeke was loading merchandise at the general store, and had said she could look around while she waited for him to finish.

The village was growing. New shops seemed to open each month. Phoebe stood at the door of the cobbler's shop and watched Mister Peterson tacking the sole onto a man's boot. She took a deep breath of the pungent leather smell, but she didn't stand there too long because she was on her way to explore the newest shop in town – a bookstore. A bell tinkled as she opened the door. The room was filled with an intoxicating aroma of ink and paper.

A man came out from behind a green curtain, wiping ink-stained fingers on his apron. "May I help you, young lady?"

"I'm just looking, sir."

"When you find what you want, come get me. I'll be done soon." He disappeared behind the curtain.

Phoebe meandered along the shelves. She ran her fingers over the spines of the hundreds of books. There were books about people, history, philosophy, travel, and politics. She was drawn to the poetry books and the story books – or novels, as the label on the shelf said. They told of faraway places, princesses living in castles, or pirates sailing the high seas.

Phoebe pulled out a book with a green cover, "The Collection of Washington Irving." She saw "Rip Van Winkle" and "The

Legend of Sleepy Hollow" among its stories. *This is the book I want.*

Phoebe walked back past the history and philosophy books to the back of the room, where the owner had gone. She pulled aside the thick curtain. The man was placing big white sheets of paper on a table. On the table was a flat box with rows and rows of tiny words, made of little carved letters. He rolled some ink on the words and carefully placed the sheet of paper over it. Then he brought down another flat table on top and pushed a lever around a big screw to make it tight. After releasing and lifting the top plate, he pulled the paper away.

Phoebe gasped. "A newspaper!"

He smiled. "Yes, that's how a newspaper is made." He wiped his hands again. "Did you find something?"

"How much does this book cost, sir?"

"Aha! Washington Irving – it came in yesterday, brand new! That one costs one dollar."

Phoebe sighed. At that price, she'd never be able to buy one. "Do all the books cost a dollar?"

"Well, it depends, of course, on which book. The newer ones are priced around one dollar, but after a few months, I lower the price to fifty cents when a batch of new ones are published. What are you interested in?"

"I like poetry and stories."

"I have a nice collection of poetry on this shelf – William Blake, Robert Burns, Walt Whitman, William Shakespeare, Isaac Watts..."

"Do you have any exciting books – that don't cost too much?"

He studied her thoughtfully, then rubbed the few hairs left on the top of his balding head, leaving a black smudge. "I've been considering something, and I think it might work. I have a crate of used books. Some of the covers are worn. Some of the pages are ragged. I was thinking of selling them for twenty cents, since they're not new, but I think if I lent them out for only a penny, it would be good for youngsters and for me. When you bring it back, you can borrow another one."

He dragged a crate of books from the back room. "Here, take a look through these." He took some out, tipping his head so that he could read the titles through his spectacles. "There are quite a few young folk books in here: *A Basket of Flowers, Maurice the Fisher's Cot, Robinson Crusoe, Original Stories from Real Life, Swiss Family Robinson*... Now that's an exciting one."

Phoebe took the book from him. It had a dark red cover. On the first page was a drawing of boy riding a zebra, with palm trees behind him. Phoebe flipped through the book. There was another illustration of a tree house. She stared at the picture. *I've always wished I could live in a tree.* "May I borrow this one?"

"Oh, yes. You will like that one. Bring me a penny the next time you come to town, and I will let you borrow that book for a month. That should be plenty of time for you to read it."

Phoebe reluctantly gave the book back to him.

"You can take it now and bring me the penny later." He held it out to her.

"Really?" She reached to take it again, but stopped. "No, sir. It wouldn't be right. I best wait until I have the money in hand."

Phoebe couldn't believe this wonderful gift of all these books at her bidding. All she needed was a penny. She could probably ask Zeke, but he had given her a penny yesterday and she had already spent it on peppermints. There must be some other way to get a penny.

"Is there anything else I can do for you?"

"No, thank you, sir." She sighed. "I'll be back soon . . . as soon as I can earn a penny."

"I understand. That's very commendable. What's your name, young lady?"

"I'm Phoebe – Phoebe Johanson."

He held out his hand. "I'm Mark Phillips. You probably know my children, Sarah and Billy. I hope to do business with you soon." The bell jangled again as she stepped outside.

Phoebe walked past the bank. She knew she couldn't earn any money there. That's where you put your money to keep it safe or borrowed lots of it to buy something big. She peeked in Mister Cooper's general store. Maybe he had something for her to do for a penny.

"What do you want?" He always made her feel like she had interrupted something important.

"I was wondering if you had a job I could do to earn a penny, like sweep your porch or straighten some shelves or wash a window."

"I don't need to pay anyone to do something I can do by myself! Now, skedaddle out of here and stop wasting my time."

Phoebe looked around at the dingy store. *He may be able to do those things, but he never does.*

She wandered over to the grist mill and watched the water wheel turn around and around for a while. Maybe the miller could use a helper for something. Inside, the mill was dusty and the noise of the stones grinding on each other deafened her to anything else. She tried to ask, "Do you have a job that I could do?

He held his hand behind his ear and leaned toward her.

"DO YOU HAVE ANY JOBS THAT I COULD DO?"

He shook his head and shrugged his shoulders. He couldn't hear her over the grinding wheels. His son carried a heavy bag up the stairs to the upper level, and soon she could see the corn falling down a chute. It came out of the side of the huge stone wheels as crushed meal. This would be ground again and then again, to make a finer flour. Some days the miller ground corn, other times he ground barley, or buckwheat, depending on the harvest.

She watched him for a while, being sure to stay out of his way. She wasn't sure what she could do to help him, anyway. She was too small to carry the bags and it wouldn't do much good to sweep.

As she stepped outside, she saw Matthew, with his ever-handy fishing pole. His mother and father were just tying up to the hitching post. "Good day, Phoebe," Deborah called. "It's a beautiful day, isn't it?"

"Yes, Ma'am. Good day, to you too, Mister Gilmore."

He tipped his hat and nodded to her. "Good day, Miss Phoebe."

She smiled whenever someone called her Miss Phoebe, like she was already a lady. She decided to curtsy to him, to return the nicety.

Deborah settled little Sally on her hip and shouted at Matthew, who was peering over the bridge at the rushing water. "Don't go far. We'll be done shortly."

"Ahh, Ma! There's a good fishing hole down the stream a ways. Can't I go down there?"

"Matthew! You mind your mother," said Mister Gilmore.

Phoebe's eyes lit up with an idea. "I'd be willing to watch Matthew and bring him home when he's done fishing – for a penny."

Mister Gilmore laughed. "A penny?" He looked at his wife. "It sounds like a right good deal to me. What do you think, my dear?"

"I'd gladly pay you a penny anytime you're willing to go traipsing off in the woods and streams with Matthew. He's forever yearning to be in the woods, but I don't have the time, and he's not quite big enough to be on his own."

"I don't mind watching him. I'll take good care of him."

"I know," said Deborah, "and I trust you, knowing that you won't get lost or do anything foolish." She fished a penny out of her purse and dropped it into Phoebe's palm. "Thank you much, dear. That takes a load off my mind."

"Let me tell Zeke what I'm doing, and then we can go fishing."

In a few minutes Phoebe and Matthew were downstream. Matthew was trying one spot after another while Phoebe daydreamed of living in a tree like the characters she saw in *Swiss Family Robinson*. She couldn't wait to borrow the book and see how they did it.

Phoebe watched a pine cone swirl and spin in the dark eddies. Her eyes followed it until it disappeared around the bend in the creek, and then she threw another pine cone into the water.

Matthew swung his fishing pole over his head to cast the line. "Ouch! OWWWW!"

Phoebe saw that he had caught the hook on the back of his leg. She shook her head and tossed the rest of her pine cones. "Matthew Gilmore, you're the most getting-into-trouble kid I've ever seen!"

"Phoebe, it hurts! I'm bleeding!"

Phoebe made her way down the bank, slipping and sliding in the muddy grass. She hung on to bushes and saplings to keep from falling into the creek herself. Squatting next to Matthew, she examined his leg. It didn't look too bad. She could probably pull it out. She reached to see how firmly it was attached.

"Don't touch it!"

"Then how am I going to help you?"

"I want a big person to take it out. You'll make it bleed more."

"It's not that bad." She reached toward it again.

Matthew scooted backwards. "Don't touch it!"

Taking care of him wasn't going to be as easy as she thought it would be. "Fine! Let's go home, and your mother can take it out." She stood up and started back up the hill.

"I can't walk home!"

"Well, I'm not going to carry you."

"Phoebe, it hurts!"

She looked at his grimy face streaked with tears. She supposed she'd have to get him home somehow.

Turning around, she said, "Hop on my back. I'll carry you."

He wiped his nose on the arm of his sleeve and clambered on her back.

"Oooph! You're going to have to stop eating so many flapjacks." She took a few steps, but kept slipping on the muddy bank. "I can't get you to the top of the ravine. You'll have to walk that far."

Carrying Matthew's fishing pole, Phoebe followed the wailing boy up the hill. She considered pulling the hook out with a quick jerk, but decided it might pull a chunk of skin with it. Then he'd really yell. At the top of the hill, Phoebe paused to consider their predicament. "Can you carry the pole, Matthew? I can't carry you and the pole, too."

"We can leave it here, and I'll come back and get it tomorrow."

"But you're still attached to it!"

"Let's break the line!"

He twisted the line around his wrists and tried to break the string, but it was tougher than he thought.

"Let me try." Phoebe wrapped it around both hands and pulled. She gnawed the taut string until it frayed and tugged again. Finally, it gave way with a TWANG!

"OWWW!" Matthew grabbed his leg and rocked back and forth on the ground. He opened his grasp to take a look at the wound. "I'm bleeding! You pulled the hook out of my skin!" He let out a loud bellowing.

"Oh hush! You sound like you're dying."

"I'm bleeding to death!"

"Don't be such a baby. You're not bleeding to death."

Taking a hanky from her pocket, she slid down to the creek again to get it wet. She climbed back up and wiped his leg clean. Holding the cloth on it for a minute, she finally got the wound to stop bleeding. "See, it's not so bad."

"But I still can't walk. I'll bleed again."

Crouching down, she let him crawl on her back. He wrapped his scrawny arms around her neck so that she could hardly breathe. She hoisted him as high as she could. He hooked one leg around her hip, but held the one with the cut straight out.

Phoebe had to stop and rest every few steps, but finally they reached the road. She set him on his feet.

"I'm not carrying you anymore. You can walk now."

Matthew took a few limping steps. He leaned over to see if it made his leg bleed. "Hey! I can see right into my muscles." Seeing he wasn't going to die, he took a few more steps. "I'll probably have a super scar when it gets better."

Phoebe fetched his fishing pole, and they hobbled home. It took three times as long as usual because Matthew stopped every few feet to inspect his leg and make sure it wasn't bleeding again.

Phoebe sighed. "If you don't hurry up, I may die before I get home."

7
THE TOWN MEETING

The next day, penny in hand, Phoebe rode into town with Zeke. There was a storm brewing in Snyders Corner. Dark clouds billowed in the hot summer air. The wind whipped the young saplings back and forth. Stinging drops of rain pelted the horses as they pulled wagons and buggies into town.

Another kind of storm was brewing too. The men of the town were meeting in the church — Zeke, Jarvis Cooper and Stanley Gilmore were there, plus Sidney Hunster, the banker, Seth Peterson, Mark Phillips, and a few of the farmers from the surrounding area.

While Zeke tethered Ol' Sam, Phoebe ran to the bookstore to rent *Swiss Family Robinson*. Mister Phillips was about to close the shop to attend the town meeting, too, but he waited while she quickly chose her book from the crate. She hurried over to the church and slipped into a back pew to read her new book while she waited for Zeke. It was her book for a whole month!

Morris Reynolds was the chairman, being the oldest resident present. "Are we all here? Let's begin with prayer before we get this meeting started." Phoebe closed her eyes and listened to him. "Our Heavenly Father, direct our meeting this evening. Give us wisdom as to which man You wish to lead our little flock. Guide our words and attitudes. We seek Your will tonight. In name of Your Son, Jesus Christ, Amen." Other "Amens" echoed his, and then there was a shuffle of feet as the men made themselves comfortable in the hard seats.

Phoebe snuggled into the corner of the pew and opened to the first chapter as Jarvis Cooper stood up. "I say we vote on a bachelor preacher. He won't cost us as much as a whole family."

"What it costs us is not as important as what he preaches," said Phillips.

"I agree," said Zeke. "If he knows the Bible and preaches the truth, that's what matters most."

"Well, I don't want a pulpit-thumping man, preaching about sin and hell all the time," argued Jarvis. "Going to church ought to make you feel peaceful and happy about being a Christian, not all worked up and feeling guilty."

"Well, maybe you have something to feel guilty about," said Morris.

"Look who's talking – someone who owes me more than his share in credit."

"I didn't say I was perfect. Besides, I told you that I'd pay up as soon as I sold my harvest and a few beef cattle in the fall."

"That's not for two or three months! How can I run my business on credit? That's stealing. That's what that is!" Jarvis pushed his red face toward Morris.

Zeke pulled on Jarvis's sleeve. "Sit down and act civilized. We'll never accomplish anything if'n you fellows keep arguing."

Stanley Gilmore stood up. He fidgeted with his hat and cleared his throat until everyone calmed down. "I was partial to the preaching of the young preacher, Seymour Thomas. I propose that we ask him to come."

Jarvis Cooper stood up. "I wasn't here the Sunday that he spoke, but from all I heard, he's still a young whippersnapper. What does he know about running a church?"

Zeke stood up, too. "Well, if you didn't hear'm speak then you don't know what you're talking about!"

"I heard enough to know that I don't want him bringing any modern heretic ideas to our town."

"You probably wouldn't like anyone new coming in our town. Well, it's not your town, Jarvis Cooper. It belongs to all of us!"

By this time, a few others joined in the discussion. Phoebe looked up from her book. She couldn't figure out how they could hear what the others were saying.

Morris thumped his hand on the pulpit. "Men! Men! Calm down! This isn't accomplishing anything."

Zeke and Jarvis sat down. Stanley waited patiently for what Morris might say about his suggestion. "I heard Seymour Thomas's sermon, and I liked it. He preached right from the Bible. He spoke the truth without fear of what people might think of his words. He has gumption to speak the truth of God. I say we ask him to come." He looked at the various faces. "What about some of you other ones? What do you think?"

There were some "amens" and grunts, but no one spoke up. Stanley Gilmore leaned back in his seat and looked at the blotch of paint on the toes of his boot. He glanced up every once in a while as if he hoped someone would agree with him.

Jarvis stood up again. "What about his age? He's a boy! Did anyone ask about his education or experience?"

Morris held his hand out to stifle Jarvis's ranting. "Yes, he attended Yale for four years, graduating with excellent grades. He assisted in an assembly in Boston for a year. This will be his first congregation, but a person's got to start somewhere."

Jarvis shook his head and threw his hands up in disgust. "I don't care. If you men want this greenhorn to practice his preaching on you and your families, go ahead and invite him into our peaceful little community."

Zeke mumbled, "Peaceful?"

Stanley chuckled, then covered his mouth and coughed.

Morris cleared his throat and stood up straight. "Alright, do we have a proposal?"

Zeke stood up. "I propose that we vote to have Seymour Thomas to be our new minister."

"Good. Do we have a second?"

Mark Phillips raised his hand. "I second it."

"Thank you. Let's vote. All those in favor raise your right hand and say, 'Aye'."

A chorus of "ayes" sounded around the room, with hands waved in solemn affirmation—hands rough from raking hay, hands stained with news ink, and hands blotched with paint.

"Any 'nays'?"

A loud "nay" bellowed from the direction of Jarvis.

Morris looked at him and scowled. "The 'ayes' take the vote. We will ask Seymour Thomas to be our new minister."

Distracted from the ship-wrecked Robinsons, Phoebe wondered which young minister was Seymour Thomas. There had been so many visiting preachers, it was hard for her to remember.

Zeke stood up and faced Morris, then looked around at the others. "Fellers, now that we have a minister, he and his wife-"

"Wife?" Jarvis jumped to his feet. "No one said he had a family! I suppose he has a whole brood of children, too."

Morris pounded the pulpit with his fist. "Jarvis Cooper, will you please control yourself?" Jarvis closed his mouth and crossed his arms across his chest. "Pastor Seymour Thomas has a wife. We haven't met her yet, but they were married only three months ago, so I can quite assure you that they don't have any children yet."

Coughs and muffled snickers ran up and down the benches.

Morris turned to Zeke. "You were going to say something?"

"Yes, I was saying, now that we have a preacher, he and his wife will need a place to live. I suggest we build them a proper parsonage on the land next to the church building. I'm not a good craftsman, but I can swing a hammer, if someone shows me where."

Jeb Simmons, a quiet man who lived on the other side of the hill spoke up. "I've built a few houses. I know how to do it. If we can round up the materials, I can organize the work."

Another man spoke up. "I've got timber on my land to use for lumber. If we all give, we can have a parsonage built before winter."

Zeke smiled and gave a little jig where he stood. He turned toward Morris Reynolds. "So? Shall we do it?"

Another chorus of "ayes" echoed in the rafters. Jarvis was still slouching in his seat with his arms crossed.

Seymour Thomas and his wife would be coming on the tenth of October. Over the next few months, someone was working on the new parsonage every evening. The new building was two stories tall, with a nice big sitting room to entertain company and a modern kitchen with an iron cook-stove and sink pump. Upstairs had two big bed chambers. They added a shed and a small barn to house a carriage and a couple of horses.

Stanley donated paint from his business and gave up other jobs to finish it before the big day. The ladies sewed curtains and made braided rugs for the sitting room and bed chambers. They stocked the shelves with dishes, and found sofas and chairs and beds that they could spare for the new minister. Soon the whole place was finished. Someone even planted some flowers near the front steps.

~ # ~

Meanwhile, after the harvest, fall classes had begun. The schoolhouse sat a half mile down the Troy Road, going north out of town. Miss Edgecomb was barely twenty years old, but she was very capable of handling a class room. She taught all the students through the eighth grade. There were fourteen students this year.

This was Phoebe's sixth year. Most of the students were quite young – only Scott Peterson and Delly were in Phoebe's class. On the first day of school, Delly glared at her for a moment and then promptly chose a seat on the other side of the aisle. Phoebe shared a desk with Priscilla, who was only in the fourth grade.

Phoebe promised the Gilmores that she would walk Matthew to and from school each day. He was in the primary grade and was so excited he was as wiggly as a fish on a hook.

After school, Phoebe plopped her books on the kitchen table. "I'm home, Maseppa."

No one answered. She opened the back kitchen door. Maseppa was gathering some apples from the old crooked tree. Phoebe wandered over and sat on the swing. Maseppa put another apple in her basket. "How was school?"

Phoebe drifted back and forth. "It was fine. I'd like it better if I could spend the whole time reading books, especially those about faraway places. I'd be perfectly content if I never had to do arithmetic, especially geometry. I can never remember the formulas for the circumference of a circle or the area of a triangle."

"I do not know about geometry, but it is good for you to go to school. I know you can learn it." Maseppa propped the basket on her hip. "I will need you to help me cook supper."

"Yes, Maseppa. I'll be in soon."

Dry leaves crackled under Maseppa's feet as she walked back to the house. Phoebe drifted back and forth. *Maseppa never went to school, and she knows a lot of things.* After the freedom of summer, it was hard to get back into the routine of being confined to a classroom every day. In two more years, she would be done, unless she went to secondary school, but that was a long ways away. She didn't want to think about growing up yet.

The sun was warm, but a cool breeze foretold of the chilly days to come. Her big toe made a groove in the dirt . . . back . . . forth . . . back . . . forth.

A yowling, flying furry ball flew from the door of the log cabin. He scrabbled at the air and rolled a few times before disappearing into the brush. Phoebe jumped up and saw Uncle Pete's big body filling the door of his cabin. "That cat has got to stay out of my stuff! It ate my sausage and licked his tongue through my butter. He's got it in fer me."

"Uncle Pete, he's just a cat. He doesn't know it's wrong."

"Well, he'll be the death o' me. I don't know if I could stand 'nother winter holed up inside with a cat."

Phoebe knew it wasn't poor little Butterball's mischief that had gotten Uncle Pete all stirred up. It was having someone else make sure he ate right and washed his clothes every few months and cut his hair and beard occasionally. Maseppa took good care of him, but he didn't like her fussing over him. Phoebe crawled into the underbrush. "Here, kitty, kitty, kitty. You're the most getting-into-trouble cat I've ever seen."

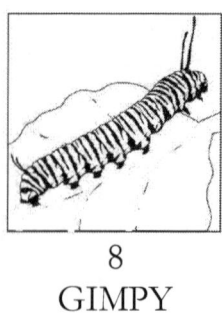

8
GIMPY

On a chilly September morning, Phoebe waited for Matthew to catch up as they hurried to school. As they passed the place where they picked strawberries last summer, Phoebe noticed some milkweed plants. She couldn't wait until the pods dried and cracked open and the fluffy seeds floated away on the breeze like snowflakes. She noticed some yellow and black striped caterpillars on the plants and picked up one. She let him hump up her arm. Matthew found one too.

"Ewww… he tickles!" Matthew moved it from his arm back down to his palm where it wasn't so ticklish.

"Don't you love their yellow and blacked striped pajamas?" Phoebe held hers up to eye level. "I think I will name you Gimpy."

"Gimpy? That's a funny name."

"He's a funny caterpillar. Besides, I think something's wrong with one of his feet. He wobbles when he crawls, like one isn't working right."

Matthew put his caterpillar back on a milkweed plant. Phoebe put hers in her pocket and picked a few leaves and added them to her pocket too. "You're not going to keep him, are you?" Matthew asked.

"Why not? Besides, I think he needs me."

Matthew shook his head. "Come on. I want to play ball before school starts."

Phoebe added a few more leaves and followed him, trying to rub the white sticky sap from her fingers.

"You're silly. How are you going to keep him at school?"

"He'll be fine in my pocket. He's all curled up in a ball. He'll probably stay that way all day."

Miss Edgecomb was shooing the last of the boys into the building when they reached the school. "Come, Matthew and Phoebe. Hurry up!" They quickly hung up their coats and found their places. Phoebe peeked at Gimpy, still curled up in a ball.

After the morning routine of pledge to the flag, Bible reading, and prayer, Miss Edgecomb passed out some papers. *The history test! I forgot all about it!* There were three instructions on the chalkboard.

1. List three explorers - their country, where they traveled, and what land they discovered.
2. Describe the Plymouth Plantation. Name two of its leaders. Tell of its struggles.
3. Describe George Washington. Write five points of his creed.

Phoebe groaned. She had paid attention in class, but she should have studied last night instead of reading about the pirates in *Swiss Family Robinson*. She hunched over her paper and began writing. The first class was standing near Miss Edgecomb's desk reciting their spelling lesson, making it hard to concentrate.

Scott and Delly brought their papers to Miss Edgecomb. Phoebe glanced up, but kept writing. She closed her eyes and tried to remember Washington's Rules of Conduct.

When a man does all that he can, though it succeeds

not well, blame him not.
Be not forward, but friendly and courteous.
Let your recreations be manful, not sinful.
Speak not evil of the absent, for it is unjust.

She only needed one more. She looked out the window. A robin tugged at a worm. That made her think of Gimpy. She peeked in her pocket and could see him nibbling the leaves. She closed her eyes to think of one more rule.

When you speak of God or His attributes, let it be seriously, in reverence.
Undertake not what you cannot perform, but be careful to keep your promise.

She skimmed over the page to see if she'd forgotten anything and took her paper up to the desk. While she waited for the other classes to finish, she took out a book to read. Suddenly Priscilla jumped up onto her desk and pointed down. "EWWW! There's a worm on the floor!"

Phoebe looked into her pocket... nothing... not even any leaves! Scott scrambled beneath the desk. He picked up the caterpillar by two fingers and dangled it in front of Priscilla. She pulled up her hands in front of her, as if she needed to push some danger away.

"Don't hurt him! He's mine!" Phoebe snatched the caterpillar from Scott and rubbed her finger over Gimpy's striped skin to see if he was fine. She carefully slipped him back into her pocket.

Miss Edgecomb helped Priscilla down from the desk. "Phoebe, may I see that caterpillar? I think it may be a monarch. Where did you find it?"

Phoebe placed the yellow and black ball in Miss Edgecomb's palm. "I found him on some milkweed plants on Snyders Hill. I think something's wrong with his foot. He crawls funny, so I named him Gimpy."

All the children giggled.

Miss Edgecomb set the caterpillar on her desk and found "Monarch" in her John Good's *Study of Nature*. She set the open book on the front desk and everyone gathered around. "It says here that it only eats milkweed. It makes its chrysalis in September, and in about two weeks, it will hatch into a butterfly. Monarch butterflies migrate thousands of miles to warmer climates for the winter."

Miss Edgecomb looked at Phoebe. "We could put your caterpillar in something and let it makes its chrysalis. It would be very interesting to observe it hatch and fly away. Do you mind if we share the experience with you?"

Phoebe looked down at Gimpy crawling on her arm. "Sure! That would be fun. What are we going to put him in?"

Everyone had a suggestion.

"A bucket?"

"A basket?"

"A crate?"

Miss Edgecomb's face lit up. "There's an old window pane behind the schoolhouse, with one broken corner. We could patch that with a piece of paper. If we put the whole thing over a basket, we could observe him without him crawling away." She looked at the caterpillar again. "What did you say you named him?"

"Gimpy, because he has a hurt leg."

Matthew raised his hand. "Should we get more milkweed leaves?"

"Yes, Matthew. Would you like to do that?"

With the big basket set on the top shelf near the window and the broken pane on top, they had a nice home for Gimpy. Matthew returned with a few milkweed stalks. Gimpy started munching right away.

Everyone returned to their desks and books. All was quiet as they worked out their arithmetic on slates or paper or the blackboard for those who needed help.

Priscilla raised her hand. "Miss Edgecomb? May I sit somewhere else? I can't think with that worm right next to me."

"Yes, Priscilla. Why don't you change places with Phoebe. I'm sure she'd rather be near her caterpillar anyway."

Phoebe peered in the basket to see Gimpy. He was happily munching away on his leaves.

Every day when they returned to school, Phoebe had more milk weed leaves for Gimpy. One morning, he didn't need them anymore. He had attached himself to the top of his basket cage and made a smooth green chrysalis with a line of gold around it. Phoebe thought it looked very elegant.

She didn't want to leave the basket there on Friday, for fear Gimpy would emerge over the weekend. Miss Edgecomb didn't think he would, since it had only been three days. Phoebe whispered, "Wait for me to come back, Gimpy."

On Monday, Phoebe hurried to school. Matthew had a hard time keeping up with her. She ran right into the school room without putting her things away first. She wanted to be sure Gimpy hadn't emerged from his chrysalis yet. She peered into the basket. *Whew! He was still in his little green pod.*

Sometimes as she studied her geography or read an interesting book, she forgot about Gimpy. It was only when history got boring or arithmetic got hard that she wished he would wake up.

When Friday came around again, he had been in his chrysalis for ten days. Phoebe worried that he'd come out while she was gone. "Wait for me, Gimpy. Don't come out yet."

On the next Monday, she looked in the basket. The color of the chrysalis seemed different today. It looked more of a milky white. "Miss Edgecomb, does Gimpy's chrysalis look different to you?"

Everyone crowded around.

"Yes," said Miss Edgecomb. "I think things are going to happen today."

Phoebe could hardly concentrate on her school work. She could see the shell becoming more and more transparent, with darker colors showing through. Gimpy was moving.

She gasped. "He's coming out!"

She could hardly move with everyone crowding close and trying to see. As they watched, Gimpy's nose slid through a crack in the bottom. Slowly...slowly he pushed through. His belly was really fat and his wings were folded all around it. He hung from the chrysalis with his tiny feet. He seemed to be resting.

Everyone talked at once. "That was spectacular!" "What a show!"

Miss Edgecomb urged everyone back to their seats. "It may take a while for it to fly. Let's get back to work."

But Phoebe couldn't work. "Hello, Gimpy. You've grown up," she whispered. "I'm going to miss you. You won't be gimpy anymore. You'll be able to fly." Priscilla looked at her, rolled her eyes, and shook her head.

Phoebe watched him stretch his orange and black wings wider and wider. He waved them around and walked over to the edge of the basket where a breeze blew in from the window that was open a little bit. As the end of the school day neared, Phoebe raised her hand. "Miss Edgecomb, may we take Gimpy outside to fly away? I think he's ready."

Everyone crowded around again. "Ooohh! Look at him!" "He's beautiful!"

With the teacher's consent, Phoebe carried the basket outside. She lifted the glass and put her hand near Gimpy. He crawled on to her finger. His little feet felt like the tickle of pine needles.

He waved his wings up and down and walked from one finger to the other. Finally, he caught the breeze and circled above their heads. Phoebe held up her hand and he settled on it again. She brought him down before her face. He seemed to be looking at her and saying "Thank you for all the love." Then with another gust, he took off higher and higher until they couldn't see him anymore.

Some of the children were jumping up and down and waving. "Good bye, Gimpy! Have a nice trip."

Phoebe didn't wave or shout. She wiped a tear from her eye. "Come on, Matthew. It's time to walk home."

9
THE PARSON'S WIFE

Finally, October tenth arrived. It was a Friday, and Miss Edgecomb let the students assist the new parson and his wife move into their new house.

The boys offered to carry boxes and trunks, showing off their muscles to the girls. The girls, not wanting to miss out, found smaller items to carry – lamps, baskets, and coverlets. Each gazed around at the big rooms and new appliances. For, until now, only those working on the building had been allowed inside.

Phoebe froze at the doorsill with a stack of books in her hand. Her mouth formed an O as she stared at the beautiful woman directing people where to put things. The woman was small with honey-colored hair piled on top of her head. Her skin looked like white rose petals, with a hint of pink on her cheeks. When she saw Phoebe, she crinkled up her nose and eyes into a smile. She motioned for her to put the books in the sitting room.

Phoebe glanced through the titles as she set the books in the corner of the room. They must have belonged to Parson Thomas – *Doctrines of the Church*, *Old Testament Times*, and *Parables of Jesus*.

Phoebe scooted back and forth with blankets, baskets, and more books through the maze of crates, sometimes feeling as clumsy as a moose. By the end of the day, Parson Seymour Thomas and his young bride, Genevieve, were settled in the new parsonage. Already it looked more like home than a house, with flowers planted along the walkway and curtains in the windows, provided by the women in the congregation. Genevieve Thomas's soft voice thanked everyone for helping. Phoebe didn't want to go yet. She hoped the parson's wife would notice her, and she did.

"Thank you for helping." She brushed a loose curl out of Phoebe's eyes. "What beautiful hair! What's your name?"

Phoebe never heard anyone call her hair beautiful before. She tugged on the rebellious curl dangling in her face. It didn't look any different to her. "My name is Phoebe Johanson."

"What a pretty name! I hope we can be good friends, Phoebe Johanson."

The town was abuzz with news of the new parson and his wife. Of course, the women of the village had their opinions of the parson's wife. Some thought her to be too timid to lead a Ladies' Aid Society, and others thought her clothes too modern to be appropriate for a parson's wife. They even thought her name and voice sounded too foreign.

Phoebe thought her to be very nice and elegant. To her, Missus Thomas was like an angel. She was so beautiful with her hair drawn up into a loose bun beneath a ruffled bonnet. She wore a long dress with a bustle and ribbons and lots of pearl buttons on the tight sleeves. Sometimes, she even wore white gloves and carried a parasol.

Phoebe loved going to church, mostly because Missus Thomas taught a children's class after the singing part of the Sunday services. There were six of them in the class: Phoebe, Sarah and Billy Phillips, Priscilla Peterson, Matthew Gilmore, and sometimes Scott Peterson, but he lived on the back side of Snyders Hill and didn't come too often. Delly Kittle and her brothers would probably be in their class too – if they came. None of the Kittles ever came to church.

The children sat around the comfortable sitting room on the sofa and armchairs. Sometimes Phoebe had a hard time paying attention because she was examining a painting on the wall or a bookcase near the writing desk.

After the children's class, Phoebe wriggled through the crowd of people that was pouring out of the church. "Maseppa, Missus Thomas has invited me to spend the afternoon with them. May I?"

Maseppa looked into Phoebe's excited face that was almost level with her own now. "Yes," she answered. "Be polite and say 'thank you' and come home before it gets dark. Yes?"

"Yes, Maseppa!" Phoebe gave her a hug and bounced away.

Phoebe stood near the minister and his wife in the vestry while they greeted the departing church members. Some of them spoke to her, and she curtsied politely. For a few minutes, she pretended that she was the parson's daughter, but then felt guilty about having such selfish thoughts.

When everyone had left, Phoebe and Missus Thomas strolled across the church lawn to their house, while the parson closed up the church building for the week.

Phoebe wandered about the parsonage examining little touches of beauty here and there. There were vases of flowers sitting on crocheted doilies, embroidered chair covers, and fancy stitched Bible verses on the walls. One read,

O GIVE THANKS
UNTO THE LORD

Phoebe fingered a pink afghan on the back of the sofa. "Did you make this?"

"Yes, I just finished last week. Do you know how to knit or crochet or embroider?"

"I learned to knit when I was little, but I don't know how to do any type of needlework."

"Oh, that's too bad. Would you like to learn? We could have our own sewing time. I'll teach you how."

"You'd teach me how to do fancy stitchery, Missus Thomas? Could I come over here every week?" Phoebe couldn't believe she just said that. *What am I saying? I don't want to be a fancy lady, pulling my skirts away from the mud and squealing at mice and worms.*

"That would be perfect. I hope we can be good friends."

When Missus Thomas served dinner, Phoebe felt like she was the Queen of England. The table was set with flowered plates and silver utensils. There was chicken and stuffing, plus mashed potatoes and buttery carrots. For dessert, a vanilla custard waited on the sideboard.

Parson Thomas made Phoebe laugh with silly jokes and asked her to tell them about herself. She told them about Gimpy and sneaking Butterball home under her apron, but her life seemed so ordinary compared to theirs.

Missus Thomas wore a sparkly ring on her finger next to her wedding band. When Phoebe looked at it closely, she could see that it was a pale blue stone set between two diamonds. The blue matched Missus Thomas's eyes. Phoebe thought it quite exquisite.

Although Phoebe would have liked to have stayed longer, she excused herself before the afternoon shadows lengthened. Missus Thomas promised to have her back again to start their needlework lessons. Phoebe felt like skipping all the way home, but thought that an elegant lady like Missus Thomas would never skip like a silly girl – especially on a Sunday.

Phoebe chattered like a red squirrel when she got home, telling Maseppa about her visit at the parsonage. "The plates were made of china and we had mashed potatoes with nary a lump and she is going to teach me how to do fancy stitchery and - "

"That is good. Now go change out of your Sunday clothes."

Alone in her room, Phoebe looked at her old clothes. They were short and plain. She peered at herself in the looking glass. Her face was tanned and sprinkled with freckles. She knew that was because she hated wearing her bonnet. Maybe if she started wearing it now, she might have soft white skin like Missus Thomas's. She looked at her hands, rough and dirty from grubbing about in the barn and woods. She wished she had white gloves to cover them. Her fingernails were chewed right down to nubs. Her hair lay in braids over her shoulders. She undid her braids and brushed out the tangles. She pulled it up and turned this way and that to see how she'd look with in a bun. She thought it made her look much older.

Maseppa stood in the doorway. Phoebe saw her in the mirror and jumped around, letting her hair fall down around her shoulders. "I was seeing if I could wear it like Missus Thomas."

"You are not Missus Thomas. You are Phoebe, still *ikweksa* . . . a little girl."

"I'm not so little anymore. I'm almost thirteen years old! I want to dress like a bigger girl. Could we get some fabric to make some new dresses?"

"I can make —"

"No! I want fancy dresses, with lace and ruffles and ribbons."

"You do not need fancy dresses for school and working in the barn."

"Well, could I have at least one for church?"

"I will think about it. It is time to make supper. *Ondàs*."

"Yes, Maseppa. I will be down soon."

Phoebe looked at Maseppa as she turned to go back downstairs. Her long black hair was pulled back into one braid down her back. She wore a simple brown dress with an apron and usually walked barefoot except when she went to town. Even then, she wore her leather moccasins.

Phoebe loved Maseppa, but she didn't want to look like her. She wanted to look like Missus Thomas. She pulled her hair up again and stared into the looking glass. She wove small braids on each side of her face and pulled them together in back. The rest of her hair hung in wavy curls down her back to her waist. She thought it made her look a little more mature. Maybe she could wear it like this until she was thirteen.

"WoooEee!" whistled Zeke when Phoebe came into the kitchen to help prepare supper. "Who is this beautiful young lady?"

"Zeke, it's me!"

"Me? Who's me?"

"I want to look older. When I'm thirteen, I'm going to wear my hair up like Missus Thomas."

"So now you want to look older. It wasn't too long ago that told me that you wished you'd never grow up. I'll never figure you out." Zeke threw up his hands in mock surrender.

Zeke opened his paper and casually said, "You do look much older with your hair like that. You're growing into a beautiful young lady."

Phoebe blushed and gave a little curtsy. "Why, thank you, sir!"

10
FRENCH CLASSES

"I'll race you!" Matthew took off before Phoebe could react.

"Hey, that's not fair!"

They huffed up the steps into the school, puffing and laughing. Everyone was bustling into the entry, hanging their wraps, and putting their lunch pails on the shelf.

Priscilla was already there and gave Phoebe the type of smile that meant she had a secret. Miss Edgecomb rang the bell and the children who were still dilly-dallying outside hurried in. Priscilla pulled Phoebe's head close so she could whisper in her ear. "The preacher's wife is coming here."

"Here – at school?"

"Yes, I heard Miss Edgecomb tell Missus Peterson yesterday."

"I wonder - "

Just then everyone crowded into the classroom. Phoebe noticed Missus Thomas sitting in the back. She gave her a quick smile and made her way to her seat. Everyone stood for the pledge to the flag, the Bible reading, and morning prayer. Instead of starting with their usual classes of arithmetic and penmanship, Miss Edgecomb stood before the class.

"Class, today we have a special treat." She looked to the back of the room. "Missus Thomas, our new minister's wife grew up in France." Everyone turned around in their seats. "She has agreed to come to our school and teach us French each week."

Everyone gasped.

Missus Thomas walked to the front of the room, all the children turned like folding back a blanket. She took little steps and smiled at different ones as she met their gaze. She faced them and smiled again. "Bonjour! That means "hello." Can you say it? Repetez, repeat after me – bonjour!"

The class mumbled, "Boojoor."

"Très bien! Repetez – Booooonjooour."

"Bojooor."

"C'est bon."

Missus Thomas walked over to Phoebe and took her hand. "Bonjour, Phoebe. Now you say it."

"Bojoor" *I sound silly – certainly not like a French lady.*

"In France, you would call me Madame Thomas." It sounded like "mah-dahm toe-mah." She stretched her arms to include everyone. "Can you say that? Maaadamme Thooomas"

"Maaa damme Thooo maaas."

Missus Thomas clapped her small hands. "Très bien!" She wrote 'MADAME THOMAS on the chalkboard. Then she pointed to herself. "Je m'appelle Madame Thomas. Repetez – Je m'appelle."

The voices were a bit louder with more confidence. "Je ma pelle."

"Oui! Repetez – Je m'appelle"

"Je m'appelle."

She walked over to Matthew and pointed to him. " Repetez - Je m'appelle Mattieu." It sounded like "mat yuh."

Matthew ducked his head, and everyone giggled.

"Would everyone like to know their French names?"

A chorus of cheers filled the room.

"I don't know all of you, so you will have to tell me your names. Sometimes there is not a French name that matches, but I will give you one for our class." Madame Thomas walked around the room, touching each child on the head, giving them French names as they told her their English names. "Philippe, Marie, Pierre . . ." When she got to the back of the room, she tapped Delly on the head.

"Adeline"

"Ahhh…c'est une belle nom francaise! You have a beautiful French name, Adeline!" She pronounced it "ah – dell – een."

Delly blushed and smiled. She pushed her hair behind her ear and sat up straighter. "Je m'appelle Adeline."

"Oui! Très bien!"

Phoebe had never seen Delly smile before. It made her look pretty. Phoebe caught her eye and smiled, too. Delly's smile disappeared. She scowled at Phoebe and turned her face away.

Phoebe felt like Delly had punched her in the heart. *Why does she dislike me so much? What have I done to offend her so?*

After everyone had a chance to say their name, Madame Thomas taught them to count to ten in French. The words felt clumsy in Phoebe's mouth. "Uh, doo, twah, cot, sank, sees, set, weet, noof, dees."

When Missus Thomas announced that she had to leave, everyone groaned, but she promised to be back every Friday. Phoebe hoped French got easier. The words sounded ugly when she said them, but like music when spoken by Missus Thomas.

11
NEEDLEWORK

The next time Phoebe visited the parsonage, Missus Thomas brought out a box covered with pink silk and white satin ribbons. When she opened the lid, Phoebe peered down into a rainbow of threads rolled into little shanks, like yarn, only smaller. Phoebe had never seen so many variations of greens, reds, pinks, and yellows.

Missus Thomas unfolded a piece of cloth with stitchery all over it. "I made this when I was around twelve years old." Phoebe could see birds and flowers and hearts around the edges. The alphabet ran across six rows, then the words, "A wise daughter will heed the words of her father." At the bottom, she saw the name *GENEVIEVE FELICIA DAILY* and the year, *1823*.

"You made all of this when you were my age?"

"Oh, yes . . . my mother started me stitching when I was about six years old. I didn't keep any of those, but this one hung in my bedroom for a long time."

"I like these flowers," said Phoebe. "These here, with the black dots in the centers."

"Yes, those are poppies with French knots in the centers. I can teach you how to make them." She pulled out a small book. "Here are some other stitches and patterns. What do you think you would like to do?"

Phoebe flipped through the pages. There were daisies and ferns, grapes and apples, hearts and stars. There were zig-zags and cross-stitches and basket weaves. There were pages of various styles of letters. She liked the script ones, but they looked a little harder with all the curves and loops.

Missus Thomas helped her pick out several beginner patterns. She chose threads of strawberry red, summer blue, leaf green, and butter yellow. They marked off a piece of linen into lines and squares.

"I think for today, I'll show you how to make several different stitches. We'll start your sampler when you're ready."

"I like this picture of a house. Is it too hard?" asked Phoebe.

"Not too difficult. I think you could do it after you learn a few basic stitches."

"Is there a proverb that talks about a home? I think "home" is one of the prettiest words. Don't you think so?"

"I'm sure we could find a piece of poem that would be fitting."

So, for the stretch of an hour, Phoebe perched on the edge of the footstool, huddled over a circle of cloth and practiced her Lazy-Daisy stitch, and the back stitch, and the cross stitch.

Phoebe stretched her arm out to pull the thread all the way through the cloth. "Oh, no! It came out of the needle." Missus Thomas patiently re-threaded the needle and handed it back to Phoebe.

Parson Thomas came in the room and relaxed next to his wife on the sofa. He closed his eyes. It looked like he might be catching a nap, but he must have been only resting because after a few minutes, he asked (without opening his eyes) "Phoebe, I haven't seen your Uncle Pete in a few weeks. Is he still around?"

Phoebe pulled her needle, carefully this time, so as not to lose her thread again. "He went out West."

"Is that so?" He sat up, interested. "What brought that about?"

Phoebe stopped sewing for a minute to answer. "Uncle Pete can't abide sitting still. Zeke says he's got a wandering spirit. Uncle Pete's got to be going and seeing new places. He heard tell of a wagon train going West that needed a guide and someone who knew some Indian."

"Uncle Pete knows how to speak Indian?"

"He used to trap furs across Canada, a long time ago. That's when he found Maseppa's tribe. But he got his foot caught in a trap, and it hurts him mighty fierce sometimes."

"Excuse me for interrupting," he said, "but what's this about Maseppa's tribe?"

Phoebe sighed. She wasn't really sure about this part of the story because no one talked about it much. "I'm not rightly sure, but near as I can understand, Uncle Pete married Maseppa's mother and went off trapping again. When he came back, the tribe had moved and he didn't know where they were. He didn't know about Maseppa being born either. Then after a lot more years, he found them again."

"Oh, so Uncle Pete is Maseppa's father?"

"Yes, he's not really anyone's uncle. When he found them, Maseppa's mother was very sick and died. He didn't know how to take care of Maseppa, so he brought her to my father and mother's house before I was born. My father was Uncle Pete's cousin."

"Aha! Now the story is coming together. What happened to your parents?"

"My parents?" She sighed again and pushed the needle down through a leaf.

"If it's too hard to talk about, that's fine."

"No, it's all right. I wish I could tell you more, but I don't know too much. When I was very little, Maseppa lived with us. My father was killed by a tree falling on him. My mother tried to get him out, and she died when her baby came too soon. So Maseppa took care of me."

Missus Thomas gasped and said, "That's so sad."

"I don't remember the baby. We have a painting of my parents, so I know what they looked like, but we don't have a picture of the baby. I do remember jumping into Papa's arms when he came home, and I remember Mama singing while she made bread." She made a few more stitches without talking. "I wish I could remember them more."

Missus Thomas whispered, "I'm sorry, Phoebe, but you can be thankful for Maseppa and Zeke."

Phoebe smiled. "Yes, Maseppa has been a good mama to me. We lived in the woods for a long time and she taught me about the animals and plants."

"And Zeke?"

With a giggle, Phoebe brightened. "Zeke found us when our wagon tipped over. It's funny that I remember that, but I don't remember the day or so before that, when my parents died. Anyway, Zeke took us to live with Granny. She's blind, but she is very smart and loving. We lived with her in the winters and traveled around in the summers. She taught me how to read and count and recite verses from the Bible."

"I thought you said she was blind. How did she teach you to read?"

Phoebe snipped the thread with a pair of tiny scissors. "She's blind now, but not when she was younger. I wrote my letters on a clay board, and she felt them with her fingers. She knew the Bible so well, that she knew when I read it right or wrong. She taught me to see people with my heart."

"Is Granny Zeke's mother?"

"Hmmm . . . no, I don't think she's kin to him either. I think his family lives in Boston."

"Ahh . . . This gets more interesting all the time. So, Granny was a matchmaker?" He winked at her.

Phoebe looked up with a puzzled frown, and Missus Thomas smiled. "Seymour, stop that!"

He asked, "Zeke thought Maseppa was pretty special, huh?"

"She is special," said Phoebe. "Zeke is special, too. He made a travel wagon for us from his old peddler wagon. It had a bunk for me, with a window that I could look at the stars with, and a little stove. We still have it behind the barn, but it's not much good anymore. Zeke found Uncle Pete and paid the taxes on our house and then he married Maseppa so we could live here."

"I've seen the way he looks at her. He loves her, and he'd do anything for her, just like a good husband should, right, Dear?" He settled back in the seat and closed his eyes with a smile.

"Seymour, you're embarrassing me." His wife said with a smirk.

Phoebe smiled. She hadn't thought of Zeke loving Maseppa, but she supposed he did. He never hugged her or kissed her, at least when she was around, but Maseppa wasn't one to hug and kiss much anyway. She thought Zeke had other ways of showing that he loved her.

Parson Thomas lit the parlor lamps with pink roses painted on their bases of milky white glass. Phoebe looked at the windows with a start. "Oh my! It's getting dark already. I best be on my way 'fore Maseppa and Zeke wonder about me."

"Do you want me to drive you home?"

"No, thank you. I know my way home. I'll even take a short cut over the hill. Maseppa and I go that way lots of times."

"You be careful," warned Missus Thomas as she helped Phoebe with her coat. "Are you sure you don't want Seymour to take you?"

Phoebe smiled. It sounded funny for anyone to call Parson Thomas by his first name. "I'll be fine. Don't worry about me."

Beyond the warm lights from the village windows, the evening seemed darker than usual. Phoebe decided not to take the path over the hill after all. She could walk much faster on the road. The western sky still had a pinkish glow behind her, but angry clouds crowded together above the blackened silhouettes of the treetops.

The air was quiet – too quiet. She couldn't even hear any birds. Phoebe wrapped her cloak tightly around herself. The pine woods seemed darker than ever. Even with no wind, the needles seemed to whisper softly. Phoebe walked a bit faster. Something rustled through the dry leaves. Then silence. Phoebe stopped. She stared into the gloom. Were those eyes peering back at her? An owl hooted, and the glowing eyes disappeared. Phoebe didn't look for them. She ran.

She ran until she could hardly breathe. She felt as though something would surely catch her if she stopped. She kept running around the bend of the road. *There's the candle in the window.* She sprinted up the tree-lined lane, up the steps to the kitchen porch and safety of home.

When she burst into the kitchen, Maseppa and Zeke turned, their faces filled with worry and surprise.

Phoebe laughed. "I'm fine. I was only being chased by my imagination." At least, she hoped it was only her imagination.

12
SKATING

It was a cold winter – a dry winter, with hardly any snow. It seemed colder than usual. Even the trees seemed to shiver as the wind blew through their bare branches. Maseppa had been extra busy selling herbs for sore throats and fevers in the last month or so, and Phoebe was often sent to the attic to fetch some of the dried plants hanging from the rafters. She sometimes lingered to breathe in their spicy, musty aroma.

On a blustery January morning, Missus Reynolds called on them, wanting a cure for a persistent cough. As usual, she had her opinion about the weather too. "If you ask me, there's plenty more ailments, when the winters are bare." Phoebe didn't know how true that might be, but she did know that the wind seemed more fierce without the softness of the snow.

One Friday afternoon, as classes ended, Sarah Phillips came up to Phoebe's desk. "I'm going skating tomorrow. Do you want to come, too?"

"Really? The ice is thick enough?"

"Yes, my father checked it yesterday."

"That sounds like fun! I'll have to bring Matthew. I told Deborah I'd watch him tomorrow."

"Sure, he can play with Billy." Sarah noticed Delly listening to them. "Do you want to come, too, Delly?"

She ducked her head and busied herself with her books. "I can't. I have chores, and my papa won't let us get near the mill pond. He's afraid someone will fall through the ice and drown."

Phoebe sighed as she watched Delly hustle out of the school. Her heart was torn between feeling relieved and feeling sorry for Delly, who seemed as crusty as a piece of old bread.

On the way home, she told Deborah about going skating and offered to take Matthew with her.

"I appreciate that, Phoebe, but be careful."

The next morning, Phoebe rushed through her chores. She fed the chickens, gathered the eggs, and fed Butch and Butterball. She was sweeping the kitchen when Matthew showed up.

"I'm almost done." She ran upstairs to put on her warm clothes.

"Phoebe, hurry up." Matthew hollered up the stairs. "I'm getting really hot!" He was wearing at least three layers of shirts and sweaters, a pair of wool pants, and of course his long woolen underwear beneath it all. He had two pairs of socks on and heavy boots and a long muffler around his neck.

"I'm coming!" She wished she was a boy and could wear pants. She wore her woolen under things with stockings and heavy petticoats. She pulled a sweater over her dress and extra socks over her feet.

Zeke had just brought her some new boots and skates from Boston, and today was the perfect weather for skating. She clunked down the stairs. "Maseppa, I'm going now!"

Maseppa was chopping up some pumpkins. "You will be careful. Yes?"

"Yes, Maseppa."

The sky was the deepest blue, and the air had a bite as sharp as old cheese. It had been below zero degrees for the last week and the ice was as smooth as pudding skin. Sarah and Billy were already gliding around on the mill pond and waved to Phoebe and Matthew. Scott Anderson was there, too – showing off by skating backwards and in figure eights.

Phoebe and Matthew scooted down behind the mill to where the land lay low to the pond. Someone had pulled a log close to the edge for people to sit on while they put on their skates. Phoebe quickly buckled the straps of her skates. She had a little trouble with one buckle and had to fiddle with it a little while to get it unstuck. Her bare fingers got numb in the cold. She was glad to tuck them back into her mittens. Matthew didn't have skates, so he scooted about on his boots.

The boys began playing a game with a rock and long sticks. Matthew was having fun with the boys, so Phoebe figured he'd be fine without her for a while. She and Sarah decided to skate to the far side of the pond, away from the boisterous boys.

Sarah glanced back to see if they were out of ear shot. "I think Scott is sweet on you."

"Me?" Phoebe looked back, and he was watching them. She turned back quickly. "Are you sure?"

"He looks at you all the time at school."

"He's a pest. He's always throwing things at me, like acorns and paper balls."

"Silly! That's just his way of getting you to look at him."

"He's got a big nose."

"Not that big! I think he's cute, especially those brown eyes."

"He never talks to me. He stands there with that dumb smile on his face whenever I ask him a question."

Sarah shook her head. "Oh, he talks! He is only speechless when he's around you. When he comes over to do things with

Billy, they talk all the time about guns and traps and locomotives and steam machines. He's just quiet around girls, especially you."

They skated behind Mister Cooper's store and the other shops. They went past the church, too. The pond was much narrower here, and the edges were darker. Sarah gave a little spin. "It's so smooth down here out of the wind." Sarah glided from one edge to the other. She stopped and then got on her knees. "Look! You can see right through it like glass."

Phoebe could see frozen bubbles in the ice. She could even see leaves on the bottom. They both kneeled on the ice and shaded their eyes. "There's a fish," said Phoebe. "It must be hard being a fish."

As Sarah moved closer to her, the ice gave a pop sound.

"It's not as thick here. We better head back," Sarah suggested.

A pine cone skidded across the ice and stopped near the girls. A rustling sound came from some bushes close by. Sarah whispered, "It's probably Billy and Scott. Let's ignore them."

A war cry pierced the air, and volley of pine cones pelted them. The girls covered their heads with their arms and tried to get away. Phoebe tried to hurry, but her skate caught on a cone and she fell down with a thud. The ice broke around her, plunging her into the icy water.

Phoebe gasped as the frigid water pricked her skin like sharp needles. She sank below the surface. Bubbles foamed around her in the murky depths – or so it felt. It was only about four feet deep, and she soon sprang up with a shriek. She kicked and splashed until she realized that she could stand. She lifted her arms and chin above the broken ice.

"Phoebe!" Sarah tried to help, but the pond cracked each time she took a step.

By now, the boys had tumbled down the bank to the frozen

pond. Scott stretched out a long branch toward her. "Grab this."

Her hands were so cold that it was hard to keep a tight grip. Between the boys pulling and Phoebe kicking, they finally got her to shore. Her hair hung over her face, and her woolen clothes weighed her down. She felt like a fat cow.

Billy said, "I'll go get help."

Sarah, Matthew, and Scott helped Phoebe along the side of the pond. Sometimes she stumbled in the rough grass. Shivering and crying, she tripped over a rock and huddled into a ball, shivering and crying. Her tears felt warm on her cheeks.

"Are you girls all right?" It was Parson Thomas with Billy.

Sarah yelled, "Phoebe fell through the ice!"

"I'll take her to the parsonage to get dry."

He picked up Phoebe, and carried her like a little child. She felt helpless and cold. When he set her down in their warm kitchen, she pushed her stiffening wet hair out of her face to see Missus Thomas's blue eyes wide with worry.

Phoebe closed her eyes. The tears slipped through her frosted lashes. *Missus Thomas must think I'm such a fool. What a mess I am! I'll never be an elegant lady like her.*

But, of course, Missus Thomas found her some dry clothes. She served them all some hot tea and asked about school and such. Soon, Phoebe stopped shivering and felt much better.

"I'll take everyone home," said Parson Thomas. "I don't want you getting chilled again."

At supper that night, Phoebe told Zeke about falling in the ice. Zeke paused mid bite. "Oh my! You younguns be careful on that pond. We don't want anyone drowning."

"Sarah and Billy's father checked it out. The ice is over six inches deep already. When Sarah and I skated up past the school, the ice was so clear we could see the bottom of the pond. I even saw a fish."

"That's closer to where it comes in from the stream and doesn't freeze as thickly. I'd rather you didn't go that far, you hear?"

"Yes, Zeke."

Maseppa gave her some pine tea and looked straight into her eyes. "Do you feel fine, Phoebe? Getting wet in the winter is not good."

"I'm fine, Maseppa."

In the middle of the night, Phoebe dreamed.

It was summer and she was swimming in the mill pond, but she had on all her winter coats and boots on. She splashed and kept sinking down. She could see the others were on the shore but they were getting farther and farther away. The water seemed to be getting cold. She could see the leaves and rocks on the bottom. A fish swam by. Bubbles floated all around her. The water was so cold. Her ears hurt. She tried to holler to those on shore, but she couldn't talk. Scott was there and he just stood there, looking at her and throwing pine cones at her. He wouldn't help. Her ears hurt.

She woke up. Her blankets had fallen on the floor. She was cold and shivering. When she stood up, a sharp pain pierced through her head. Her throat and inside her ears felt like they were burning. She wrapped a blanket around herself and shuffled down the stairs to Zeke and Maseppa's room.

"Maseppa?" She touched her shoulder. "Maseppa?"

Maseppa turned over in bed.

"My ears are hurting mighty fierce."

Maseppa put some bits of garlic in some oil and warmed it

slightly on the stove. When it was warm to the touch, she poured a few drops in each of Phoebe's ears. It felt good. Maseppa stuffed them with cotton gauze.

"May I sleep down here? It's cold upstairs."

Maseppa helped her make a bed on the sofa in the sitting room and stirred up the fire. It hurt Phoebe to lay her head all the way down, so she propped herself up with a few pillows.

"You will be fine now?"

"Yes, Maseppa. Thank you."

When Maseppa went back to bed, Phoebe lay looking at the fire. The dream came back through her mind. *So Scott likes me? He didn't act like it in my dream. Why do boys show that they like a girl by being pests? That's silly.*

The first thing she heard in the morning was Zeke filling the wood box. The sticks of wood rumbled like thunder in the box. She sat up quickly and then grabbed her hurting ears. One cotton ball had fallen out in her sleep. She found it eased the pain if she pressed on her ears. She moaned a bit and tears came to her eyes. She was a big girl and didn't want to cry.

"Still hurtin', huh, Angel?"

She gave a slight nod, but winced at the pain.

"Maseppa's out milking the cow. She'll be back soon."

"I don't think I can go to church today."

"No, you stay right here. You need to get better. I've heard that sometimes ear aches can get so bad that the ear drums burst." He put his hand on her forehead. It felt cool on her skin. "You feel warm." He tucked her in, and she snuggled down on the sofa.

All the noises of the house seemed louder. When Maseppa set

the tin pail in the sink, the clank seemed to be like a church bell in her head. She closed her eyes and held her hands over her ears. It wasn't long before Maseppa returned with more warm garlic oil for her ears and a cup of tea.

"What's in this?" Phoebe puckered after the first sip.

"It will take away the pain and help you sleep."

Zeke made sure they had whatever they needed and left for church. He gave Phoebe a kiss on the forehead and said he'd pray for her.

Phoebe watched Maseppa carding some wool into long roves that would soon be spun into yarn. The soft steady thumps made her sleepy. Maseppa stopped to fetch another stick for the fireplace.

Phoebe took this moment to ask, "Maseppa, how did you know that Zeke liked you?"

Maseppa paused and gave a slight smile. "Zeke is a good man."

"Yes, I know, but when did you first know he liked you?"

Maseppa nodded. "I know Zeke liked me when he gave us the wagon at Granny's house."

"I remember. I thought you were angry with him."

"I did not know what I felt. He was so good to me. I did not know why. I thought I was *madji* – bad luck. I thought I would be bad for him. I did not want him to like me." She wound the thread a few more times. "But I liked him."

Phoebe lay back on her pillows. Butterball curled up next to her and began purring. She closed her eyes and let the steady thumps of the carding paddles carry her off to happy memories and, hopefully, better dreams.

13
MASEPPA'S CALF

On a chilly morning in May, Maseppa began the preparation for a new piece of cloth. It started with winding more thread for the loom. She dragged a winder from the sitting room into the kitchen. Its long turning arms made the room crowded, but she liked being near Zeke while he read the newspaper and drank his morning tea. After assembling the contraption and gathering her skein of wool thread, she paused and looked around the room to be sure nothing needed her attention before starting the tedious job.

Zeke turned a page in the newspaper. "Is Phoebe awake?"

"Yes. She is feeding the animals."

Zeke set down his paper and leaned his chair against the wall. He put his feet on the table, but quickly moved them to a chair when Maseppa scowled. He sipped his tea and watched Maseppa untangle a knot in the wool thread.

The kitchen was quiet with only the soft noises of the whispering fire in the stove and the rhythmic squeak of the thread winder. As Maseppa wound the soft creamy yarn around the spokes, she swayed from one foot to another. *My heart is happy. It feels like sunshine on meadow flowers.*

Zeke had closed his eyes, but Maseppa had a feeling that they weren't really closed – that he was still watching her. Her bare feet glided back and forth as she worked.

"Zeppa, you are beautiful."

She smiled and continued winding the thread. "You are the only one who tells me that."

"Then everyone else is blind." Reaching out, he stood and drew her to himself. She stood before him with her head down and her hands still clutching the yarn. He lifted her chin to look into her eyes. "When I look at you, it's like looking into a deep woodland pool — so mysterious and beautiful."

She turned away. "I do not feel beautiful. I feel different and dirty. I am not pretty with fancy dresses and white skin."

Zeke pulled her close again, swaddling her in his strong arms. He leaned his forehead against the top of her head. "Mmmm . . . your hair smells like a summer wind." He deposited the skein of yarn on the thread winder and positioned her arms on his shoulders. Wrapping his long arms around her waist, he whispered, "Trust me, Zeppa. You are more than all of that. I don't care about fancy dresses or hairstyles or creamy skins. You have a tender heart and hard-working hands. I wouldn't want you to be any different than you are now."

She pulled her arms down with her palms on his chest. He held her closer, and she laid her cheek against him. She could hear his heart beating and closed her eyes—not moving, not speaking, but not resisting. Zeke leaned back slightly and lifted her face again. He kissed her forehead. He kissed each eye and the tip of her nose. Then, with the touch of a pussy willow, he brushed his lips to hers ... He waited ... She responded with a return pressure as soft as a kitten's paw, but he felt it and smiled.

The shed door flew open with a bang. "Molly's having her ca-"Phoebe's mouth froze mid-sentence at the sight of them in each other's arms. Maseppa pulled away quickly and picked up the skein of yarn again. Zeke rubbed his hand over his face and gave Phoebe a silly grin.

"What's this 'bout? Molly? Is she calvin'?" Zeke grabbed his hat and jacket and followed her out to the barn.

Maseppa put away her yarn and looked beyond the closed door in her thoughts. *I do not know this kind of love. I know Phoebe's mama and papa loved each other. I want love like that but I do not know how.*

She followed Zeke and Phoebe to the barn, where she could hear Molly's bellowing. Inside the barn, the noise echoed in the rafters. The horses nickered and paced in their stalls. The chickens skittered around underfoot. Butterball sat on a thick beam, watching with rounded eyes.

Zeke kneeled next to the uncomfortable cow. "It's alright, Molly. We'll help you with this." He examined the position of the calf. "Zeppa, I'm going to need you." He found a strong cord and tied it around the little hooves already emerging.

Maseppa sat close to him in the hay. Phoebe cradled Molly's head and rubbed her forehead and nose. Zeke gave Maseppa the end of the cord. "When she has her next contraction, we need to pull hard. The front legs are stuck."

Molly lifted her head and moaned. "MOOOOO!"

"Pull! Pull! Come on, Molly, push out this baby!"

Inch by inch the little legs showed. It seemed to take hours. Finally, with a horrendous bellow, Molly pushed, Zeke and Maseppa pulled, and a slippery blob fell at their feet. Maseppa rubbed it with a grain sack, while Zeke quickly untied the rope and helped Molly to her feet.

The mother cow licked the wet sack from the spindly calf until it was all soft and clean. She nudged it with her nose. It lifted its hind end up on its back legs, but they wobbled and it fell again. Phoebe giggled.

Zeke laughed. "It's a girl! Thank you, Lord. We could do with a new milker."

They sat on the barn floor on the side of the stall watching

Molly tend her baby. It finally got on all four feet, looking like a sack of grain propped up by some toothpicks. Zeke put his arm around Maseppa. "So, Zeppa? What are you going to name your baby?"

"It is for me? I never gave a name to a cow. I do not know a good name."

"You don't have to name it today. Think about it. I'm sure you'll think of a special one."

The calf stumbled a few steps over to Molly and found her teats, dripping with milk already. It sucked for a few minutes before crumpling again to the floor. Molly licked the light brown hair as the calf fell asleep in the hay.

Phoebe hugged her knees and leaned her chin on top. "Do I have to go to school? I'd rather watch Molly and her baby all day."

"Of course, you need to go to school. She'll be fine. It's best to leave them alone for a while. I'm sure you'll want to tell all your friends about her anyway."

Phoebe jumped to her feet. "I hadn't thought about that!" With a final pat on the head for Molly and the calf, she scurried back to the house. Zeke and Maseppa sat there looking at the tiny creature. Zeke's arm was still around her shoulder; she leaned against him.

Zeke pulled her closer and kissed her forehead. She looked up and he kissed her on the lips, a firm and long kiss that told of all the love in his heart. He smiled and looked in her eyes. "Do I have to go to work? I'd rather stay here and watch you all day."

Maseppa gave him a playful shove and got up. She gathered the dirty straw and grain sack, while Zeke laid more clean straw around the stall. After he closed the barn door, he reached for Maseppa's hand, and they walked back to the house together.

After Zeke and Phoebe were off to their duties, Maseppa resumed winding the yarn on the winder. She was alone with her thoughts. *Is it still the same day?* So much had happened that it seemed to be days later. *My own cow. I never had my own cow or any animal. What will I name my own little cow?*

She put more wood in the stove and pumped water to wash clothes. The sun was shining brightly and there was a slight breeze, the perfect weather for doing the washing. All the while she thought about what she might name the calf. Every once in a while, she peeked in the barn to be sure all was well. As the hair dried, it softened into a creamy tan color. It made her think of churning cream into butter. It also looked like the color of her mother's doeskin tunic. *I have not thought of my mother in a very long time. I am living another life now. I am not afraid. I have Jesus God now. I have a home for Phoebe. I have Zeke.*

With that thought, she smiled. Feeling her face grow warm, she put her palms on her cheeks. All of a sudden she couldn't wait for him to come home tonight. She wanted to make a good supper for him as a wonderful surprise.

Within a few hours, Phoebe was home from school. She thumped her books on the table in the sitting room. "Mmmm ... something smells delicious!" She followed her freckled nose into the kitchen. Maseppa was pulling a golden brown pie from the oven. "Mmmm ... what's it for? Who are you giving it to?"

"It is for us for supper."

"Why? Is it Zeke's birthday or yours? I know mine has already passed." She lifted a lid from a bubbling pot on the stove. "Is this chicken soup? You've been busy today, Maseppa. What's the reason?"

"No reason. I wanted to make a pie and a good supper today."

"How's the baby calf? Is it walking around? I can't wait to see it." She opened the shed door, but not before nibbling on some scraps of pie dough on the table and the curly apple peelings.

"You need to change your clothes before you go in the barn."

Phoebe sighed and closed the shed door. She ran through the house and up the stairs, two steps at a time. In less time that it takes to say "Rumplestilskin," she was back down the stairs and out the door.

Maseppa cleared away the flour and apple skins and cores from the table. She threw them out in the slop pile behind the barn. She noticed that the lilac bush was beginning to blossom and picked a few twigs of them.

She gathered the dry bed sheets from the clothesline and carried them to their room. She tucked the sheets around the feather ticking and gave it a final fluff. The blue and white quilt was one that Granny had given them.

Her heart pounded with a mixture of excitement and anxiety. She slipped off her dirty dress and put on a pale yellow one that made her skin and hair seem darker. She undid her braid and brushed her long hair. She pulled it up on top of her head like the other women, for a moment, then let it fall again and twisted it into her usual thick braid down her back. With one last look at the room, she closed the door.

Maseppa put a white cloth over the table and lit the oil lamp. Immediately, the light filled the room with life and blocked the growing darkness of the evening. The lilacs filled the room with their spring fragrance. She set bowls and spoons around the table. She got some coffee perking and cut some thick slices of bread. She went out into the cold pantry in the shed for some butter and pickles. When everything was on the table, she looked out the window for Zeke.

Phoebe came in the shed door. "Wow! Everything is beautiful, Maseppa! Are you sure it isn't a special day? It sure looks like a party!"

"It will be the time for supper soon. Wash the barn smells from your hands and get ready for supper."

Phoebe looked at Maseppa and cocked her head sideways. "Something is different about you. You sound different. You changed into your church dress. Do you want me to change too?"

"You may change if you wish, but it is not needed. Maybe you could brush your hair. It is a mess and has some straw in it." She picked a piece from Phoebe's braid. "Were you lying in the straw with the calf?"

"She's so cute, Maseppa! I love her soft hair. She let me touch her head and sucked on my finger."

"You go now and get ready."

Maseppa heard Zeke's wagon before she saw it pull into the yard. Her heart pounded, and she smoothed her skirt with her hands. She knew he would be putting Ol' Sam up for the night, giving him some oats and brushing him down. Zeke would take a look at the new calf before coming in the house. She couldn't wait to see him. She poured some coffee in his cup and filled his pipe with tobacco. While she was looking for something else to do to occupy her hands, he opened the door.

As he took off his hat, her heart skipped a beat and her eyes watered. He took a whiff of the savory air and glanced at the table, but his eyes lit up when he saw Maseppa. "WoooEee! You are more beautiful than a daylily!" He crossed the room in two steps and took her hand in his. Bending low, he kissed the back of her hand. "I will return, my Lady, as soon as I clean up a bit."

At the supper table, Phoebe chattered on and on, while Zeke and Maseppa carried on their own conversation with their eyes. Phoebe grabbed a slice of bread and spread a thick coating of butter on it. "Zeke, Maseppa says all this isn't for a birthday or nothing. When is your birthday, Zeke? Mine is April fourth, right?"

Zeke slurped a spoonful of soup. "I haven't done nothin' for my birthday, since I was a youngster. I was born on September twentieth, so today's not my birthday. Zeppa, do you know when you were born?"

She cocked her head and looked from his face to Phoebe's. "I do not know. My mother did not tell me."

Phoebe wiggled on her chair. "You could choose a birthday, Maseppa! What time of year do you like?"

Maseppa looked at Zeke and then around her. "I think I choose the time of summer. It makes me feel happy to walk in the trees and listen to the birds and animals, to find leaves and berries."

Phoebe smiled. "Yes, that is the best time for you, Maseppa. What do you think, Zeke? Is she more a July or August person?"

His eyes twinkled. "I'd say Zeppa is an August person. Do you have a favorite number?"

"Number? I will say three. One for Phoebe, one for Zeke, and one for me. That is three."

"WoooEee!" Zeke waved his napkin over his head. "I declare August third the birthday of Zeppa Ernstein." He lifted her hand to his lips and kissed it.

Phoebe grinned.

Maseppa quietly smiled. "I have thought of a name for the new baby cow. It is the color of my mother's dress. I will call the calf Doeskin. It is good, yes?"

"Perfect! It fits you and the calf, too."

Maseppa brought the apple pie to the table and served it. The rest of the evening was filled with laughter and fiddle music. Soon it was the time to turn down the lamps and bank the fires. Phoebe skedaddled up to her room. Zeke went to the barn to bed the animals down for the night.

Maseppa's heart thumped like a rabbit's hind leg while thinking of Zeke as she waited beneath the sun-scented sheets. *I do not know why I am afraid. No, I am not afraid. I am happy. It is a good feeling.*

Soon she heard him whistling while he washed his hands in the kitchen. His footsteps thudded through the sitting room and down the hall. At the door, he stopped and gazed at her for a moment. Removing his boots and trousers, he slid in beside her and cradled her head in the crook of his arm. "You've been busy today, my love. Now why is today so special? It's not my birthday, nor Phoebe's, nor yours." He kissed her warm lips.

"This is a special day because this is the day I know love."

14
LUCKY THE CHICK

It was Phoebe's chore to gather the eggs every day. She didn't mind. It was a fun game to search in the corners of the hay mow and the grass around the barn for the hens' favorite places.

"Maseppa, did you know that Sissy is brooding under the back step? I think she has at least eight eggs."

"Yes, it is good that we will have more chickens."

"How long does it take?"

"It will be about twenty days, but she has been sitting already for five days. I made lines on the wall of the barn."

Sissy gave a low gravelly caw whenever Phoebe peeked under the step. Phoebe made sure there was plenty of grain and water nearby. When it rained, she draped an old blanket over the edge of the steps to protect the hen and her eggs.

Finally one morning, Phoebe noticed Sissy was very restless. She kept standing up and peeking under her feather skirt. One time when she stood up, Phoebe could see a yellow bit of fuzz. She sat nearby and waited. Once in a while a little head with beady eyes poked out between Sissy's wings.

Soon Sissy couldn't keep them contained any longer. She stepped out into the sunshine. Seven little pom-poms scurried here and there around and between her long skinny legs. Sissy gave a constant low chatter, keeping the babies close to her. She scratched the dirt and pecked. The little chicks ran to her and tasted the dirt. Once, she found a worm. Two chicks tugged on each end and broke it in half. They pecked at the wiggling string, not really sure how to eat it.

When Phoebe knew Sissy was far enough away, she crawled over to the step and peeked into the shadows. A jumble of empty shells was left in the nest. There was one more egg that didn't hatch. Phoebe picked it up. It was already getting cooler. She held it to the bright light of the sun, then shook it gently and held it to her ear. She could hear a tiny peeping. It was still good!

She held it between her hands and thought of how she could keep it warm. She knew the sunshine would be warmer than under the steps. She wrapped it in her skirt and sat on the steps, thinking. Sissy wandered back to her nesting spot. Picking up the broken shells with her beak, she scattered them in the dooryard and cleaned up the nest with a few scratches of her feet. Sometimes a little chick would get in the way and be knocked backwards by his mother's foot.

Sissy cackled to the chicks, and they settled under her wings for a nap. Phoebe gently poked the last egg under Sissy's warm breast feathers.

"Maseppa, will Sissy take care of that last chick? I'm afraid it won't hatch."

"Maybe it will hatch tomorrow."

In the morning, Phoebe leaned over the end of the step to look at the egg. Sissy and her chicks were already out for their morning stroll, finding bugs and worms and bits of grass. She reached in and felt the egg – it was still warm. There was a tiny hole on one side. She could hear a tiny pecking.

She waited and watched. The hole got bigger, and soon a chunk of shell fell out. She could see the little beak.

Maseppa came out of the house. Phoebe lifted her head and whispered, "It's hatching." She leaned over the edge again and resumed her vigil. Maseppa crouched and looked underneath, too.

The little chick seemed tired. Its head leaned against the opening with its beak open and breathing hard.

"You should not touch him now. He needs to do it himself. It will make him strong."

Phoebe felt sorry for him. "Come on, little fella. You can do it."

He seemed to find more energy and tackled the shell again. Finally, it broke into two pieces and he tumbled out. His skinny neck wobbled about. His gangly legs sprawled in different directions. His damp feathers were plastered on his scrawny neck. He lay in a heap, breathing hard.

"Ahhh . . . he's so beautiful! I'm going to name him Lucky."

Maseppa looked at Phoebe. "I would not say he is beautiful right now, but he looks healthy. He will live."

"May I pick him up yet?"

Maseppa looked to see where the mother hen was. Sissy was still on the other side of the barnyard scratching food for the other chicks.

"He's shivering, Maseppa. He's cold."

Maseppa reached her long arm under the step and pulled him out. She let him rest in her lap. As he sat in the sunshine, his feathers dried and began fluffing out. He had a tuft of black on the top of his head. He peeped and tried to move around.

"May I hold him?" Phoebe held out her hand. He was so soft and cuddly. She brushed his downy feathers against her cheek.

"See if the mother hen will take care of him," said Maseppa. "It is better that way."

Phoebe cupped the little chick in her hand and set him close to the ground. Sissy came running to see if she had a treat for them. The little chick huddled on the ground, but Sissy didn't seem to notice him. She continued her scratching and pecking in the dirt. The other chicks ran around and over him. When they wandered to another part of the yard, he followed them peeping the whole way.

"Oh, Maseppa. He's scared. I feel so sorry for Lucky."

"I think he will be fine soon. We will wait to see if he learns to eat with the other chicks."

Phoebe didn't do much that day but sit on the back step and watch Sissy and her chicks wander around the yard. Lucky followed them, peeping the whole time. When Sissy rested, he made his way under her feathers to get warm with the other chicks.

Something else was watching them, too. Butterball ducked his head as he crouched in the grass. His tail switched back and forth. He watched as Sissy stepped and scratched closer and closer. With a flying pounce, he flew into the middle of the chicks. Sissy squawked and attacked the cat with her sharp claws. Feathers and fur, meows and cackles filled the air. Phoebe ran to rescue the chickens.

"Noooo! Stop it, Butterball!" She reached into the fight and grabbed the cat and tossed him aside. "Don't attack our chickens!" He ran off toward the barn, his fur all ruffled.

Sissy called her chicks and scuttled under the step. Lucky scurried after her. One chick lay on the ground. Phoebe picked him up. His head flopped to one side. She caressed his soft feathers and put him close to her ear. She lay her finger against his chest and couldn't feel his heart beating.

She walked slowly to the barn, her eyes blurred with tears. She pulled open the barn door and found a spade leaning in the corner where it belonged. Butterball cowered behind the grain bin. Finding a spot of soft soil under the apple tree, she dug a hole. She wrapped the limp chick in some ferns and laid him in the hole. She clenched her teeth and willed the tears to stop. *It doesn't do any good to cry. It's only a chick, and a cat doesn't know any better.*

Butterball had followed her out into the yard. He rubbed against her legs and meowed. Phoebe put down the spade and picked him up. He purred and rubbed his chin against hers. "I'm sorry I yelled at you, but you can't eat the baby chicks."

She put the spade back and put Butterball up in the hay loft. "Go eat some mice. That's your job." She closed the barn door, knowing Butterball could get out another way if he really wanted to, and maybe, in the meantime, he'd forget about the chicks.

On her way back into the house, she peeked under the step. Sissy was huddled way back as far as she could go. She rumbled a warning to Phoebe, so Phoebe left her alone and went into the house.

"What was all the noise, Phoebe?"

"Butterball attacked Sissy and her chicks. There was quite a fight. He killed one of the babies. Sissy scratched him up pretty badly, too, so I think he'll keep clear of her for a while." She got a drink from the pump with the tin ladle. "I'm worried about Lucky. He can't stay close to Sissy. I hope Butterball doesn't get him."

"It is the way of animals."

"I know, but I don't want it to happen to my animals."

Butterball did keep his distance from Sissy, and the hen kept her eye on the cat. She'd cluck to her chicks whenever he was in the yard, and he kept a wide berth of her activities. Phoebe relaxed her watch over them. Little Lucky did fairly well at keeping up with the rest of the clutch. He'd come at a run whenever Sissy clucked to them, to see what treat she found.

The chicks were getting quite big and their feathers were coming in well. There were six hens and two roosters. Phoebe thought Lucky was the prettiest. He was growing a nice wattle and comb. She could even see a few green feathers in his tail.

He didn't forget her. When she clucked, he was the only one to come running to her side. She liked to find a berry or bug to give him for a treat. He'd follow her around the yard as she gathered eggs. He'd even let her stroke his glossy feathers.

One afternoon, Phoebe was hoeing the garden and paused to watch the chickens. She gave a cluck, and Lucky flapped his wings and crowed. She bent to find a worm for him, and he sprinted across the yard.

"AWWWWK!"

A big bird swooped from the sky and grabbed Lucky by the back of his shoulders. Phoebe dropped the hoe and chased after the bird. She picked up a rock and tossed it at the hawk. Whether she hit him or he didn't have a good grip on Lucky, the hawk dropped the rooster to the ground.

"Luuuuckyyyy!" She ran to where he landed. There was blood everywhere and he lay on his side. She scooped him up in her hands and saw that he was still alive.

Running back to the house, she hollered, "Maseppa! Help! Lucky's hurt!"

They washed his neck and saw that only the skin and feathers had been ripped off. His flesh was exposed, but his spine and neck seemed to be fine. Maseppa noticed that his leg was hurt and wrapped a bandage around it to strengthen it.

Zeke shook his head and smirked at the bald bandaged rooster in the kitchen. "You are the unluckiest rooster I've ever seen."

For a week, they cleaned the wound on Lucky's neck. He stayed in a crate in the shed while he healed. When he could walk again, Phoebe let him wander around during the day, but put him back in the crate at night. When the skin on his neck healed, he was ready to go back outside with the other animals.

He followed Phoebe everywhere, now that he had spent time in the house. He must have thought he was better than the other animals. He still had a bald spot on the back of his neck, but he was fit as a fiddle.

Lucky also developed an irritating habit of strutting around the house at four o'clock in the morning, crowing as he went. Zeke yelled out the window, "Lucky, be quiet! If you weren't Phoebe's pet, you'd be stew."

Phoebe knew Lucky was a very lucky rooster after all.

15
FRENCH FAIRY TALES

Phoebe was making good progress on her embroidery lessons. Each week, when she went to Missus Thomas's house, she learned how to make lazy-daisies, French knots, and many other stitches. Finally, it was time to make her own sampler.

She stitched the alphabet at the top in red threads and put a border around the edges with hearts, leaves, and flowers, with French knots in the centers. In the middle of it, she wanted to make a house and add a poem by John Howard Payne.

Mid pleasures and palaces
Though we may roam,
Be it ever so humble,
There's no place like home.

One Sunday afternoon, while Phoebe waited in the parlor for Missus Thomas to join her, she couldn't help but look at the books on the shelf beside her. Most of them looked boring to her, having to do with theology, and a few were in another language, which she assumed was French. One book, a large red one on the bottom shelf, looked interesting. She pulled it out to see an illustration of a little elf sitting on a cloud beneath a canopy of hanging flowers.

Missus Thomas entered and set her sewing on a low table. "I see you've found my *Contes des Fees* – my fairy tale book by Charles Perrault. My mother gave that to me when I was about your age."

Startled to be caught snooping, Phoebe quickly tried to put it back.

"You may look at it. Each story is written in both French and English. Would you like to borrow it?"

Phoebe gasped. "But this must be a very special book to you." She thumbed through the pages, pausing at illustrations of a castle, a girl talking with a wolf, and a cat wearing boots.

"It is special, but I know you'll take very good care of it."

Phoebe hugged it to her chest. "I promise." She set it near her cloak, so that she would remember it when it was time to go home.

Returning to the parlor, she chose a black thread to outline the roof of the house. She was getting better at keeping her needle threaded, but it was still hard for her to make her stitches follow a straight line. Sometimes the thread twisted. She turned her cloth over to untangle the knot. "Oh, fiddlesticks! This is such a mess!"

Missus Thomas lay her work down to help Phoebe. "You must be patient and gentle with your threads."

Phoebe's face flushed in shame at the difference between their hoops. The back of Missus Thomas's cloth looked almost as beautiful as the front. Tiny colored stitches lay in neat rows and petite dots. Phoebe's was a hodge-podge of tangled strings and knobby knots. The edges of the cloth were crumpled and frayed. It was a mess! She felt like throwing it away.

Missus Thomas pulled out the tangle and handed the hoop back to Phoebe. "Bon! You are doing well."

"But it doesn't look like yours at all. It's horrible!"

"Ah, no! It is very good for your first one. Of course, your stitching doesn't look like mine. You are still learning. As you practice, it will get better and better. You will see."

Phoebe sighed. *Practice? I don't think I'll ever want to do this again.*

"When you finish, I will show you how to wash it and iron it and put it in a frame." Missus Thomas picked up her own handwork. "My first sampler looked worse than yours."

"Really?"

Phoebe took a deep breath and poked the needle into the cloth. Missus Thomas had certainly had a way of making a person feel better. Maybe she could finish the sampler by the end of the month – if she didn't spend too much time reading her new book.

~ # ~

It became harder and harder to concentrate on school lessons when warm breezes brought scents of honeysuckle blossoms and sounds of birdsongs through their classroom windows. Every minute of recess of the warm sunshine was a treasure.

Some played marbles, other jumped rope, but Phoebe perched on the school steps with a book on her knees, more specifically *Fairy Tales of Charles Perrault* that Missus Thomas had let her borrow. She read the stories first in English, and then puzzled over the French words of "Cinderella," "Puss in Boots," "Sleeping Beauty," plus more.

Matthew called, "Phoebe! Stop reading, and come play with us." He was standing in a circle with some of the other younger children, too young for a game of rounders with the bigger boys.

She looked up. It took her a few seconds to bring herself into this time and place, back to the schoolyard, leaving the world of castles and fairy godmothers. She sighed, put a scrap of paper in between the page, and shut the book. "What are you playing?"

"Punchinello! You choose the funniest actions, Phoebe."

It was really a silly game that never ended, but the younger children loved it. They played it day after day.

They chanted and clapped hands, while the one in the center of the circle performed a repetitive action, such as tapping the top of his head.

"What can you do, Punchinello, funny fellow?
What can you do, Punchinello, funny you?"

Everyone then mimicked the action.

"We can do it too, Punchinello, funny fellow.
We can do it too, Punchinello, funny you."

The one in the center closed his eyes, extended his arm, and turned about until the end of the stanza. The person to whom he pointed was the next one to stand in the center, and it started all over again.

"Who do you choose, Punchinello, funny fellow?
Who do you choose, Punchinello, funny you?"

"Phoebe, will you get in the middle, please?"

While they chanted and clapped, she hopped on one foot and flapped her arms like a bird. The children all laughed with glee. When it was time for them to join in, they wobbled and stumbled and swatted each other with their waving arms.

Phoebe closed her eyes and slowly walked in circles. When the song stopped, the bell rang. She shook her head to clear the dizziness and quickly went inside.

Halfway through geometry, she remembered the borrowed book. She raised her hand. "Miss Edgecomb? I left something outside. May I go get it now?"

"Make haste. You tend to procrastinate on your arithmetic more often than necessary."

Phoebe scurried out and looked on the bottom step, where she had been sitting. It wasn't there. She looked over near the oak tree, where they had been playing Punchinello. It wasn't there. She even looked in the outhouse although she was sure she hadn't taken it in there. It wasn't anywhere!

Where can it be? It's not mine. I've got to find it.

Phoebe returned to the schoolroom. She looked in her desk. *No, it wasn't there. Where could it be?*

"Phoebe Johanson, is there a problem?"

"Yes, Ma'am. I was reading a book during recess, and now I can't find it."

"Class, Phoebe has misplaced her book... What is the name of the book, Phoebe?"

"It's *Fairy Tales of Charles Perrault*, but it's not really mine. I borrowed it from Missus Thomas. I have to find it!"

"Has anyone seen the book Phoebe was reading?"

No one had an answer. They all looked at her with sympathy and disappointment, except for Delly. She kept working on her arithmetic and acted as if she hadn't heard Miss Edgecomb at all.

The primary class resumed their recitation and the others went back to their work, but Phoebe couldn't focus on her geometry at all. *Would Delly take the book?* She shouldn't think ill of anyone without proof, but it surely looked suspicious. She'd have to find out after school.

Phoebe tried hard to make her obtuse and acute angles fit into her circle graph, but they just wouldn't cooperate. She gladly put her books and slate away when Miss Edgecomb gave the signal for the closing song and prayer.

When she finally got outside, Delly and her brothers were already half way down the hill. "Delly! Wait for me!" but she never looked back. Phoebe looked around the schoolhouse one more time before heading home.

"I'm sorry about your book," said Matthew as he fell in step beside her.

"Me, too . . . mostly because it's not mine, but I think I know where it is."

"Where?"

"I think someone took it."

"Who?"

Phoebe took a breath and almost told him, then stopped. "I don't know for sure, so I better not say." She thought of the Kittles' house. There wasn't much to be called pretty in that house. She didn't remember any books.

When they got to Matthew's house, Deborah was outside planting flower bulbs in her garden. "Good day, Phoebe. How was school?"

"It was fine."

"No, it wasn't, Mama. Someone stole Phoebe's book."

"We don't know for sure, Matthew," interrupted Phoebe. "I was reading it at recess, and I set it down to play Punchinello. When I went back to get it, it wasn't there."

"Really? Oh my! That's too bad. Well, I hope you find it soon."

"Me too. It wasn't mine. I borrowed it from Missus Thomas."

"Don't fret, child. It will show up eventually. I'm sure she will understand." She brushed her hair from her forehead with the back of her dirty hand and got up from her knees with a grunt. Rubbing the soil from her palms, she invited Phoebe in for a glass of milk and a slice of fresh bread.

"No, thank you, Ma'am. I ought to be getting home."

Phoebe trudged step by step along the road, not noticing the ducks overhead or the trees bursting with new leaves. She was thinking. She was glad she didn't have to pass the parsonage on her way home from school. She certainly didn't want to face Missus Thomas right now.

I know Delly took it. I have to get it back!

She considered telling Maseppa about it, but decided she better know the truth first.

When she got home, she found Maseppa in the kitchen cutting rhubarb. She crunched on the end of a sour stalk. "Maseppa, I need to go over to the Kittles' house."

Maseppa frowned. "Why do you need to go there?"

"I have to ask Delly something about school."

Maseppa was quiet. Phoebe had learned to wait patiently for her decisions. "I do not feel good about that family, but you may go if you come back before it gets dark. Take Butch with you."

"Yes, Maseppa."

"You should not wear school clothes."

"I'll change," hollered Phoebe as she ran upstairs two steps at a time. She slipped on her everyday dress and tugged off her shoes. Calling her pup, she flew off the porch and down the road to the connecting path. She felt so free when she was barefoot in the woods. It was like the days when she and Maseppa gathered berries and roots. It was like being a deer or a squirrel, leaping and living among the trees. Butch bounced around in anticipation of an adventure.

Before she emerged from the woods on the other end of the

path, she slowed to a walk. "Oh Butch, I'm a bit scared. I'm glad you're with me, but you have to mind me, you hear?"

As before, Phoebe could hear the Kittles' house before she saw it. Stafford and Ross were shooting slingshots at a tin kettle. In between clangs, they argued as to who made which dent. Their hound, the first to notice Phoebe, began barking and growling at Butch.

Phoebe grabbed the scruff of her dog's neck and whispered, "Shhhh, Butch. Don't mind him."

Mister Kittle burst from the door with a musket in his hand. "What's all the ruckus goin' on out here?"

Phoebe gulped. "Good day, sir. I've come to see Delly."

Right then the hound lunged at Butch, and he leapt up to meet the growling dog. Phoebe tried to grab him, but they were twisting and biting and tumbling, so that she couldn't get close. Mister Kittle shot the gun in the air, and the hound ran off yelping.

"Now, what was you after, young'un?"

"I've ... I ... is Delly home?"

"DELLY, there's some'un to see you!" he hollered into the house. Soon she appeared beside him.

"Hello, Phoebe," she said. Her eyes narrowed, daring Phoebe to speak.

"Um ... I ... do you know where my book is?"

"How should I know? It's not my book."

"No, it belongs to Missus Thomas. She let me read it. I thought maybe you knew what happened to it."

Delly gave a glance up at her father then twisted her lips into a sneer. "You think I took it, don't you?"

Mister Kittle's eyes grew big and he raised his shoulders. "Are you calling my little girl a thief? Get out of here! Get off our property and take your dog with you. If I ever see your dog on our property again, I'll shoot him!"

Phoebe's heart thumped and her eyes stung. "Come, Butch." As they fled up the road, she heard them laughing. She didn't know if the pounding of her heart was from fear or anger. *How can people be so heartless and cruel? I know Delly took my book. I hate her. I hate her pa. I feel like -*

Immediately, her conscience pricked her heart. Some Bible verses came to mind: "Love your enemies" and "Overcome evil with good." She squeezed her eyes shut and clenched her hands. *God, I know I'm not supposed to be mean back, but it's so hard to be kind to the Kittles! They're such a mean bunch of folks. I don't know if I can do it.*

It was much harder walking back. Phoebe probably should have gone the long way around on the road, where there weren't as many trees and it would be brighter, but she just wanted to get home. Besides, she'd have to pass close to the church if she went by the way of the road, and she didn't want to meet Madame Thomas, perchance, in town.

As she passed through pine woods, she glanced out of the corners of her eyes and back over her shoulders. Every little rustle of leaves made her jump. When a crow screeched overhead, she couldn't help but run the rest of the way. Butch passed her and disappeared in the trees.

It wasn't as dark once she came out onto the road, and she paused to catch her breath. With steady steps, she trudged up the steps to the porch. Butch greeted her with a wagging tail as if he had been there all along.

"You rascal! You almost got yourself shot today. Don't scare me again like that." She rubbed his head and gave him a hug around the neck. She leaned against the kitchen door as she pushed down on the handle. A savory aroma swirled around her and calmed her heart. "What are we having for supper? It smells wonderful."

"Good. You are home. Help Zeke with the milking and feeding the animals. Supper is almost ready."

All at once, Phoebe knew it was time to tell someone about her problem with Delly. She gladly headed out to the barn. She could see Zeke's lantern and heard him whistling. The barn had an earthy farmy scent. The smell of hay and cows and grain all mixed together. It smelled safe and warm. Zeke would know what to do.

16
DELLY

Phoebe dreaded going to church on Sunday. She just knew Missus Thomas would know the book was lost. She almost begged Maseppa to let her stay home, but she couldn't think of a good enough reason.

Phoebe, Maseppa, and Zeke were the first ones to arrive. The parson was just opening the doors. His wife, holding up her pale blue dress with a ruffle around the bottom edge, was tip-toeing across the grass. Phoebe wished there was some place to hide or someone else there for Missus Thomas to talk to.

"Good day, Phoebe." She tugged on her white gloves and laid them neatly on the front pew. "Are you coming over this afternoon for another embroidery lesson?"

Phoebe's head lifted quickly. She had forgotten! "Um . . . I don't think I can come today." Her heart dropped. She really wanted to go. "I have something I have to do." *Like find her book.*

"Oh, I'm sorry. Maybe it will work out next week. I have some nice designs for you to choose from." Missus Thomas opened the front of the organ and arranged some music sheets on the top. "Have you started reading *Charles Perrault's Fairy Tales* yet? How do you like it? That has always been one of my favorite books."

She knows! thought Phoebe. "Yes, I've read the English parts, now I'm trying to learn some of the French."

"Oh, c'est bon! That is good!"

Other members of the congregation began arriving and filling in the pews. Phoebe gladly excused herself and sat next to Maseppa in their pew. She hoped and prayed that she would find that book before next Sunday. This feeling was torture.

Monday morning was cold and wet. The gray clouds hung so low that you could hardly see the rooster wind vane on the top of the barn. Zeke drove Phoebe and Matthew to school in the covered buggy. The cold rain blew in the sides, so they still got wet. They waved good-bye to Zeke and raced up the steps.

The air in the coat room smelled musty and damp. Slick mud covered the floor boards. The pot-bellied stove was pumping out as much heat as it could to the shivering children circled around it. Miss Edgecomb tapped a ruler on her desk and everyone scattered to their desks. Phoebe noticed that none of the Kittles were there.

The rain pelted the window panes and roof, making it hard to hear anyone read or recite. The warm stove made the room feel safe and cozy from the fierce rainstorm outside. Phoebe's eyes felt heavy and she couldn't concentrate on travels of Magellan. Just as she felt her head nod, the back door banged open and a scuffle of feet could be heard.

Everyone turned to see the Kittle children tumble into the room. They all wore floppy leather hats, but those must not have been much protection against the blowing rain. They tromped and sloshed and dripped to their various seats.

"My goodness!" said Miss Edgecomb. "Did you children walk all the way from your house in this rain? I didn't think you'd come today." She helped Ross remove an oversized shirt and stood him near the stove. "You children must be freezing. Why didn't you stay home today?"

Stafford said, "Pop said we had to come, or – "Delly gave him a sharp look, and he closed his mouth.

"Well, tell your father that if the weather is blustery, you may stay home."

"I'll tell him," said Stafford, "but it don't matter to Pa what the weather does. He likes us to get out of the house when he's sleepin'."

"Hush!" whispered Delly.

"Well, at least you can get dried off now. Hang your wet clothes on my chair, and stand near the stove to get warm."

Stafford took off his flannel shirt, clomped up to the stove, and turned his back to it. Delly went up too, but stood on the other side with her shawl still wrapped around herself. She clutched at the front. Puddles of water formed around their shoes.

Miss Edgecomb tried to get Delly to take off her sweater, but she clutched the front even tighter. Giving up, Miss Edgecomb said, "All right, children, let's get back to our studies. Will the second class come up to the front for their spelling lesson?"

Phoebe tried to return to the history of Magellan, but she kept looking at Delly and Stafford and Ross huddled around the stove. *What kind of father would make his children walk to school on a day like this?* She caught the eye of Delly, who quickly looked away. Phoebe noticed that her shawl looked square, like there was something underneath it.

After the spelling lesson, Miss Edgecomb looked at her watch that hung around her neck. "Phoebe, would you please help the younger girls to the outhouse and then fetch their lunch pails so they can eat in here? We'll have to have our recess inside today."

Annie and Jemmy put on their coats and bonnets to face the blowing storm for the few feet to the outhouse. They each grabbed one of Phoebe's hands and squealed with mock fright as she raced with them across the soggy yard. The wind whistled through the cracks and even up the hole. No one ever dilly-dallied in the outhouse, but especially not on a day like today.

Even though the storm meant being trapped indoors all day, there was an air of excitement and adventure. Children scurried up and down between the desks. Some of the boys began leapfrogging over them until Miss Edgecomb promised a sing time. She also decided to allow them to sit with their friends instead of in their normal assigned spots. Annie and Jemmy pulled Phoebe to sit with them, so Phoebe squeezed into the seat next to the little girls. She looked around the room and noticed Delly sitting alone.

"I'll sit with you another time," she told the little girls. "I promise."

She stood near Delly's desk. "Would you like me to sit with you?"

Delly looked up with squinted eyes, "Why would I want that? Maybe I like being alone."

Phoebe stared at her. Her eyes stung and her throat tightened. Her breath came fast and hard. She turned on her heel and plopped in the bench at her own desk. *Grrrr . . . That Delly can be so . . . so . . . difficult! Doesn't she recognize when someone is trying to be nice?*

Phoebe ate the bread and cheese and apple pie that Maseppa had packed for her, but it tasted bland and dry. She loved to sing, but today she didn't feel like it. She'd be glad when their lessons were done and Zeke came to pick them up. She lifted the lid of her desk and froze.

There was the book! The red coloring from the binding was spreading to her papers. One edge looked smeared, like mud had been wiped off. She glanced over at Delly, but she was bent over her desk with intense concentration. She glanced up at Phoebe and then looked back at her work.

Miss Edgecomb was collecting papers from the third class on the other side of the room. Phoebe took the book and walked quickly to the coat room. She wrapped it in her cloke and put it under her lunch pail. Just as she was slipping back into her desk, she heard Miss Edgecomb. "Phoebe Johanson, please sit down and resume your studies."

"Yes, Miss Edgecomb."

The schoolroom returned to the normal sound of rustling papers and books. Phoebe glanced at Delly, who was staring at her. Phoebe and Delly held each other's gaze for a few seconds. Phoebe smiled and there was a little twitch at the corner of Delly's lips.

Phoebe was glad that Zeke was there when school let out at three o'clock. She told Matthew to get ready while she went to ask Zeke something. She explained about the Kittles, and just like she knew would happen, he offered to take them home. She ran back through the stinging raindrops.

"Delly, Stafford, and Ross, you don't have to walk home. Zeke said he'd take you home. We'll have to squeeze together, but that's alright. We'll stay warmer that way."

Matthew, Stafford, and Ross sat on the floor of the buggy, while Delly and Phoebe squeezed in the seat next to Zeke. There wasn't much room for their feet.

Delly whispered, "How come you didn't tell on me about the book?"

"I don't know. I guess I felt sorry for you, being all wet and all. I want to be your friend."

Delly's face clouded. "I don't need no charity friends," she hissed and turned her face toward the passing, wet landscape.

Phoebe glanced to her left to see if Zeke was listening. He was whistling and didn't seem to be paying attention to them. The boys were on their knees and talking about Ol' Sam.

Zeke dropped off the Kittles, and Delly stomped through the rain without so much as a glance backwards. Phoebe felt frustrated and ashamed, but mostly confused.

After Matthew got out, she and Zeke headed home. The rain pattered on the buggy roof, and Ol' Sam slopped steadily through the mud.

"Zeke?"

"Yes?"

"Sometimes it's hard being nice, isn't it?"

Zeke lifted his hat and scratched his head. "I heard you and Delly talking. Let me tell you something. She's hurting and embarrassed about her life. She's pushing folks away 'cause then they'll see how things really are."

"I know it's not her fault that her pa is like that. I just want to be her friend."

He smiled at her. "I know, Li'l Angel. You've got a big heart." He thought for a minute. "There's a place in the Good Book that talks about 'heaping coals o' fire' on folks' heads to show you care."

"Coals of fire?"

"Granny called it 'coals of kindness.' It's showing so much love to them that their shame makes them uncomfortable and they can't help but be sorry."

Phoebe thought on that for a while. *It isn't easy to be kind to the Kittles. It's like trying to hug a porcupine!* Phoebe cocked her head and faced Zeke. "Do you think you could take me over to the parsonage 'fore we go home? I've got something that I need to tell Missus Thomas."

17
COALS OF KINDNESS

"Butch, go home! You can't come with me."

Phoebe wagged her finger at him, and he stopped. She turned around and continued on her way to the middle of town. Every few seconds, she looked back to see that he hadn't moved. By the time she reached the turn in the road, he had disappeared. She hoped he had gone home.

With a light skip in her step, she made her way up the street to the general store. Maseppa needed some molasses and soap. Phoebe had always loved general stores, with their bins and jars of so many colors and smells and objects that she had never seen before. But Mister Cooper's store gave her the creeps. It smelled musty and dusty. Everything felt gritty and slightly greasy. Plus, it seemed dark. It wasn't a place she liked to look around in very long. She usually asked for what Maseppa needed and any mail they might have gotten, and left without wandering around the store.

She got the molasses and soap and chose two cents' worth of peppermints, which she planned to take to Delly and her brothers.

Zeke pulled in with his wagon of freight just as she left the store. "Hello, Phoebe. Do you need a ride home?"

"No, thank you, Zeke. I'm going over to the Kittles' house. I'm going to try some of that 'coals of kindness' we were talking about. I bought some peppermints for them. I don't think they get candy very often. Could you take these things back to Maseppa?" She handed the molasses and soap to him.

"Sure enough. I hope your 'coals of kindness' works this time."

He hefted a fifty-pound sack of oats onto his shoulder and carried it to the storage room behind the store.

As Phoebe strode out of town toward the Kittles' house, she lifted her face to the sun. The sky was as blue as could be. It felt good to be alive on such a fine day. She waved at Feona Reynolds, who was hanging towels on her clothesline. A wooden peg clenched between her teeth kept her from saying anything.

As Phoebe neared the Kittles' house she heard rustling in the dried leaves on the side of the road. The nose of a dog peeked out of the bushes at her. When he saw that Phoebe saw him too, he trotted up to her with a gleeful prance that seemed to say, "There you are! Now, we can walk home together!"

"Oh, no, Butch! Mister Kittle doesn't like you." She wished she had a string to tie around his neck, but she didn't have anything. She sat him at the end of the path and wagged her finger at him. "You have to stay here. I'll be back really soon, you hear me?"

He hung his head, but as she turned, he stood up as if to follow.

"No! You have to stay here, Butch." She made him lie down and tapped him on the head.

He put his muzzle on his paws and watched her walk away.

Knocking on the Kittles' door, Phoebe was surprised that she couldn't hear any noise: no barking, no crying, no yelling, no nothing. It was eerie. She was turning to leave when the door opened. Mister Kittle staggered against the door frame, his eyes red and his shirt half open and in his right hand he held his musket.

"What do you want?" he growled. At the sound of his voice, the hound bolted past him and leaped at Phoebe, knocking her down. A snarling, drooling mouth of sharp teeth leaned over her face. As she pushed its head away with her hands, a streak of fur came from the side and knocked the hound off her. It was Butch.

The dogs circled and growled, biting, and yelping. Phoebe tried to grab Butch's tail to get him away, but she was afraid of the hound's teeth. An explosion blasted her ears, and she instinctively covered her head and fell to the ground. The hound ran off behind the house, and Butch lay there... not moving.

"I told you I'd shoot 'im if he came 'round 'ere again!" he muttered and disappeared into the shack.

Phoebe crawled over to Butch. He lifted his head at her. There was blood on his neck and side. She didn't know if he was shot or if the blood was from being bit by the hound. She wasn't sure if she could carry him all the way home, but she couldn't leave him there.

Cradling him like a baby, she hefted him as best she could. She got as far as the short cut, but couldn't go any farther. "Butch," she whispered. "I'll be right back. I'm going to get help."

Running as fast as she could, she sprinted back to the Reynolds' farm. Missus Reynolds was hanging the last shirt and seeing Phoebe coming, hurried to meet her. "What's wrong, child? I heard the gun. Is someone shot?"

Phoebe tried to talk. "He... He ... shot Butch. ... I can't ...carry him..."

Missus Reynolds followed Phoebe, her basket still in her hands. Running ahead, Phoebe could see that Butch was still alive, but he didn't raise his head to greet her.

"Please help him!"

Together they lifted the dog into the wicker basket and carried him back to the house. In the kitchen, Missus Reynolds packed cold wet rags on his wounds.

"I don't know how deep these go. If they only scraped the skin, then he'll be fine, but..." Her voice trailed off, and Phoebe was glad she didn't finish her sentence.

"Maseppa knows herbs." Phoebe stroked the trembling dog. "She'll know what to do. Please, can you watch him while I run home?"

"I will see if Morris will ride after Maseppa. I'd prefer that you stayed here with me."

Phoebe sat on the floor next to the basket and patted Butch's head while they waited. There was too much going on at once. Her head hurt if she tried to think about it all. She leaned back against the wall. She wondered where Delly and her family might be. Soon they heard Zeke's wagon rattling into the dooryard.

Maseppa and Zeke hurried into the Reynolds' house. Maseppa had brought herbs and made a poultice to put on the dog's wounds. She made a willow bark tea and poured it down his throat spoonful by spoonful. The whole while, Missus Reynolds complained about the Kittle family until Zeke hushed her by saying, "I reckon they have their problems, but it isn't right to blame the whole family for one man's actions. I reckon the wife and the children have enough troubles without making more."

"Zeke?" said Phoebe. "There wasn't anybody around except Mister Kittle, when I knocked. Where do you think they might be?"

"I'll take a walk over there and see what's going on." He and Morris left together while the ladies nursed the dog.

Butch seemed to be breathing more calmly. Missus Reynolds offered them some milk and raisin bread. Soon the men returned.

"The family was out gathering hickory nuts today," reported Zeke. "The mister denies he shot anything today."

"I heard it!" Missus Reynolds pointed to herself.

Phoebe burst into tears. "I just want to go home."

18
THE CAVE

On Friday, Delly asked Miss Edgecomb if she could share a desk with Phoebe, saying, "so as we can study together better." Miss Edgecomb agreed and switched her seat with Priscilla's.

As soon as the classroom settled into its normal routine, Delly leaned over and whispered, "I'm sorry about the book."

"It's okay. I forgive you."

"Will you be my friend? I never had a friend before."

Phoebe's head jerked up. *Friend? So the 'coals of kindness' did work.*

Miss Edgecomb gave a sharp look in their direction. "If you two girls continue to talk instead of studying, I will move Delly back to her original seat. Can I trust you to behave?"

They both answered, "Yes, Miss Edgecomb."

Phoebe turned the page of her history book and focused on the French Revolution. Except for the storming of the Bastille, it was downright boring with all those strange names and battles. The exam was next Monday, the last one of the school term, and it was going to be the hardest one. She felt a nudge from Delly. She tried to ignore her. She had gotten into enough trouble from talking to her. Delly pushed a piece of paper under Phoebe's book. Waiting until Miss Edgecomb turned the other way, Phoebe pulled it out and opened it on her lap.

*My Pop is home and angry
I am not going home.*

Phoebe looked up in surprise at Delly, but she was pretending to be working hard on her report. Phoebe turned the paper over and wrote on the back.

Where are you going?

She slid it back. Delly waited while Miss Edgecomb walked by. She scribbled her answer.

I found a cave.

Phoebe's eyes grew wide. *A cave? I didn't know there any caves around here.*

Will you show me?

Delly couldn't reply because it was time for their Latin lesson. She stuck the note in the desk and they went up to conjugate verbs into the past imperfect tense. Then it was time for Phoebe to listen to Jemmy read to her. She liked teaching the little ones to read. It was exciting to see them progress in their pronunciation and comprehension.

At recess time, Delly sat next to Phoebe on the steps. Phoebe shared some of her molasses bread with her and asked, "When are you going?"

Delly looked around to make sure no one was near. "I aim to go right after school. I told my ma that I'm staying at your house. She don't mind. She likes you, and she's right glad I have a friend."

"But what will happen when you don't come home?"

"I reckon my pa will get angry, but then he'll drink some more and won't even notice who's there and who ain't there. He gets so drunk he don't know his own name."

Phoebe fingered her braid thoughtfully. "Delly, how about I tell Maseppa that we're going camping, and then maybe we could stay in the cave together. There's no school tomorrow, since it's Saturday, so she won't mind us coming back late."

"No one can know where we are, or they'll tell my folks."

"I won't tell exactly where we're camping. I promise." Phoebe felt a twinge of guilt for being so secretive, but also a tingle of excitement. *This is going to be a great adventure.*

"I ain't comin' back," said Delly. "I'm goin' to live there. I can take care of myself."

"That's silly. What about school?"

"I don't need school neither."

Phoebe sighed. *This is more than an adventure. I wish I hadn't promised not to tell.*

All afternoon, she tried to think of a way to convince Delly that it wasn't so bad to stay home, but Delly's home was pretty bad. It wasn't that they didn't have much food or clothes or that she had to sleep on the floor, it was that her father could be pretty scary when he got drunk. She couldn't think of a good reason for Delly to go home. At least she could see where Delly's cave was.

After classes were dismissed, Delly walked home with Phoebe. They found Maseppa behind the house, beating a braided rug. "Maseppa, Delly and I want to go camping. Is that all right with you?"

Maseppa paused a second before sending another puff of dust into the air.

Delly sensed Maseppa's hesitation. "My ma likes Phoebe. She says it's good for me to have friends."

Maseppa nodded. "Yes, it is good to have friends. Phoebe, you be careful. You hear me?"

"Yes, Maseppa."

Butch limped out from behind the woodstove. Phoebe stopped to pet him, and Delly rubbed his head. "My pa told me that he shot Butch. "I'm sorry. I'm glad he didn't die."

Phoebe swallowed. "It wasn't your fault." It still hurt to think about that day. "I'm not angry anymore." Just saying those words made her feel better. She even felt like forgiving Mister Kittle, just like Missus Thomas forgave her for damaging the book.

Phoebe stood up. "Let's get my things to go camping."

The girls scampered upstairs, where Phoebe grabbed a warm sweater for each of them and her little pocket knife that Maseppa had given her a long time ago. She wrapped them all in a blanket and bundled them on her back. They clattered back downstairs, where Maseppa was washing her hands at the sink. "May we have a bit of cheese and biscuits, too?"

"Yes, you may take some food with you."

They raided the pantry, stuffing raisins and crackers and pickles into Phoebe's pack. She wondered how they would build a fire. She wished she could take some coals in a fire pot. "Maseppa, may we take a lantern?"

Maseppa nodded.

Phoebe found a lantern in the shed and lit it from the fire in the stove. They scrambled out of the house, eager to be on their way.

"Now where is this cave?" asked Phoebe.

"It's down in the ravine behind our land," said Delly, "down near where you first saw me."

Phoebe thought back to that day and giggled. "You didn't like me, did you?"

"I didn't like anyone."

They chattered as they galloped through the shortcut. Phoebe was glad that there weren't any houses along the path. They'd have to be careful to avoid people once they got to the road on the other end.

"I know another path," said Delly. "No one will see us."

It wasn't much of a path. They had to climb over a dozen fallen trees that were too low to crawl under. Phoebe imagined that the trees had deliberately fallen in their way to make their progress more difficult. At least it would be hard for anyone to follow them.

Soon they came to the ravine, where the stream, full of recent run-off from the spring rains, rushed along its way. In the late afternoon shadows, down at the bottom of the ravine, Phoebe could barely see Delly ahead of her. Suddenly, she couldn't see her anymore. She held up the lantern and scanned the roaring water.

"DELLLLLLYY!"

Something grabbed her leg, and Phoebe screamed!

She looked down to see Delly laughing at her. Delly was half under a giant rock. She disappeared into a hole. Phoebe leaned down and put the lantern near the hole. She could see that it opened up into a larger area.

Sitting down, she slid into the hole, pulling the bundle of clothes and food with her. The lantern's light flickered on the walls. Glistening spears hung from the ceiling and other cones reached up to meet them. She could stand up straight and couldn't even hear the stream anymore.

Delly stood there grinning. "Isn't it great?"

Her voice echoed in a dark tunnel . . . "great"

"It's wonderful!"

The echo repeated . . . "wonderful"

"I could live her forever."

"forever"

Phoebe wasn't so sure about that. They could at least sleep there one night. She opened the blanket and spread it out. She looked around for something to burn, but there were only rocks and dirt. "We need wood."

They crawled back outside. A warm wind whipped through the trees, stirring up the dead leaves on the forest floor. Phoebe found a few dry limbs. They didn't have a hatchet or saw, so they'd have to bring the whole branches with them. She grabbed a few handfuls of dry leaves for kindling.

Inside she looked for a place where the smoke could escape. She realized that there was a draft blowing toward a dark crevice at the back of the room. That would be better than putting the fire near the door and having their escape hole blocked. She stacked the dry leaves and smaller twigs. Lifting the lantern's shade, she caught a stick on fire and inserted it into the pile. Soon the leaves began smoking, and she gently puffed on them until a little flame appeared.

In a few minutes, she had a fire snapping warmly. The smoke drifted toward the back and out the tunnel. Delly leaned her head into it. "I wonder how far it goes. It must go all the way outside for the smoke to be pulled that way." She leaned closer. "I hear something. It almost sounds like water."

The sound grew louder and louder. She backed up, keeping her eyes on the hole. A fluttering, squeaking rush of black creatures flew from the tunnel, filling the room, and finally escaping to the outside.

When it was quiet again, Phoebe looked around. She had backed up against one wall, and Delly was against the other. The lantern was knocked down somehow, but the campfire was flickering enough to finish setting up their gear.

Phoebe started laughing. "I guess the smoke scared them out of there"

"I hope they don't come back!" Delly flinched at a shadow on the wall.

"Are you sure you still want to sleep here tonight?"

"What? – let a few measly bats scare me off? Let's eat supper."

They ate the food Phoebe had raided from the pantry and went outside to get a drink from the stream. They gathered a few more dead limbs to last through the night. After arranging their bedding, they lay there talking and laughing.

"Phoebe, you are the luckiest girl I know."

Phoebe didn't answer. She had never thought of herself as lucky. She had always thought of herself as not having much – not having a real family, not having a home . . . well, not until last year.

"Are you still awake?"

"Yes, I'm awake. I just never thought of how much I have." She turned over on her stomach and looked at her friend. "Delly, it doesn't matter what you have on the outside or what kind of family you have, it's how you are on the inside. That's the part that God sees, and that's the part I see in you, too."

Now, it was Delly's turn to be quiet. The burnt branch broke and a shower of cinders floated up to the shadowy ceiling. Delly whispered, "I never had a friend that saw the inside of me before. Thank you, Phoebe, for being my friend." Her brown eyes glistened in the reflection of the firelight.

Soon the fire died down and both girls fell asleep.

Phoebe felt something shaking her. "Phoebe, Phoebe, I hear something."

She sat up and listened. She couldn't see anything at all. There was no light at all – nothing.

"Where's the lantern?" asked Delly.

"I don't know, but it won't do any good without any fire," said Phoebe. "Maybe I can stir up a few coals." She carefully felt her way toward where the fire had been. She didn't want to burn her hands. She felt the branch, but the ashes were cool. She broke off a stick and stirred them, but still couldn't see even a spark.

"Phoebe, I'm cold. I hear something skittering behind me. I don't know what it is! Let's go back."

"Where?"

"I don't know. I don't want to stay in here, in the dark."

It was hard to find their things in the dark, but they gathered as much as they could. They could always come back in the daytime to get them.

Phoebe grabbed Delly's arm. "I think if we follow this wall, we'll come up to the hole that leads outside."

They were surprised to find that, once they were outside, they could see the tops of the trees in the little light given by the stars and the half moon. They back-tracked along the stream, climbed over the fallen trees, and came out onto the road.

"I know where we can sleep," said Phoebe. "There's a nice loft in our barn. We can sleep there."

After dragging their woolen blankets and scooting through the woods in the wee hours of the morning, they bedded down in the soft hay, comforted by the warm familiar sounds of Ginger snuffling and Molly chewing her cud.

"Phoebe, are you awake?"

"Yeah"

"I reckon I could go back home if you'd keep bein' my friend."

19
PHOEBE'S CRITTERS

School finally let out for the summer season. Phoebe was glad to be done with history and mathematics. She'd rather be reading, traipsing through the woods, or playing with her animals.

Butch was never quite the same after that day at the Kittles' house. He didn't like to follow Phoebe on her walks through the shortcut anymore. He either slept behind the stove or in the sun patch when the sun warmed the front porch. He greeted Phoebe in the morning and when she came home from school, but didn't seem as perky as he used to be.

Butterball, on the other hand, was always in trouble. You would never know that he once had a broken foot. He especially was interested in Maseppa's loom. He would jump up and sit on the bar, and before long would swat at the threads as she alternated the warp threads or the shuttle as it came shooting through the tunnel toward him. It was quite common to hear the rhythmic thumping stop and Maseppa say, "I will put you outside if you get on my weaving loom again!" Then you would hear a softer thump as she very deliberately deposited him on the floor. After two or three of these, she would take him to the door and toss him outside until she was done.

Once Phoebe heard Zeke yelling from the back shed. "Phoebe, come get your cat!"

She ran out there to see him holding a very sticky, wet kitten. "What is that all over him?"

"It's turpentine! This silly cat must have rubbed against my jar of paint brushes." He switched the squirming cat to the other hand. "He can't lick himself clean or he'll die from poisoning. You'll have to give him a bath."

"How?"

"Get one of Maseppa's old kettles and fill it with warm water." As Phoebe ran to do that, he added, "Don't forget some good lye soap too."

What an escapade! That cat did not want to be washed. While Zeke held him by the scruff of his neck, Phoebe doused him with water and rubbed soap all over him. He meowed and screeched and scratched. When they thought they had rubbed soap over enough of his fur, Zeke poured a bucket of water over him while Phoebe tried to hold him still. If Butterball thought the soap was bad, cold running water over his head was worse. With mutterings under his breath, Zeke tossed the wet cat out of the barn into the sunshine to finish the process. Poor Butterball and poor Zeke! They rarely stayed in the same room together after that.

Another day, Phoebe saw Butterball crouched in the grass watching something. Her gaze followed his sight. There was something fluttering under the lilac bush. She stepped closer. It was a baby bird. Looking above it, she saw a nest in the branches with other babies in it. A female robin chirped on a branch nearby.

Phoebe gently picked up the little fellow, holding his stubby wings folded close. She could feel his heart pounding under her fingers. His yellow beak opened wide and he gave a weak squawk. She tried to put him back in the nest, but he flopped out – tumbling through the lilac branches all the way to the ground.

Butterball's tail twitched.

Phoebe couldn't leave the little bird on the ground for Butterball to attack. She cradled him in her hands again and carried him to the house. "Maseppa, look what I found. What do baby birds eat?"

Maseppa looked in her hands. The bird's downy feathers fluffed out on his breast and under his tail, but the top of his head and wings and tail were smooth with new feathers. He opened his beak again in a dry peep. "He needs to drink water."

"I'll make him a nest with rags in something."

"Use the old milk bucket, with the hole. It makes a mess when it leaks."

"Will you hold him while I make the nest?" She transferred the tiny pitiful creature to Maseppa's strong hands and ran off to the shed to find the bucket and rags. Soon the robin chick was snug in his new home.

With steady movements, she dropped water into the open beak one drop at a time. Its throat quivered with each swallow. Soon its eyes blinked, and it hunkered down to sleep.

"I wonder what they eat. I know grownup robins eat worms. Do you think baby robins will too?"

"I think it would be good," answered Maseppa. "It will be a lot of work to take care of a baby bird."

"I know, but it needs me. It needs a home."

Phoebe found the spade and dug in the pile of rotten cabbage leaves and food garbage, out in the chicken yard. She had to be quick to grab the worms before the chickens did. Soon she had three grimy, wiggly worms.

By the time she got back in kitchen, the baby bird was cheeping in his bucket. She held one end of a worm and the bird stopped peeping long enough to gobble it down and peep for more.

"You're a pig, not a bird!" One after the other the worms disappeared, and Phoebe gave him another spoonful of water, one drop at a time. He flapped his stubby wings and squirted a white blob on the brown rag.

"Ewwww! I'm not going to change your bed every time you do that! What am I going to do with you?"

Every hour or two the bird let everyone know he was awake and hungry. Before the sun even shone through the kitchen window, he was squawking for breakfast. Soon he was hopping to the edge of the milk pail and getting even more demanding whenever someone was nearby.

Maseppa had enough. "It is time to take your baby bird out of the house. He is dirty and noisy."

Phoebe claimed a corner of the barn for him. She hung his pail from a hook on the wall and hoped Butterball couldn't reach him.

Phoebe was getting tired of digging for worms. It was getting harder and harder to find some good spots. The chicken yard was a lumpy mess of potholes. She decided it was time for help.

"Maseppa, I'm going to the Gilmores' house, all right?" Without waiting for an answer, she ran off.

Deborah told her that Matthew was in the barn. Phoebe thanked her and went to find him. He was leaning over a fence out back. "Hey, Phoebe, look. We got a goat!"

"A goat?"

"Yeah, Pa says he's just for meat, not a pet. He said not to name him, but I did. I call him Bucky."

Bucky was adorable with his brown floppy ears. Phoebe fed him some grass, and he bounced around in his pen. She couldn't imagine eating him, but she knew that was the way with animals on a farm.

Matthew, would you like to see something special at my

house?"

"What?"

"I've got a baby bird. He fell out of a tree."

"Really?"

With his mother's permission, Matthew scampered back with Phoebe over the foot-worn path between their homes. Matthew peeked into the bucket. The little bird lifted his head and opened his beak – hoping for a snack. "He's kind of ugly." Matthew reached toward him.

Phoebe pulled his arm back. "You can't touch him – not yet."

"Ahhh . . . he's so small. What do you feed him?"

"Worms . . . but I'm running out of them. Do you know where to find any?"

"Of course! I dig them all the time to go fishing. Can I help you feed him?"

"I'll pay you a penny for twenty worms."

"Twenty worms! That's a lot. I say five worms.

"Ten worms and you can help feed him – and I suppose you can touch him, but you have to be gentle."

"Deal." He rubbed the soft head. "What's his name?"

"I haven't decided yet. I think I'll name him Peeper."

"That's a good name."

For the next month, Phoebe and Matthew dug and fed Peeper hundreds of worms. They watched him sprout glossy feathers and giggled at his feeble attempts to fly with his stubby wings.

"He think you're his mother." Matthew laughed as Peeper followed Phoebe around the yard.

Phoebe sighed. She knew that it was up to her to make sure Peeper could find his own food before he could survive on his own. He sat on her shoulder while she turned over the dirt in the old manure pile, but made him pull out his own meal. She set him on the fence post and made him fly down by himself.

By the end of summer, Peeper blended in with the other robins in the neighborhood, with his handsome red bib and black cape – until he saw Phoebe and came squawking across the yard to perch on her shoulder.

Phoebe loved every animal on their farm. Of course, there were the horses, Ginger and Ol'Sam, and Molly the cow. They had Sissy, Lucky, the other chickens, and a couple of ducks, too, named Wibble and Wobble. Besides the regular livestock, she always had some kind of wild critter in the corner of the barn – a half-drowned chipmunk, a blue jay with a broken wing, or an orphaned coon. Zeke refused to let her raise a nest of field mice. "We can't be adding to the mice population. There are too many eating our grain already! I'd rather you raise a critter that would get rid them."

"Like a fox?" Phoebe clapped. "Oh, I'd love to have a pet fox."

"A fox?" Zeke slapped his hand on his head. "Then we'd have to worry about the chickens!"

20
CAMP MEETING

One evening, Zeke shook the newspaper to fold it backwards. "Listen to this." He laid it on the table.

"Camp Revival Meetings, August 8 through the 14th, New Lebanon, New York, with Reverend Charles G. Finney, lawyer, theologian, and president of Oberlin College. There will be preaching and singing and praying every day and evening. Room is provided for tenting."

Phoebe looked at it with him. "What's a camp revival meeting?"

"It's a church meeting in a big tent. People gather together and and have meetings for a whole week."

"A whole week? Who would take care of the animals?"

"Well, I could come back each evening to feed the stock. We can take the cow. Maybe one of our neighbors who isn't going would be willing to help out for a week."

Parson Thomas encouraged his congregation to attend the meetings and to invite all their neighbors. There were posters on the store walls. The men worked out a plan to take turns coming home to feed each other's animals. Everyone was excited to spend a week together at the camp meeting. Finally August 8th arrived.

It was a sweltering day. They packed blankets and pots and fire wood and food in the back of the wagon. Phoebe peered around the pile of blankets in her hands. "What about Butterball, Maseppa? May I bring him?"

"No. It would be best for him to stay here."

"But who will feed him?"

"He can find his own mice. Butch will come with us."

On Saturday afternoon, they headed out. Zeke and Maseppa sat up front. Phoebe sat in back. Butch limped as fast as his injured leg could go from this side of the wagon to the other. He knew they were going somewhere and didn't want to be left out of the adventure. Phoebe finally got him to jump up into the wagon with her. Molly was tethered behind.

About ten wagons were at the camp meeting field already. People from the surrounding towns had begun pitching their tents on one end of a long pasture. A huge tent was set up at the other end with poles and ropes to hold the huge tarpaulin in place.

Inside the big tent stood a pulpit and about sixty benches made of planks set on chunks of wood. Sawdust was spread all over the floor. Phoebe even saw a pump-organ up front near the pulpit.

"*Ondàs*, Phoebe"

Reluctantly she followed Maseppa to where Zeke had already starting to lay out their tent. Nearby was a place to corral their horses and cows. Phoebe led Molly and Ol' Sam over there. On her way back, she noticed the people in the other tents. One family had about eight children running around and helping. She could hear them calling each other names like Caleb and Anna and Micah. A girl around her age waved at her.

Phoebe helped Maseppa make the beds and gather rocks for a fire pit. Soon their site was done and she was free to wander around. She tied Butch on a string and walked back to the tent with all the children.

One of the children approached her. "Hello, is that your dog?"

"Yes, his name is Butch."

"I'm Anna. What's your name?"

"Phoebe. Have you ever been to a camp meeting before?"

"Yes, we came last year. I was born-again then."

Phoebe scrunched up her face. She wasn't sure what that meant. "We go to church meetings every Sunday."

"All that is good, but you'll hear about being born again at the meetings."

Phoebe and walked with her around the field. Anna waved at some of people. Most of them seemed to know her. "This is my new friend, Phoebe." They nodded or shook Phoebe's hand. The two girls looked inside the big tent where men were shoveling sawdust between rows of chairs.

"Why do they put sawdust on the ground?"

"That's so it won't get really muddy with all the people walking on it every day."

By the time evening came, around fifty tents had been set up. Organ music began playing. Each family lit a lantern and gathered in the tent. Zeke and Maseppa and Phoebe sat on the left side about half way down. Phoebe leaned this way and that trying to see the organist between all the heads.

A man got up front and taught them some new songs. It was exciting to sing with so many people altogether.

> "We're marching to Zion,
> Beautiful, beautiful Zion;
> We're marching upward to Zion,
> The beautiful city of God."

Then Reverend Finney stood behind the pulpit. He opened his Bible and held it in one hand while he walked back and forth and gestured with the other. Phoebe wondered why he needed a pulpit. He started with the creation story in Genesis, telling how God created a perfect world until sin entered. He told how God was a holy God and could not let sin be unpunished. Phoebe wished they were sitting closer so she could see him better. He was very interesting.

At the end of the sermon, they sang "Amazing Grace" and the preacher invited anyone who hadn't gotten his sin taken care of, to come forward to the front row. Quite a few people walked down to the front. They kneeled in the sawdust and got their hearts right with God.

It was beautiful seeing all the lanterns flickering around the field as everyone walked back to their tents. Some people who lived nearby rode home in their buggies.

Phoebe snuggled down in her bedroll. The tent had a musty smell. She could hear babies crying, the horses nickering, and a cow mooing. Butch crawled under the side of the tent and buried himself under her blankets.

She thought about the preaching and Anna's questions. It was hard to remember, but she did recall her father telling her about the Good Shepherd and how He wanted her to be His sheep. She remembered praying, but she was a little girl. *Did I really understand? Did I really mean it? I don't want to be condemned to hell because I haven't been born again.*

The next day, Reverend Finney started with a prayer, his voice carrying all the way to the back of the tent and outside to others who might be nearby. "Almighty Lord, we praise Thy name this morning for all Thy blessings to us. We thank Thee for Thy bounteous mercy to us while we were yet sinners. Lord, I pray for each soul here this week that they will examine their hearts and see if they are ready to meet Thee today. Save souls this week. Revive hearts to be willing to give their lives for Thy service. In Your

Gracious Name, Amen."

In his sermon, he taught them about the sinful fall of Adam and Eve and Cain and Abel. After a break for lunch, he taught about Noah and the flood that destroyed the sinful earth. He taught about the covenant with Abraham and the promise to send a Savior.

Phoebe had heard these stories before, but Reverend Finney taught how God used each man in His plan to save sinners from an eternity without Him in hell. It was so interesting that she was surprised to find that two or three hours had passed.

Tuesday evening, the last song "My Blessed Savior, Is Thy Love" was sung by the young lady,

> "So great, so full, so free?
> Behold, I give my love, my heart,
> My life, my all to Thee,
> My life, my all to Thee."

Phoebe went down the sawdust path to the front. She kneeled at the bench. She was crying, but didn't care.

"Lord God, I don't know if I did this as a little girl, but I want to be sure. I want You to take away my sins and wash me clean. I want to be born again. I want to belong to You. Amen."

The preacher kneeled down next to her. "Bless you, child. Do you want the Lord to cleanse you from your sins?"

"Yes, sir. I just prayed and told Him so."

"Bless you, child." He clenched his hands together and squeezed his eyes shut. He lifted his face and prayed loudly. "Almighty God, we thank Thee for saying, 'suffer the children to come unto me and forbid them not'. Lord bless this young girl. Teach her Thy ways. In Jesus's Almighty Name, Amen"

When she stood up, she saw that Maseppa and Zeke were

kneeling at the bench, too. When they were done praying, they stood up. Zeke gave them both a big hug. Phoebe saw that Maseppa had been crying, too. *Maseppa? She never ever cries!*

On Wednesday, Zeke left early to tend the animals again. When he returned, he had the whole Kittle family with him. Phoebe and Delly hugged each other and jumped up and down. "I'm so glad you're here, Delly." Zeke helped them set their tent in time for the evening meeting.

After they all sang, "We Are Bound for the Promised Land," Reverend Finney got up and spoke of Jesus's teachings. He told how the Pharisees thought they were religious but didn't realize that it was all useless without God's redemption. He told of Nicodemus who came to Jesus by night. "Ye must be born again." It was such a touching sermon, that if she hadn't gotten saved the night before, she would have wanted to that night.

Delly fidgeted next to her. Phoebe began praying for her. She heard Delly gasp and looked up. Mister Kittle was walking to the front, crying like a baby. Missus Kittle burst into tears, saying "Thank you, Lord! Thank you, Lord!"

Phoebe whispered to Delly, "Don't you want to get your heart right with God, too?"

Delly clenched her skirt in her hands. "I don't know how."

"Do you want me to go with you?"

"Yes!"

Phoebe went with Delly to the front and kneeled at the bench. "Just tell God that you're a sinner and want to belong to Him."

That was all it took. Delly poured her heart out to the Lord, telling him that she had not believed because He hadn't answered her prayers about her father. But now she saw that God could save a man like her daddy and that she was sorry that she didn't believe. She wanted things to change. She wanted to belong to His family.

She wanted to be a good girl...."

Phoebe was so happy for Delly and her whole family.

The rest of the week was like heaven. Dozens of people got right with the Lord each night. The song singing was wonderful. Phoebe sang with gusto. Most of the time it was off key, and she got a few funny looks from those around her. She didn't care. She was redeemed! She was a born again Christian!

The week finally ended. Anna and Phoebe promised to write each other and hoped to see each other again next summer. Parson Thomas met with them and others from their congregation. They talked of having a baptism soon within the next few weeks.

Phoebe felt free and clean. She wanted to fly like the gold finches flitting from tree to tree chirping and singing for joy. She hummed and sang the new songs. Zeke laughed. "You ain't no canary, Phoebe, but you are as happy as a lark today."

"I can't help it, Zeke! I feel as bubbly as a spring of water."

"Me, too, Li'l Angel. I asked Jesus to save me a long time ago when Granny told me about being saved by faith. But this week has shown me that I was being selfish about it. I want to tell others. That's why I brought the Kittles back with me. Look what the Lord did! I want to go back to my family in Boston. I want to tell them about the Lord, too."

Phoebe looked at Maseppa. "How about you, Maseppa? What did you learn?"

Maseppa was quiet for a while. Ol' Sam's hoofbeats filled in the silence. Phoebe waited patiently for her answer. "When I was caring for Phoebe and the wagon burned, I needed God. I decided to follow the path of Jesus, but still I am afraid. Sometimes I am angry at my father for leaving or other people who do not like Indians." She smoothed her dress with her hands and sighed. "I have not been a good wife to you, Zeke. I want to be a good wife and mother." She wiped her eye.

Zeke put his arm around her. She leaned on his shoulder, and he kissed the top of her head. Phoebe heard him whisper, "I love you, my sweet Zeppa."

21
THE BAPTISM

Matthew tossed a stone in the pond and watched the circles get bigger and bigger. "Phoebe, why are you getting' baptized?"

Phoebe looked over the edge of the bridge. Her reflection wiggled in the ripples. Every time she looked at herself, it reminded her of her parents. Maseppa said that her mother had curly hair mother and her father had blue eyes like her. She wished they could see her get baptized. *I wonder if they can see me from heaven.*

"Phoebe, you're not listening to me. Why are you gettin' baptized?"

"It's the right thing to do. Parson Thomas said it wasn't enough to follow God on the inside. We should show others that we belong to God."

"When did you belong to God?"

"I was a wee child, about your age –"

"I'm not a wee child! I'm almost eight years old!" He jumped to his feet and stood as tall as he could.

"You're getting taller, but you're not as big as I am, Matthew Gilmore!"

"I think getting baptized would be like swimming. I like swimming."

"Well, I'm going to get wet, but it's not like swimming. We're going to have it over at Sand Lake where it won't be so mucky at the bottom. There's going to be about ten people baptized. Zeke and Maseppa are getting baptized too."

"So, how do you do it . . . just jump in the water?"

Phoebe grinned. She could picture herself pinching her nose and doing a cannonball with a white robe on.

"No, silly. Parson Thomas will preach a little. Then he will ask me to walk out in the water with him. He will say a blessing over me and lower me down in the water and pick me up... and it will be all done."

"That's it?"

"Well, I reckon we'll sing some songs and he'll preach some more, but that's all I have to do."

"But you can dunk under like that down at the swimming hole anytime."

"Oh Matthew, you don't know anything."

"I do too! I just never heard of anyone getting baptized before! You're mean. I'm going home!"

He stomped off and then turned with a scowl and stuck out his tongue.

Phoebe sighed. Sometimes Matthew just didn't understand.

Ever since the camp meetings, the Kittles had been coming to church. They came late and sat in the back pew, but they were there every week. Ross and Stafford fidgeted a lot in the children's class, but Delly seemed to drink in every word, like they were cool drops of rain on a hot day.

Missus Thomas explained to her class what baptism meant. They talked about the baptism of Jesus and then how the disciples baptized people when they repented.

The parson planned a gathering down at the lake the last Sunday in August. He asked the congregation to consider obeying the voice of the Lord and letting the community know that they were taking a stand for the Lord. Phoebe, Zeke, and Maseppa all planned to be baptized, plus some of the other members of the church. Delly and her parents were, too.

Finally the day arrived. Phoebe wore her white Sunday dress, Maseppa wore a yellow dress with white stripes, and Zeke wore his wedding waistcoat and tie. Maseppa brought a bundle of extra clothes and towels, plus a basket of food for the picnic afterward.

They didn't have a Sunday school class this week, because Missus Thomas knew that her husband would be preaching on the meaning of baptism and new life in his sermon. She wanted her students to hear it.

Parson Thomas looked around his congregation. "Being baptized doesn't save you, it shows to others that you have chosen to put away your sins and your old life and that you now want to live by faith in your new life. You are a new creature, created in Christ Jesus."

Phoebe looked at Zeke, who was nodding in agreement.

After everyone was dismissed, they left in their buggies to meet again on the beach of Sand Lake for the baptism and picnic.

About twenty people stood in a semicircle around Parson Thomas. Mister Kittle was the first to be baptized, then his wife, then Delly and others who had committed to taking this stand of faith. Each waded out until the water came to their waists. The parson would say their name and baptize them in the names of the Holy Trinity.

Parson Thomas called Zeke to join him in the water. "Hezekiah

Erstein, I baptize you in the name of the Father, and the Son, and the Holy Ghost!"

With that he grabbed Zeke's shoulders and dipped him beneath the water. Zeke shook his head when he came up, and water sprayed about in the sunshine. He smiled at the Parson with joy.

Phoebe stood near Maseppa, and she could feel her tenseness. Phoebe knew that Maseppa didn't like to be in the middle of attention. This would be very hard for her. Next the Parson called Maseppa's name. She hesitated, and Zeke waited for her at the water's edge.

"Parson, could I assist with the baptizin'?"

"I'd be blessed and honored."

Zeke walked out with Maseppa. The parson said the blessing and Zeke put his arms around Maseppa and baptized her. Deborah met her on shore with a warm towel and a hug.

"Miss Phoebe?" Parson Thomas reached out his arm. "Are you ready?"

"Yes, sir."

The water became colder as she walked step by step into it. Her dress felt heavy as it soaked up the water. She stubbed her toe on a rock on the bottom and almost tripped and fell, but Parson Thomas caught her hand and helped her stand.

"Phoebe Johanson, I baptize you in the name of the Father, and the Son, and the Holy Ghost!"

She grabbed her nose as her face submerged beneath the cold water. Her hair swirled about her as she went down and then she felt herself being pulled up into the sunshine again. She wiped the water from her eyes and smiled at Missus Thomas waiting for her at the shore with a towel. Since she was the last one, the Parson came out of the water too.

"Lord, we thank you for these souls who have today taken the stand to say that they belong to You. Help them to obey You and follow Your will for the remainder of their days. Keep them from the evil one and his temptations. Now bless us as we partake of this food that You have so bountifully given to us. In the Name of our Lord and Saviour, Amen."

Matthew came trotting over next to her. "Phoebe, you're all wet. Was it fun? Was it like swimming?"

"No, Matthew, it's not like swimming. You'll see when you get baptized someday."

Phoebe not only felt wet, but she felt older. She knew that she had showed others that she had made a grown up decision and she meant to live up to its convictions.

22
BUCKY

By the end of summer, Bucky, Matthew's goat, had become a headache for both Matthew and Phoebe, because most of the time they were chasing him out of people's gardens. He was heavier than both of them put together and meaner than a cross-eyed bear.

Phoebe was supposed to take Matthew fishing, but before they could gather his pole and jar of worms from the barn, his mother hollered to him. "Matthew! That goat is in the garden again!" Deborah ran out of the kitchen door, flapping her apron at the rebellious goat. "Shoo! Shoo!"

The goat lifted his head and backed away from the flailing white cloth. His chin hairs wobbled back and forth as he chewed.

"You ate all my chard and beets! Out of here, you big brute!" She tried to grab the dangling rope, but he trotted out of reach and continued grazing. "Matthew!"

Little Sally tottered after her mother. She took a few wobbly steps and plopped down. Crawling on her hands and knees, she giggled in the grass as she tried to keep up. She saw something interesting on the ground and picked it up in her chubby fingers.

Deborah gave up chasing the goat and returned to Sally. "Oh, no! That's not good to eat, Sally! Those aren't raisins! Those are goat poops! Blech! Spit them out! Blech!"

Bucky wasn't a cute little kid anymore. He weighed over a hundred pounds and sported two long horns. Each morning, Matthew would slip the loop on the end of the rope over the top of a tall iron pole, and Bucky would munch on the grass and shrubs around it, clearing a circle each day. Every two or three days, they would drive the big stake into a different part of the yard. It was a good way to keep the lawn looking trim—as long as Bucky stayed tied.

Recently, Bucky had been getting loose and feasting on Deborah's vegetables and even the neighbor's – if he could escape unnoticed. He was getting so big that it took all of Matthew's strength to pull him away. Sometimes, Phoebe was there to help. She'd push from behind, and he'd pull from the front until they got him closed in the barn. Bucky didn't like being in there. He'd bang his head against the wall and bleat loudly over the injustice of being separated from his food.

Matthew couldn't figure out how Bucky was getting loose. The rope wasn't broken or chewed. The knot of the loop was still intact. He decided to watch to see how the goat was escaping, but that silly goat acted very mild and obedient while Matthew sat nearby. He would calmly graze around and around the stake and sometimes find a shady place to lie down for a nap and chew his cud. Matthew didn't want to waste his time watching a sleeping goat, but he knew it wouldn't be long before his mother was hollering again about Bucky being in the garden.

Phoebe thought they ought to spy from a crack in the shed. Matthew's father had moved the long stake to the back field behind the shed, where there was plenty of new grasses and flowers for Bucky to eat. He seemed content with his new surroundings, so Phoebe and Matthew decided to wait until the next day when most of the grass would be gone.

"Here's a good wide crack to watch him, Matthew." She leaned her face against the rough boards.

Matthew scooted a crate next to her. "Let me see." He gave a peek and then sat back. "This is going to be boring."

Bucky lifted his head and looked toward the shed.

"Shhhh, he heard us." Matthew whispered.

Bucky could see the garden behind the barn. He stretched the rope as far as it could go, but it didn't come close to the carrot tops at all. He pivoted around and ran straight toward the pole.

"He's going to butt it!" Matthew exclaimed.

But Bucky ran past the stake until the tension of the rope yanked on his neck, pulling his front feet off the ground. He turned and ran past it again, yanking on the rope the other way. He did this eight or nine times until the pole loosened in the ground and leaned at an angle. Then Bucky walked deliberately to it. He nudged the loop over the end of stake, and he was free. He proudly strutted off to eat his fill of carrots and cabbages.

Matthew slapped his hand on his knee. "That stupid goat is pretty smart!"

Phoebe giggled. "I wouldn't have believed it if I hadn't seen it. I guess we better go get him before your mother finds out."

Bucky didn't want to be caught. He tromped through the green beans and peas, nibbling as he went. Whenever Phoebe or Matthew came close, he'd run off a few feet. Matthew tried to step on the trailing rope, but was pulled on his backside as Bucky ran farther. "OWWW! Come back here, you stupid goat!"

Phoebe found some wild clover and picked a handful. "Come, Bucky. Look what I have for you." She waved the bouquet in front of the goat. He took a couple steps toward her. She backed up and he followed.

Matthew whispered, "Hey, keep going, Phoebe! He likes that." Matthew stood up and brushed the dirt from his hands. "I'll try to grab the rope while he's watching you."

"Come on, Bucky. Come get the delicious clover."

Matthew crept forward with exaggerated slow motion steps

until he reached the end of the rope. He grabbed the loop and twisted it around his arm. "I got it, Phoebe!"

Bucky wasn't going to be caught that easily. He jumped and pulled and twisted and began running across the yard, pulling Matthew behind him.

"HEELLLPP!" Matthew's feet dragged through the thistles and burdocks and rocks.

Bucky pulled him around the house all the way to the front porch, where the steps stopped Matthew from going any farther. Matthew stood up and reeled the rope around his arm as he walked up the steps toward the cornered billy-goat. "I've got you now."

Bucky lowered his head and plowed into Matthew's stomach, sending him sailing through the air. Phoebe arrived around the corner just in time to see him land head downward on the ground. She heard a CRACK!

"OWWWW! I'm dying! I can't move my arm!"

Deborah ran out of the front door with little Sally on her hip. "What happened?"

Phoebe answered, "Bucky pushed Matthew off the porch. I heard a crack. I think he broke something."

"OWWWWW!" Matthew rolled back and forth on his back, holding his left arm. "My neck is paining me! I think I broke my neck! I'm going to die!"

Deborah put Sally down and tried to calm him down. "You're not going to die. Stop yelping and let me see if you're bleeding anywhere."

"Am I bleeding? OWWWW!"

Phoebe shook her head. "What a baby!" But then she realized that Matthew couldn't turn his neck. *What if he is really hurt? What if he is crippled?*

"OWWWWWW"

Deborah sat him up. "Phoebe, run to get help. Stanley is working at the parsonage. If he's not there, get Maseppa or Zeke or anyone you know."

Phoebe jumped up and started running. She sped up the path over Snyders Hill. She took another shortcut through the trees to reach the church. Branches slapped her face and rocks bruised her feet, but she knew Matthew was hurt. He needed a doctor.

"Mister Gilmore! Mister Gilmore!" She ran around the work site. Parson Thomas was on a ladder.

"What's wrong, Phoebe?"

"Matthew's hurt. The goat pushed him off the porch."

Parson Thomas put down his hammer. "Stanley went to Troy to get another load of bricks. He should be back soon."

Phoebe shaded her eyes as she looked up at him. "Please, can you come help?"

"Is Matthew unconscious?" he asked while climbing down the ladder.

"No, but he can't move his neck or arm. He thinks he's dying, but Matthew can be that way."

Parson Thomas chuckled. "Have Deborah make him comfortable, and I'll be right there." He opened the door of the parsonage. "Let me tell my wife where I'm going, and we can meet Stanley on the way."

"Thank you, Sir." Phoebe took off back up the trail but ran all the way to her own house. "Maseppa! Maseppa!" She burst through the back door. "Maseppa, do you have teas to fix bones?

Matthew got hurt."

Maseppa stopped weaving. "Is he bleeding?"

"No. The goat pushed him off the porch, and he hurt his arm and neck. I heard a crack. I think he broke a bone. Do you have some leaves that will make him feel better?"

Maseppa went to the pantry. She pulled out some sacks of herbs. She crushed them and sniffed. Taking a couple of bags, she followed Phoebe outside. "I do not have comfrey, but these will take pain away."

By the time they got back to the Gilmores' house, Deborah had Matthew inside on the sofa. His eyes were closed and his cheeks were wet with tears. When he heard them come in, he tried to sit up, but fell back with a yelp. "Owwww!"

Phoebe told Deborah, "Your husband went to get bricks, but Parson Thomas is coming to take Matthew in his buggy until we meet your husband on the road."

Maseppa said, "I have herbs to take the pain away. Do you have hot water?"

"Yes, I'll get some right away." She took the teakettle off the stove and poured some into a cup. Maseppa crushed some dried raspberry leaves in the palms of her hands.

"The parson is here already." Phoebe called from the front window. "Matthew won't have time to drink any tea."

"If he chews the leaves, it will help," said Maseppa.

Matthew made a face. "It doesn't taste good."

Deborah met the minister at the door. "Thank you, Parson. I appreciate this."

"Good day, Deborah. How's the little feller?" He took off his hat. "Good day, Maseppa."

Phoebe tapped Deborah's arm. "Where's Sally?"

"Oh goodness me! She's napping!"

"I can take care of her, while you take Matthew to the doctor."

"Would you? Thank you, Phoebe. I don't know how long we'll be."

Maseppa said, "Could we bring her to our house when she wakes?"

"Of course, that would be fine."

The minister carried Matthew to his buggy and Deborah followed. "When we meet Stanley, I'll swap buggies with him. He can take mine, and I'll drive the bricks back."

Maseppa and Phoebe watched them drive away, with Matthew in the middle looking small and pitiful. "Do you think he'll be fine?"

"I think so. I hope he did not hurt his neck. A hurt arm is not so bad."

"I wonder where that silly goat is." Phoebe walked around the house. "Just as I thought, you old fool!"

The goat was happily munching in the middle of the garden. He looked at her and waggled his ears at her. She gathered another clump of clover. "Come on, Bucky. You've made enough trouble for today."

He was interested in the clover and followed her right into the barn. She shut the stall door and locked it. "You're staying there for a long time. I don't think Matthew's going to mind butchering you now!"

Sally woke within an hour. She cried a little when she didn't see her mother, but put her arms out to Phoebe. Sally put her head down on Phoebe's shoulder and stuck her thumb in her mouth.

Maseppa put wood on the fires and closed the dampers. They shooed the chickens in the barn for the night. "I think I should milk the cow. They may not be back until late." When they had done all that was needed, they closed the doors and walked home.

Sally waved to the house. "Ba-ba –ba-ba"

"Come, Sally. Let's pretend we're a horsey!" Phoebe galloped a few steps and Sally giggled.

It was fun taking care of Sally, but Phoebe had to watch her every minute. Whenever she'd find anything on the floor, she'd put it in her mouth. "Don't eat that, Sally! Blech!" Butch was very curious with someone down at his level. He licked her face all over. Sally giggled and followed him around the house. Butterball wasn't thrilled. He hid upstairs, away from the new creature making funny noises.

"Maseppa, she stinks. I've never changed a baby's pants before."

"I changed your pants when you were a baby. I will show you how."

They found some soft towels and undressed Sally. "Phew! You stink, Baby!" Sally giggled and kicked her feet. "Maseppa, it might be better if she took a bath in the sink."

"I think it would be good, too."

Maseppa mixed a little hot water with the well water from the pump. They set Sally in the sink. She loved it! She splashed and kicked and got everyone wet. They cleaned her all up and dressed her in some clean diapers.

Zeke arrived home. He laughed at the bunch of them dripping

water everywhere. They told the whole story about the goat and Matthew and Parson Thomas taking them to the doctor.

Zeke made Sally giggle with some silly faces and tossed her up in the air. She pulled his beard. "Hey, that's mine!" After eating some corn meal and milk, she fell asleep in Maseppa's arms.

Phoebe touched the soft curls. "Maseppa, did you ever want a baby of your own? I love babies. I can't wait until I'm grown up and married so I can have a baby. But you are married now, so you can. Isn't that great?"

Maseppa didn't answer. She looked at Zeke, and Phoebe thought she saw his cheeks turn a bit pink.

"It's been a long time since a baby has been in this house," said Zeke. "In fact, you were the only baby that lived here, Phoebe."

"I'd thought I'd like a baby brother, but Sally is so much fun. Maybe a baby sister would be nice. Can we have a baby girl?"

"If God chooses to give us a baby, I don't think we can choose what kind He will give us."

Maseppa looked at Zeke again. He winked at her, and Maseppa blushed this time.

It was quite dark before they heard a buggy pull into the yard. Stanley came in the kitchen. "Good evening, folks. Thank you for taking care of Sally. Matthew's broke his wrist and his collar bone, and he might have had a concussion. He is bandaged up and has to be quiet for a few days."

"That's too bad," said Zeke. "If you need any help with your barn yard chores, let us know."

"I milked your cow tonight," added Maseppa, "and put the chickens in the barn."

"Oh, thank you very much!"

Sally hardly woke as Maseppa handed her to her father. "Good night, folks. I know one thing we're doing soon. We're going to have goat stew. He's done more damage this last week than he's worth!"

23
BUILDING TRUST

Not everyone was convinced that Roster Kittle had turned his life around. He had changed on the inside, but the outside was taking a little longer. His language was still coarse, and giving up whiskey was harder than he thought. So was finding a steady job.

Zeke knew that he had changed. He wished Roster could help him with hauling supplies, but that was up to Jarvis Cooper. Jarvis said that one worker was all he could afford or need. It seemed to be the same with every other place in town.

There was plenty to do around the farm, and Zeke never had enough time to do it all. Zeke had put off repairing the shingles on the roof, and Maseppa was complaining about leaks in the kitchen every time it rained. Also, they needed a new outhouse – which included digging a big pit and constructing a two-hole facility, plus filling in the old one with rocks and dirt. Of course, the winter's supply of wood needed to be split and stacked. There was plenty to do. So until something better came along for Roster, Zeke put him to work on their farm.

The first time Roster Kittle came to the house to begin work on the shingles, Butch's fur bristled on his back. He stood guard on the porch and growled whenever Roster approached.

Roster stopped a few feet from the front steps. "I don't blame you, Butch. I'd be 'fraid of me, too." He looked at Phoebe, who was trying to calm her dog. "I'm sorry for the way I acted back then. Whiskey does horrid things to a man's mind. I hope you forgive me."

Phoebe nodded, but wondered if she could ever forgive him for trying to kill her dog. She knew Zeke trusted him, but sometimes she could still feel the fear and anger rise up in her chest

After a few weeks, Phoebe got used to seeing Mister Kittle around the place. He'd show up soon after sunrise, and Zeke would get him started on a project. Maseppa would bring him some food for dinner, and he drank from the well. He politely kept to his work and never came into the house. Butch didn't bark at him as much, but he still didn't want Roster to get too close.

When fall classes started, Delly and her brothers came with their father and walked to school with Phoebe. At the end of the day, the Kittles would all go home with her. Little by little, God was changing their father. It was good to see him laughing with his children and sitting with his wife at church. Phoebe thought he even looked like a different man, especially when he smiled.

The snows came early that year. By mid-November, a foot of snow covered the ground, and it kept on coming. There would be no ice-skating that year. The mill pond was no more than a hollow place in the white drifts behind the village shops. The children found other ways to fill their time.

The children loved the snow. Every recess became a snowball war, the yard became a giant circle for a game of Fox and Geese, and the hill behind the schoolhouse sloped perfectly for sliding. The children brought sleds, skis, and even old tin basins, if they didn't have anything else. Strings of mittens and hats hung across the coat room – hopefully getting dry before being used again.

Every home changed the wheels on their buggies and wagons to runners. The town of Poestenkill had a snow warden who pulled a huge heavy cylinder through the county roads to pack the snow. If there were places where the wind blew it bare, they would shovel more snow onto the road to keep roads smooth for the cutters and sleighs. Covered bridges were also filled with snow to remain usable in the winters.

Zeke preferred driving his route in snow. He could get travel on runners in about half the time. He and Roster took Ginger and Ol' Sam to the blacksmith in Poestenkill for their spiked winter horseshoes. "You know, Roster, you ought to learn blacksmithing. We need one around here."

Roster watched the smithy pull on the bellows and pound the hot metal. "I just might do that." After talking with the owner, he was hired to be an assistant. While they were there, Zeke helped him purchase a strong horse and a used wagon.

Roster's face beamed as he adjusted the reins in his big hands. "I'll pay you back as soon as I can, Zeke. I 'preciate all you're doin' for me."

Zeke shrugged. "Everyone needs a leg up sometime."

Hardly a week went by without another big snowstorm. Sometimes, the snow would be blowing so hard that they didn't even have school. Phoebe didn't mind too much. It gave more time to curl up near the crackling fireplace with a good book or her embroidery stitching. Sometimes, she'd spend time in the barn, talking and petting the animals. Her favorite spot was up in the hayloft. If she opened the little window, she could see way past the mill and the pond – all the way to the hazy-blue mountains. It made her think of the big rock that she used to climb on when she and Maseppa lived in the woods. *That seems like a lifetime ago.* It was hard to believe that she and Maseppa and Zeke had been living here for only three years. *It seems like this has always been my home.*

One night, Phoebe lay on her bed, listening to the wind. It

sounded angry, like it was throwing a tantrum because it couldn't get inside. *I wonder what happens to the chickadees and little birds in the storms. Maybe they hang on to the branches really tightly, and the wind twirls them around like a spinning jumping jack toy.* She smiled at the funny picture in her mind. *They probably huddle together under a fir branch. They'll be hungry if the snow covers all their seeds.*

Later than night, she woke. The storm had stopped, and all was quiet. She got up to use the chamber pot under her bed. The window was all frosted. She blew on it and rubbed it to make a hole. She peered out to see how much it had snowed. There were three deer under the apple tree, nibbling the apples and bark from the lower branches. One buck was resting his hooves on the trunk to reach a little higher. She stood there watching them until her toes felt numb.

A few days later, Zeke stomped his boots as he returned from his morning chores. "Good morning, Li'l Angel!"

"I'm not so little anymore," she said, but blushed at the attention.

"Would you know anything about the grain all over the ground under the apple tree?"

As she stirred her oatmeal, Phoebe glanced at him out of the corner of her eye. "The birds were hungry." Once she started, a cascade of words poured from her thoughts. "It's so cold out there in the wintry wind, and the snow has covered up all the seeds. The chickadees were crying and crying, like they were hungry. You ought to see how happy they are with the grain. They were so excited, twittering and chirping, and calling their family to have some, too." She looked back down at her porridge, not daring to see Zeke's reaction.

Finally, after a long pause, she faced him. She was surprised to see his face all crinkled and his eyes twinkling; he was not being able to contain his laughter. "I should have known it! Of course, I should have known you were feeding all the animals in Rensselaer County! The news is probably being sent by carrier pigeon to all the mice and deer that they can get a free meal at Phoebe's house."

"I saw some deer under the apple tree last week," said Phoebe.

"I told you so!"

"I'm sorry, Zeke. It's just that I don't like to hear them crying when they sound so hungry." Her shoulders drooped and she hung her head over the steaming bowl.

"You've got the softest heart of anyone I know," said Zeke. "I'll make a deal with you. I really don't want you putting out the horse and cow grain for the birds, but if you want to, I'll let you have the stuff that gets left in the corners of their feeding box or dropped on the floor. I usually sweep it down in the dung pit. You'll need to help me clean out the stalls to get it though."

With renewed joy, she jumped up and gave him a squeeze around his neck and a smack on his whiskery cheek. "Oh, thank you, Zeke! I knew you'd understand!"

~ # ~

The snowy winter was finally over, and the world was waking up from its long sleep. Phoebe hummed as she hurried through her morning chores one Sunday morning. She dressed quickly to be sure to be on time for church, especially the children's class at the parsonage. Ginger must have been glad for spring, too, because she trotted along at a quicker pace than normal without her heavy winter shoes.

As the others arrived, Phoebe paused to look at Missus Thomas's Bible, with its shiny edges and her named stamped in gold on the front cover. *Genevieve Thomas* She had told them that her husband bought it as a gift to her when they were first married.

"Do you have a Bible, Phoebe?"

"No, Ma'am. Well, I have my papa's big Bible at home, but it's not as pretty as this, and it's much too big to carry to Sunday class."

Missus Thomas looked around at her students. "I have a great idea! If you memorize one hundred verses from the book of Psalms before the end of the year, I will give you a Bible of your very own."

Phoebe jerked her head up, her eyes widening. *My own Bible? A hundred verses isn't very hard. I've learned poetry for school.*

"You've all heard Psalm 23 many times. That one should be easy for you. Psalm 1 and Psalm 100 are also quite familiar."

Matthew blurted out, "What's the shortest Psalm?"

Everyone giggled, and he stuck his tongue out at them.

"Psalm 117 is the shortest – it only has two verses, but I'm not counting chapters, I'm counting verses."

Matthew wiggled on the bench. "I know, but I want to learn it anyway."

Mary raised her hand. "May I learn one hundred verses of chapter 119?"

"Yes, but that is not an easy chapter to learn. Many of the verses are similar, so it is easy to get confused."

Phoebe raised her hand.

"Yes, Phoebe?"

"Do we have to say them all at the same time – or may we say a little each week?"

"You may say what you have learned that week to me at Sunday class, but I would like each of you to recite some at the Christmas program in December. Today is May twenty-fourth. That gives you about seven months to work on them."

"I can't learn a hundred verses in seven months!" Matthew threw his hands up in the air.

Missus Thomas smiled. "That's about four verses each week. If you put your mind to it, you can do it."

That night, Phoebe took out her papa's big Bible and opened it up on the sitting room table. "Ezra, Nehemiah, Esther, Job, Psalms." Psalm 23 looked fairly easy, and so did Psalm 100. That made seventeen verses. She only needed eighty-three more. Psalm 119 had one hundred and fifty verses. She stood up and flipped one braid over her shoulder. "Whew! That's a long one!"

She turned back a few pages to Psalm 1.

"Blessed is the man that walketh not
in the counsel of the ungodly,
nor standeth in the way of sinners,
nor sitteth in the seat of the scornful."

She leaned over and read it again. "Blessed is the man that walketh not in the counsel of the ungodly." She repeated it a couple of times. It reminded her of Maseppa telling her that she shouldn't listen to others and follow them if they are doing wrong. She needed to think for herself and do what was right even if she was the only one.

She found a piece of paper to copy the verses from Papa's Bible so that she could put them in her apron pocket and study them anywhere.

Maseppa watched Phoebe pacing back and forth and mumbling to herself. "Phoebe, what are you saying? I cannot hear you."

"I'm learning some verses so I can get a Bible. Missus Thomas said that if we could learn one hundred verses by the end of the year, she would give us our own Bible. I've already learned Psalm 1 – that's six verses."

"That is a good thing to do. I think your mama and papa would be happy to know that you are learning God's Book."

Phoebe's evening chore was washing the supper dishes. She poured some boiling water in the tin basins and added cold water with the pump. With each up and down stroke, she said a word: down – "The," up – "Lord," down – "is," up – "my," down – "shepherd." She paused as the last word triggered a memory. "Maseppa, did my papa say those words? It makes me think of him."

"Yes, he told you about the Shepherd when you got lost in the woods. He said you were like the sheep that was lost. Do you remember?"

"A little." The memories all seemed fuzzy, like she was seeing them through the morning mist.

She tried to say a whole verse while washing each plate. "The Lord is my shepherd. I shall not want." She grabbed another dish. "He maketh me to lie down in green pastures; He leadeth me beside the still waters."

"Phoebe, it will take you all night to wash the dishes, if you don't work faster than that."

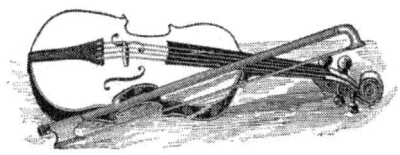

24
FIDDLING AROUND

Now that school was out for the summer, Phoebe had plenty of time to memorize the verses. She said them while feeding the chickens, while weeding the garden, and while sweeping the floors. Of course, when she was lost in reading an exciting book or gallivanting through the woods with Matthew or Delly, she forgot all about learning verses. Even so, by July, she had already learned fifty of them.

One warm evening, Phoebe sat on the top step of the porch with the Bible open on her knees.

> "The heavens declare the glory of God
> and the firmament showeth His handiwork.
> Day unto day uttereth speech
> and night unto night showeth knowledge . . .
> Let the words of my mouth and the meditations of my heart
> be acceptable in Thy sight, O Lord,
> my strength and my Redeemer."

When she finished reading the Psalm, she closed the Bible and sat there for a few minutes. Maseppa and Zeke sat on the swing. Zeke had his arm around Maseppa, and Maseppa had Butterball on her lap. No one said anything. They sat there for a while watching the blinking fireflies and listening to the summer sounds –the rushing creek, the birds, and the peepers all singing their evening songs.

"Zeke, did you know that peepers are tiny little tree frogs?"

"Really? I knew they were frogs, but I didn't know they lived in trees! You're a smart girl. What do you think you'll do after you finish the eighth grade?"

"I think I'd like to go to the girls' school in Cokesbury and maybe become a teacher. Miss Edgecomb has us listen to the little ones read. I really like that. It's satisfying to see them learn new things."

"That's a great thing to – Hey! Did you see that shooting star?"

"Yes! There's another one! Are they really falling stars? Delly said that when someone dies, a star falls, but I don't believe her."

Zeke chuckled. "I've heard that too, but I don't believe it either. I heard that it is a kind of rock that flies through the earth's air. It's going so fast that it burns up before it hits the ground."

"Really? Wow! I think they're pretty no matter what they are."

Butch trotted around the house and joined them on the porch. Phoebe scratched behind his ear. "Look, there's Orion's belt. We learned about that last month in school."

"Yeah, and there's the Big Dipper. See it?"

Phoebe had to lean way over to see the whole thing. "Miss Edgecomb said that if you follow that path of the two end stars, it points you to the North Star. That's the tail star on the Little Dipper."

Maseppa said, "My mother taught me to look at that star when I walk at night. The other stars move around the sky, but that star does not move."

Phoebe added, "It always points north, right?"

"Yes," said Zeke. "I've heard tell that the slaves who are looking for freedom follow that star to the north. It's their guide to freedom."

Phoebe said, "We've been talking about the Confederate States at school and how they want to be their own country. They don't want the northern states to tell them what to do. Miss Edgecomb says there might even be a war about it. Do you think so, Zeke?"

"There might be. I hope not."

"Would you fight in it?"

"I don't know. I hope I don't have to, but it might be the right thing to do."

Butch's ears perked up, and he gave a low growl. He stood up and began barking.

Phoebe rubbed his back; his hairs stood on edge. "What is it, boy?"

Zeke looked out into the darkness. "Probably a raccoon or skunk waking up from their winter sleep."

Whatever it was, it must have kept on going. Butch thumped his tail on the porch as Phoebe rubbed his head. "It's nice out here tonight, isn't it?"

"It sure is. Why don't you fetch me my fiddle? I'm feeling like playing a few tunes tonight."

Phoebe hopped up and disappeared into the house. Soon she was back with Zeke's fiddle case. He laid it across his lap and unbuckled the straps. Even in the dim light, Phoebe could see the gloss of the smooth wood. Zeke lifted out the instrument and the thin bow. Standing up, he tightened the horse-hairs on the bow and tucked the round end of the fiddle under his chin.

Phoebe looked up at him expectantly. He played a few squawky notes and gave the tuning keys a few twists. Soon a cascade of trills spilled from his fingers. He set his foot on the porch railing and let the fiddle sing!

Phoebe clapped and thumped her heels on the step. She couldn't sit still anymore. In her bare feet, she flew over the front lawn, twirling and gliding in time with the music. She felt like a leaf floatng down the creek in the springtime, spinning in the current, splashing over the falls, and spraying high in the air. She felt like a snowflake before the winter wind, flying high over the trees and housetops.

While Phoebe danced with the fireflies, Butch barked and nipped at her heels. Maseppa's toes tapped in time to the lively jig. Faster and faster the music swirled. Right when Phoebe could hardly breathe, Zeke ended the song. She laughed and clapped her hands. Maseppa clapped, too. Zeke held his arms out widely from his sides and gave a big bow.

Zeke began another song. This one swayed with a waltzing rhythm. Phoebe sat on the swing next to Maseppa. Butterball crawled on her lap and purred as Phoebe stroked his orange fur. She closed her eyes and could feel herself rolling over the hills on their wagon. She could almost hear Ginger's hooves clip-clopping in time with the tune. It made her feel homesick, but she was home . . . so it couldn't have been that. She felt lonely for days gone by, the days when she was a very young child, when life didn't seem so complicated.

A horse trotted by pulling a buggy. It was Parson Thomas. Zeke nodded to him and played the refrain one more time. He paused for a minute and tuned a couple of strings again. "Here's one to remember Granny." The next notes brought tears to Phoebe's eyes. It was the hymn "Fairest Lord Jesus." She could picture Granny closing her blind eyes and tipping her head back to sing the words in German. The long bold notes floated through the darkness up through the stars to heaven. Butch sat on his haunches and howled. The melancholy feelings overwhelmed her heart and tears filled her eyes. *I miss Granny. I wonder if she misses me. I reckon I could write her a letter and let her know how Maseppa and I - and Zeke - are doing . . . and thank her for teaching me to see with my heart.*

Zeke let the last note drift away until it blended with the wind in the trees. He leaned over and patted the dog. "You ain't partial to my fiddlin', Butch?"

"Do you think I could learn how to play the fiddle, Zeke?"

"Well, I don't see why not. Here, let me show you how to hold it." He handed Phoebe the long neck of the instrument and helped her tuck the base under her chin. Then he showed her how to hold the bow. "Now pull the hairs gently over the strings."

SCRAWEEK!

Phoebe winced and pulled the bow away. "Oooo . . . that's awful!"

"Well, you can't learn in one night. I'll show you more another time. Right now, it's time you went to bed."

~ # ~

A few days later, Delly and Phoebe leaned against the bridge railing as they watched Matthew fish in the mill pond. "You're not fooling me, are you, Phoebe?"

"No, I'm not. Zeke's teaching me how to fiddle."

"Do you think he would teach me to play too? I've always had a hankering to learn the fiddle."

"It's not as easy as it looks. I don't think I'll ever be able to play it like Zeke." Phoebe tossed a pebble into the pond and watched the ripples spread across the water. "See if your ma will let you stay at my house tonight, and we can ask Zeke about teaching you, too."

With the proper permission, the girls made plans for as much fun as they could fit into one evening. Maseppa fixed chicken and dumplings, and they popped corn in the fireplace. Zeke told some funny stories about his travels, and they giggled at him. They giggled about everything.

As usual, they ended the evening with a reading from the Good Book. Phoebe brought out the fiddle. "Zeke? Will you show Delly how to play the fiddle, too? She always wanted to learn."

"I don't see why not." Zeke winked at Delly, and she blushed. He helped her set it on her shoulder exactly right and hold the bow. She pulled the bow across the strings... and it was beautiful! It didn't sound like Phoebe's first try. Zeke lifted his eyebrows with wonder. "Have you ever done this before, Delly?"

She put down her arms and shook her head. "No, sir. This is the first time I've ever touched a fiddle."

She raised the bow again and tried another string. Again the instrument hummed, but with a deeper resonating voice. She smiled and pushed the bow slowly back and forth over each string. Sometimes the strings squeaked, but not very often.

"You're a born natural at this!"

"Could you show me how to put my fingers down?" She wiggled her hand at the top of the neck.

Zeke lifted his face and laughed. "WoooEee! You're chomping to learn the next lesson already!"

Phoebe sat on the sofa and watched Zeke show Delly where to put her fingers. Delly played the new note, pulling and pushing the bow up and down. She beamed at Phoebe. Phoebe smiled back.

Delly handed the instrument back to Zeke. "Thank you, Mister Erstein, for letting me try your fiddle."

"You're very welcome, Delly. I hope you can learn more. You are a born natural at it. That's for sure!"

That night, as Phoebe and Delly snuggled under the quilt, Delly said, "You're awfully quiet tonight. Are you mad at me?"

"No"

"Then what's the matter?"

Phoebe didn't know what to say. She sighed. "I'm guess I'm jealous of you doing so well on the fiddle. I shouldn't be. I'm happy for you. I can't play hardly at all. Every time I do it, the strings screech and squawk. I thought I was getting better and would be able to learn some different notes soon. Zeke says I need to practice making them sound smoother first."

"I'm sorry, Phoebe. I can't help it. It just came out that way."

"I know, but you are really good! I can't sing either. Butch howls every time I sing."

"Phoebe, you can't be good at everything."

"But I'm not good at anything!"

"Yes, you are. You can climb to the top of a tree."

"Huh! What's so special about that?"

"I can't! I'm scared that I'll fall and break my neck."

"I don't know who I am anymore. I'm not the little girl that ran wild in the woods. I don't always like playing with Matthew. I only do it to earn a penny. Sometimes I want to wear pretty clothes and learn to do fancy stitching and bake a cake. I used to think that was prissy stuff."

Delly giggled. "Me, too. Remember when you first saw me?"

Phoebe giggled. "Yes, you almost punched me in the nose!"

The next Sunday after meeting, Parson Thomas shook Zeke's hand and said, "That was some nice fiddling you did the other night."

Zeke's mouth dropped open. "You heard me?"

"The whole village heard you. It was beautiful. I play the bass fiddle myself, and I know of some others who can play some tunes. Maybe we could get together some time."

"I'd like that!"

The next week, they met in Morris Reynolds' barn. There was Parson Thomas and his bass fiddle, Morris with a banjo, Roster Kittle with a harmonica, and of course, Zeke with his fiddle. At the first rehearsal, they only compared what songs they all knew. They played reels and waltzes and folk songs.

Word got around, and the following week, the musicians had an audience. Stanley and Deborah brought their children. The Kittle family came, too. Maseppa wasn't enthused about socializing, but she liked to listen to Zeke play his fiddle, so she came along. Delly and Phoebe and some other young ones sat up in the hay mow listening to the music, clapping, and singing along. Zeke pointed his bow up at Delly. "See that young lady right there?" The other men turned to where he pointed. "She's going to be the best fiddler around. She picked up my fiddle for the first time, and it sounded like she was born with it in her hands."

The men smiled, tipped their hats at Delly, and then went back to plucking and bowing and tapping their feet to the music. Phoebe couldn't sit still. She hopped down to the barn floor and swirled and spun around and around until the song ended. Little Sally followed Phoebe around, but fell down when she got dizzy. Phoebe took her little hands and they danced together, swaying this way and that and turning around together. Morris Reynolds laughed. "It looks like we've set a butterfly into motion. That was right pretty, Miss Phoebe."

On the way home, Phoebe said, "That was fun."

"It sure was."

"Zeke, I'm not any good at singing or playing the fiddle."

"We all have our strong talents."

"I know yours is playing the fiddle. Maseppa makes baskets and knows herbs and things. Missus Thomas knows how to crochet and do fancy stitchery."

"It's not always things we can see or make. Sometimes, it's how you treat others."

"What do you mean?"

"Look at Maseppa here." He put his arm around her and gave a quick hug. Maseppa smiled. "She is steady. She doesn't let things upset her, and she doesn't get too excited over something new. I like her even and calm personality. That's one of her beautiful talents."

Maseppa gave him a playful shove with her hand. "You do not know what is in my head. Maybe I am very angry with you right now!"

They all laughed at her silliness.

Phoebe grew serious again. "But I don't know what my talent is, Zeke. I'm not good at anything!"

He smiled. "You've got plenty of good talents. I think you've got one of the biggest hearts I've ever known. Don't worry your head about it. Think of others instead of yourself and you'll do fine."

25
THE TREE FORT

It had rained for a whole week. Everything felt soggy and moldy in the damp air. When the sun finally pushed away the clouds, everyone was anxious to get out of their houses – especially Matthew.

Phoebe was giving the porch steps a good sweep when he ran up their lane. "Phoebe, come see my new fishing hole."

"I thought you could go by yourself now."

Matthew had finally convinced his parents that, since he was almost eight years old, he was now big enough to go fishing by himself. That meant Phoebe wouldn't be getting a penny to watch him anymore, but there were days when she would rather stay home and read a book than ramble through the woods. But the sun was shining and Matthew was so excited that she agreed to see what all the hubbub was about.

"Matthew, wait up!" Phoebe pushed through the underbrush. Matthew wanted to show her his new secret fishing spot, claiming the old one was too close to the road. "Everyone fishes there!"

Phoebe stopped to catch her breath. She couldn't hear him crashing through the bushes. "Matthew!"

She heard a faint call up ahead, but the stream was gurgling over some rocks, making it hard to hear anything else. She pushed ahead. A fir branch poked her in the eye. In one place, where the trees grew right on the creek bank, she had to walk up around them. *It's too bad that I'm not earning a penny for all this.*

"Matthew! Where are you?"

"I'm over here!"

She saw him standing on a big rock, waving his arms. "So is this your new fishing hole?"

"No, but look!" He pointed downstream to a place where the creek divided. "It's an island!"

There was a long piece of land in the middle of the stream, big enough to build a house on it, if you wanted to. He ran along the water to get a closer view. She could see why he was so excited. It was a wild, unexplored territory – their own discovery.

"Phoebe, do you know how to make a raft? We could float over there and no one could bother us."

She wasn't too sure. "What if the raft got loose and floated downstream? How would we get home?"

"Oh, we wouldn't let that happen. We'd be really careful."

"I know who has an old boat."

"Who?"

"The Kittles. I saw one behind their house in a pile of junk." Phoebe looked over at the island and down at the rushing water. At that point, the creek was too deep to wade across and too wide to make a bridge with a log. It was too swift to swim across, at least right now after the rain. "But, if we ask the Kittles for the boat, we'd have to include them in the secret, you know."

Matthew sighed. "I suppose we could let them play with us." He sat on the rock and stared at the island. "I wonder why they have a boat. It's not like they live near a lake or river or anything"

"I don't know. Let's ask them tomorrow."

When Phoebe stopped by the Gilmores' house with Matthew, they told his parents of the island and their plans to explore it. His father wasn't as excited as they were. "I'm quite sure that's on the Reynolds' land, so you ought to ask them if you can play there."

Matthew's shoulders drooped. "After we tell everyone, it's not going to be a secret place anymore."

"Sorry, son. Sometimes, we have to think of safety before fun." He turned to Phoebe. "Would you mind keeping an eye on things? I'd be willing to pay you again."

"No, you don't have to pay me. I'm interested in exploring this island myself."

The next day, Phoebe and Matthew hiked through the shortcut, past the pine grove, to the Kittles' house. The children were delighted to be included in the adventure. Delly didn't think their parents would mind about the boat. "Our pa got that in a trade with a bunch of other stuff, like a table and beds. Some man was moving and wanted to get rid of everything. We don't ever use it."

"I hope it doesn't leak."

Their pa didn't care if they used the boat, and their ma was glad to get it off the property, but like most mothers, she worried about the dangers. "You younguns be careful now!"

Mister Reymolds gave his permission to play on the island along with another warning. "Don't do anything foolish. Be careful, ya hear?"

Finally they were off on their adventure. Matthew grumbled. "Grown-ups sure worry a lot. I don't ever want to grow up."

With Matthew, Ross, and Stafford pulling on the rope and with Phoebe and Delly pushing from behind, they slid the boat down the path to the stream. Sometimes they all had to work together to lift it over a fallen tree or rock. Phoebe couldn't see any big holes in the boat, but it looked pretty old. She hoped it didn't leak after all this work.

Finally, they reached the creek just above the island. They slid the boat down into the water with a splash. The current pulled it, and it took a few of them to hold it tight. Nearer the island, the water spread out and calmed down.

"It's floating!" cheered Matthew. "We'll need some poles to push us along."

They looked for long sticks or branches that would work.

Matthew held up his hand. "I think I ought to be the captain since it was my idea."

Ross disagreed. "But it's our boat. I think I ought to be the captain. You can be the governor of the island." He stood close to Matthew and looked down his nose at him.

Phoebe pushed them apart. "Neither one of you is going to be the captain. I'm the oldest, and Matthew's parents have put me in charge. I don't think we ought to get in all at once. I'll take two of you over and come back for the others." She tied the rope to a tree and climbed in the boat. It rocked back and forth as she made her way to the bow. "Matthew, you and Ross can go first. Delly and Stafford will wait here."

Delly untied the rope, and the boat drifted off from the shore. Phoebe pointed to the island. "Let's aim for that big birch tree on the point." They all paddled and pushed. When they got out farther, the current pulled them downstream. They paddled harder, but they slid past the birch tree. As they neared the island the current slowed, and they were able to reach the lower end of the island. Matthew jumped out and cheered.

Phoebe shouted to Delly, "I can't go back up stream! Meet me down a ways." She pushed off and tried to paddle upstream. It was much harder all by herself. By the time she made it back to the creek bank, she was a few hundred feet downstream. Delly grabbed the rope, and they both pulled it back upstream to where they had started before.

"Phoebe, I think we ought to start even farther up. You almost missed the island the first time."

All this was taking much more effort than Phoebe thought it would. By the time they all got onto the island, it would be getting dark, and they'd have to go home. Stafford sat in the bottom of the boat, while Phoebe and Delly pushed and paddled. This time they landed on a shallow spot on the upper side.

It didn't take long to explore the whole island. It was about two hundred feet long and about fifty feet wide. There were berry bushes everywhere and lots of trees. The biggest tree was a big pine with two wide branches about halfway up. The children sat side by side on the branches.

Matthew looked up through the needles. "Do you know what we need?"

"What?" Ross asked as he tossed a pine cone toward the water.

"A fort. A tree fort!" He pointed around him. "We could nail boards from here to that branch over there and make walls that go up to here with a tarpaulin for a roof."

"We'd need hammers and nails and saws," said Ross.

Phoebe had climbed to the top of the tree. "I can see the church steeple from here."

Delly hugged the trunk. "Phoebe, you're going to fall. Don't go so high."

"Ah, don't worry about me. I've been climbing trees since I was a little girl."

She came down anyway. "I think I know where we can get some boards. Zeke tore down the old outhouse. Maybe he'll let us use the lumber. I'll ask him tonight."

Delly wrinkled her nose. "An outhouse?"

"The boards don't stink."

The boat did leak, and by the time everyone got back to shore, a puddle had formed in its bottom. Phoebe added a tin can to her mental list of things to bring next time.

That evening at supper, Phoebe told Zeke and Maseppa all about their adventure and plans for the summer. "We want to make a tree fort on the island. What are you going to do with the lumber from the old outhouse?"

"A tree fort?" He scratched his head and smiled. "I suppose I could share some boards with you. How are you going to put it all together?"

"We need some hammers and nails . . . and saws, too. Do you have any old ones that we can use?"

"I have some, but I don't really want them lost in the woods or creek."

Maseppa paused in her sweeping. "There are many hammer things in the log cabin."

"She's right! I haven't been in there for a while. We can take a look in the morning."

"Do you want to see the island?"

"Yes, that sounds dandy. I'd love to see what you youngsters have been up to. You make sure you do your chores," Zeke said. "I don't want this tree fort to make you a lazy girl."

She smiled. "Yes, Zeke. I'll do my chores."

Phoebe wrapped her arms around his neck and squeezed. "Thank you, Zeke."

He sputtered and coughed and waved his arms and legs around. "Ackk! I can't breathe! I can't breathe!"

Phoebe giggled and let go. "Good night, Zeke." She gave Maseppa a hug. "Good night, Maseppa."

The next morning, just as he promised, Zeke turned the key in the old padlock and pushed open the heavy door of the old cabin. Something scurried in the shadows and a musty odor greeted their noses. Phoebe stepped into the dark room and slowly turned in a circle. She hadn't been in there since Uncle Pete left. "Did you know that my pa lived here before he met my mother?"

"Yes, I did know that. He was a good craftsman." Zeke inspected the stack of unfinished furniture in the corner. "I wish I could carve like this."

Phoebe ran her hand over a carved post. "This looks like my bed, only mine has an acorn at the top."

"Maybe it wasn't finished." Zeke stepped to the workbench. "Here are his chisels and mallets. These are worth a lot of money. They ought to be put away for you to pass on to your children and grandchildren."

"Zeke! I'm not even married yet."

"But you will be some day, and you'll want something that belonged to your pa as a legacy to them."

He moved some crates around. "Here's some stuff we can use." There were some hammers and crow bars and saws. "They don't look too valuable. Even so, don't lose them in the woods. Learn to keep track of things you borrow."

"I will."

"Also, be careful with that saw. I don't want any missing fingers."

"Yes, Zeke, we'll be careful."

Next they walked over to the pile of old boards. Zeke tugged at a few and tossed them to the side. "There are a lot of good nails in those boards. You can pound them out and straighten them and use them over again."

Over the next few weeks, each child contributed to the cause with boards and ropes and whatever they could find at home that nobody wanted. Every day, after their chores, they met at the island.

Matthew held a bent nail on a flat rock with his left hand and tapped it with a hammer. "OUCH!" He jumped up and popped the sore thumb in his mouth. Pulling it out, he saw some skin had been scraped away. "OWWWWW!"

Phoebe hopped down from the tree. "Let me look at it."

"Do you think it's broken?"

"No, it's not broken!" She watched as the skin turned purple. "Put it in the cold water. That should make it feel better. Matthew, you are the most hurtin'est person I've ever met."

Within a few days, they finished building the tree fort. There was a nice floor, some crude walls, and even a window to keep a lookout for intruders – although the only intruders were in their imaginations. Delly and Phoebe pulled the canvas tarp over their heads. There wasn't as much room as they had hoped, but enough for all five of them to sit inside.

Phoebe said, "We should name it CASTAWAY ISLAND, and pretend that we've been shipwrecked, like Robinson Crusoe." The others agreed that it was a great name.

Ross's stomach growled. "We should've brought some food. I'm hungry."

Matthew looked over the side of the wall. "I could probably fish from here."

"I don't want raw fish."

"It wouldn't be raw. We'd cook it."

Phoebe stood up. "We need to go home soon anyway. It's almost time for supper. I promised Maseppa that I'd help her make biscuits."

She climbed down the boards nailed to the tree like a ladder. Delly, Matthew, and Stafford followed her. Ross grabbed the rope and swung down to the ground.

Matthew laughed and clapped his hands. "Hey! That's dandy! I want to try that too."

They all climbed up and tried the rope one at a time, except for Delly. She said she'd rather stick with the ladder. Phoebe began gathering the hammers and tools.

"Where's the saw? I told Zeke I'd take good care of it."

Ross said, "I tossed it down after cutting the last piece. It should be over here." He began scuffling in the dead leaves to look for it. The other children joined him.

"OWWWW!" Matthew wailed. "I found it. I stepped on one side and the other side jumped up and scratched my leg. See? It's bleeding. Owwww!"

Phoebe inspected his wound. "You'll live." She helped him wash it in the stream and let him go back to shore in the first boatload. Tired, but contented with their accomplishment, the children scattered to their homes.

With the inspection and approval of all their fathers, the children spent many summer hours on the island – fishing, swimming, and imagining adventures.

One day, when Phoebe joined Maseppa in her herb-gathering traipse through the woods, she persuaded Maseppa to see their tree fort. Phoebe got in the boat first and bailed out the bit of water in the bottom.

"I can see it from here. We do not need the boat."

"Of course, we need it. You can't see it very well from here. I made a stone fire pit like we had when you and I lived in the woods. I even made a fish trap with twigs like we had. I want you to see it, Maseppa."

Maseppa sat stiffly in the middle of the boat. Her knuckles turned white as she gripped the sides. When the current bumped them against a submerged rock, she gasped and held on tighter. "This is not good, Phoebe. I think I will swim back to land when we come back."

Phoebe smiled.

She showed Maseppa their campsite and tree fort. Maseppa showed her some edible plants that grew nearby. While they were on the far end of the island, Maseppa leaned over and examined something closely. "There is a mark of a man's foot in the ground."

Phoebe leaned over. "Maybe it's Zeke's footprint or Mister Gilmore's, but I don't remember them coming to this end of the island."

The summer weeks flowed by as swiftly as the river current. As the gardens and farm animals grew, so did the chores. Everyone was needed for harvesting, canning, and butchering to have enough food for the coming year. Sometimes the children were too busy helping to spend much time on the island, but before school resumed in the fall, the children convinced their parents to let them camp overnight.

Each one brought a bundle of bedding and a sack of whatever food they could find. Delly didn't want to sleep up in the tree. Matthew didn't think there would have been enough room for all of them anyway. So after they ate supper, it was decided that the boys would sleep up in the fort and that Delly and Phoebe would bed down around the campfire.

Phoebe looked at the other faces in the glow of the firelight. These friends had become almost like brothers and sisters, yet she knew it wouldn't be like this forever. She knew that life had a way of changing things. She felt herself changing. This might be her last summer of running barefoot through the woods, climbing trees, and being a child.

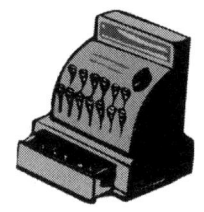

26
RISING PRICES

Sometimes Phoebe rode along with Zeke on his deliveries. This day, he was taking her to Albany with him as he purchased stock for Jarvis Cooper's store. As Zeke and Phoebe entered the store, the bell rang over the door. "Have you got your order ready, Jarvis? I'd like to head out early today." Phoebe wandered over to the display of ribbons. Their colored strips fluttered like a rippling rainbow. She liked the blue one but didn't want to spend her pennies on it today.

Jarvis Cooper scribbled a few more items on his paper. He looked back at the shelf behind him, shifted a few things around, and wrote down one more thing. He handed the paper to Zeke. "That should be all. When do you think you'll return?"

"I'm hoping to let Phoebe do a little shopping in Albany, so it won't be until evening."

Jarvis paused. "Could you take some crates of nails back to Robertson Hardware Company with you? The whole shipment was rusted when it arrived."

The bell jangled, and Stella Simmons came in. Zeke nodded his head. "Good day, Ma'am."

"Good day, Zeke." She removed her shawl from her head and shifted her basket to her other arm. Zeke began carrying the crates to his wagon. Phoebe continued wandering around the store while she waited.

Jarvis nodded to Stella and disappeared behind the display case. She meandered through the store picking up things occasionally, sometimes putting them in her basket, sometimes returning them to their place. After a few minutes, she made her way to the cash register and put her basket on the counter.

Jarvis pushed his sleeves up. "Did you find everything you wanted?"

"I was hoping for some bayberry soap, but you don't seem to be carrying it anymore."

"Well, I'm trying to keep up with the times and buy the new products. Have you tried the Castile soap? It comes all the way from England and is very good for the skin."

"I'm sure it works well, but it costs twice as much. In fact, everything that I buy goes up in price."

"The cost of living goes up every year, Ma'am. It costs more for me to buy it, so I have to pass on the cost to my customers. I've got to make enough profit to live, you know?"

Stella sighed.

Zeke paused in his work while watching the transaction between Jarvis and Stella. He scratched his beard. Phoebe could tell that something was bothering him, but he didn't say anything.

Jarvis rang up each item on the big black-and-brass register. Little tabs with numbers popped up in a window at the top. With a flourish, he punched the TOTAL key. "That will be four dollars and eighty-six cents, please."

"That's outrageous! I only got a few items."

"Sorry, Ma'am. I told you the prices of things are going up."

She looked at her items. "I suppose I could put back a couple of spools of thread and a bottle of maple syrup. How much is it now?"

"That knocks it down to two dollars and seventy-six cents."

She fished around in her purse. "I only have two dollars. I'm going to have to put the rest on credit until Jeb sells some crops."

Jarvis's forehead puckered into a V, bringing his bushy eyebrows together. He opened a book filled with columns of numbers and muttered, "I can't run a store on credit."

Stella counted the money and put her purchases in her basket.

Jarvis scratched her credit in his book. "Your credit is nearing its limit, Ma'am. If you don't pay up by the end of this month, I'll have to refuse service to you."

Blinking back tears, Stella pulled her shawl over her head and bustled out the door.

The jangling bell mocked Jarvis's attitude. "Have a good day, Ma'am."

Zeke cleared his throat. "It seems you ought to be grateful for your customers and treat them fairly."

Right then, they heard horses galloping into town. A man with a crooked nose burst into the store. He had a rifle slung over his shoulder and a pistol at his side. Jarvis's mouth opened to reply to Zeke, but stopped at this interruption. Phoebe backed up behind a display of braided rugs.

The man hitched up his pants as he glanced around the room. "I'm lookin' for a run-away darky. Anyone 'round see anything?" Phoebe noticed that he was missing some fingers.

Zeke spoke up. "New York is a free state."

The man growled under his breath at that. "No matter, if you're a free state or not. I've a right to bring 'em back. If you don't give 'em back, I could have you arrested."

Jarvis shook his head. "I haven't seen anything, and if I did, I wouldn't hide it. You can count on me."

Seeing Phoebe, he took a step toward her. "What about you, girl? You seen a darky around here?"

She shook her head. "N . . . no, Sir."

The man stomped out of the store in three loud steps. He swung up on his horse, and both men galloped away in a cloud of dust and spray of gravel.

Zeke said, "Jarvis Cooper, do you mean to tell me that if you found a runaway slave you'd turn him over to a slave hunter?"

"You heard him. It's the law. You can be arrested if you hide a slave. I'm a leader in the community. It wouldn't be good to be seen having the law arresting me."

"Wouldn't be good?" mumbled Zeke. "What about what's good for the slaves? If they are running away, it must be because something wrong, something bad is going on. I've heard some mighty horrible stories of them being whipped and taken from their wives and children. I couldn't give them back to the slave hunters."

"Well, Mister Big and Mighty, if you ever decide to smuggle one of those slaves through this village, you better not let me see you, because it's my duty to report it."

Zeke clamped his teeth shut and motioned to Phoebe. "Come, Phoebe. Let's get going."

~ # ~

Stella Simmons wasn't the only one feeling the pinch of prices. Feona Reynolds wasn't as quiet as her friend and grumbled to everyone she met about how expensive it was to live anymore. A few weeks later, she stopped in to ask Maseppa for some mint to help her upset stomach – or so she said.

"If you ask me, it's getting so a person can't afford to buy anything anymore. Candles have gone up three cents each in just this last month . . . and oil for my lanterns, I had to pay ninety-five cents for a gallon! Now, if you ask me, that's robbery!"

Zeke paused in lighting his pipe. "What did you say you paid?"

"Ninety-five cents for a gallon."

Zeke scratched his head.

Feona sputtered and shook her head around till a hairpin came loose. "It's robbery, I say. Someone should report him to the authorities. We need a sheriff around here."

"Now hold on to your bonnet, Feona. Let me do some investigating. If I find anything fishy, I'll find someone with authority to set things straight."

"If you ask me, that's outright stealing from the poor folks."

"Now don't you go talking to anyone, Feona. You need to let me check things out."

"I'm not the only one, you know. There's other folks been complaining about prices being too high and cheating them on their credit. I think he even steals our mail. I never did get a letter this spring from my sister in Virginia, and she always writes at least two or three times a year."

"Whoa! That's going a bit too far, Feona! I don't think Jarvis is stealing your sister's letters."

"Well, sometimes she sends some money. If you ask me, I think he took it."

Zeke shook his head. "You need to be quiet about this. It's

serious business to accuse someone of theft without cause."

Feona huffed out the kitchen door. "It's going to be mighty hard to keep quiet when I'm being robbed right in my own town. I'll keep mum for a while, but I'll be hard pressed to do any more business there."

The room seemed extra quiet without Feona Reynolds there. Zeke fingered his scraggly beard and gazed into space. Phoebe looked at him. "Zeke, do you think Jarvis is stealing from people?"

"I hope not, Phoebe. He's not the softest person to deal with, but I'd hate for him to be accused of this. I can't decide whether I should get more evidence before I confront him or go straight to him before Feona goes gossiping around the village." He looked at Phoebe with a smirk. "You know as well as I do that she won't be able to keep her lips sealed any more than a pickle jar in the hot sun. I've got to act quickly."

He looked at Maseppa and Phoebe. "Not a word to anyone. Hear me?"

Phoebe shook her head. "I'm not sure what it means anyway."

~ # ~

The next morning, Zeke wanted to get to the store before it opened so he could talk with Jarvis without being interrupted by customers. As he approached the shop, he could hear thumping in the storeroom. Zeke hitched Ol' Sam to the post and breathed a prayer as he walked around back, "Lord, this isn't going to be easy. You're going to have to tell me what to say."

Jarvis looked up with surprise. "Zeke! You're heading out early. I wasn't expecting you for a couple of hours. I haven't got my order ready yet."

"I didn't come to talk about orders. I have something else on my mind."

Jarvis settled on a nearby barrel. "What's going on?"

"I have a question about your prices recently. I know –"

Jarvis interrupted him. "Prices are climbing. You know that."

"Yes, I know what you pay for things that I bring to you each week. I know that oil is only sixty cents per gallon. I pay you seventy-five cents to allow you some profit, but I hear tell that you charged someone ninety-five cents for a gallon. How do you figure that?"

Jarvis chuckled. "Zeke, I'm a business man. I know which ones can pay more and which ones can't. I get the money where I can. Besides, you work for me, so I give you a better deal on your purchases."

Zeke stiffened his back. "That's not fair business ethics, Jarvis. I should know. If you are not fair, then you are going to lose all your customers."

"Who's going to know?"

"I know! It ain't right! Besides people talk. They're apt to compare prices if they're complaining about them."

"Zeke, mind your own business. This is none of your affair. You better shush or you may be out of a job. I'll find someone else to do my driving. You best keep quiet, if you know what's best for you."

"Is that a threat?"

"Take it any way you want." Jarvis turned his back to Zeke and continued stacking crates.

"Jarvis –"

"You best leave, Zeke, before I lose my temper."

"Jarvis, don't do this."

"I'm done talking with you. In fact, don't bother getting my order today. I'll find another driver." He turned back to counting boxes.

Zeke looked at the back of his head for a few seconds. "I'll be praying for you, Jarvis."

"Ha! Don't bother, Zeke."

Zeke let Ol' Sam set his own pace on the way back home. *This problem is bigger than I can figure out. Lord, I need your wisdom.* A little thought poked up its head and wiggled about in Zeke's mind. He could run a general store. He'd been a good peddler. He knew what people needed and wanted. He'd be a good store manager. Maybe someday, when the time was right, he'd get his chance.

27
THE COUGAR

Zeke wasn't worried about losing his job. There was always someone who would hire help during harvest time. He and Roster finished roofing the house and the barn. Then they spent from sunrise to sunset helping Morris Reynolds on his farm – haying, butchering, and such. Morris's rheumatism was acting up, and he appreciated the help, paying them a fair wage for their work.

One evening, Zeke got home later than usual. "Morris Reynolds lost some pigs last night. It looks like it might be a cougar."

Maseppa paused while pouring his coffee. "I heard the scream one night, but I did not think it would come close to a house."

Phoebe's eyes widened. "Matthew told me that they lost a few chickens last week."

Zeke nodded, "Yes, Stanley told me that, too." He took a bite of stew. "That's why I was late. I've talked to the men of the town. There are others who have also lost livestock. We're going to gather at the crossroads tomorrow to plan a hunt before the cougar does any more damage." He looked at Phoebe. "We're telling all the women and young'uns to stay home until we find it."

The next day seemed really long. It was hard for Phoebe to keep busy without school and without being able to go anywhere. She had finished reading *The Blind Farmer and His Children* by Barbara Hoffland and wished she could go to Mister Phillips's store to get another book. She counted how many verses she had learned, and it was still only seventy-two. It seemed to get harder to learn them. *I don't think I'll ever reach a hundred!*

She wiggled a string for Butterball to chase and scratched Butch behind his ears when he got jealous of the cat getting too much attention. Being trapped inside on a nice September day was much worse than being snowed-in on a day in February. She stared out the kitchen window toward the road. *It sure is a pretty day out there.*

Deborah Gilmore was coming up the road with Sally on her hip. Her face was red, and every few steps, she broke into a half run.

"Maseppa!" Phoebe called. "Something's wrong!"

Maseppa came into the kitchen right as Deborah stumbled up the porch steps. Phoebe opened the door for them. Deborah put Sally on the floor and plopped into a chair. She lay her head back to catch her breath. "Is . . . Matthew . . . here?" she asked between breaths.

Phoebe shook her head. "No. I haven't seen him since yesterday."

"He's gone." Deborah brushed some loose hairs out of her face. "He wanted to go fishing, but I told him it was too dangerous today."

Phoebe shook her head. "I think I know where he is. There's a place near the island that he thought would be a good fishing spot, but he didn't have his pole with him."

Deborah's eyes grew large. She turned to Maseppa. "What are we going to do? Stanley's in town with the other men." She began crying. "He's only a little boy." Sally must have sensed her mother's fear because she began whimpering. Her mother picked her up and held her close. "I'm so scared!"

Maseppa said, "Phoebe and I will go to town to tell the men."

After Phoebe and Maseppa walked Deborah to her house, she began crying again. "What if the cougar gets him? What if he gets lost? What if – "

Maseppa put her hand on Deborah's back. "It does not help to think of trouble that has not happened. I will stay here with you." She looked Phoebe in the face. "You stay on the road and go into town. Find Zeke or Stanley or someone to help. Do not look for Matthew by yourself. Do you hear me?"

"Yes, Maseppa."

Phoebe flew down the road. She didn't slow down until she got to the crossroads. No one was there. She paused to think, *Where would they be? . . . the church!* Her legs and arms pumped as she ran to the church building. A couple of wagons were parked outside, but the horses were gone. She opened the big doors. No one was inside. *Where now?*

Phoebe ran back into town. She tried each shop, but everyone had closed up to help with the hunt – all except the general store. The bell clanged as she burst through the door. "Is Zeke here?" she blurted.

Mister Cooper looked down from his ladder, where he was stacking some tins on the top shelf. "No, he and the other men are out hunting for that cougar. I'll be glad when they get it so this town will get back to normal."

"Matthew Gilmore is gone! I think I know where he is, but I need help." She paced back and forth. "He found a good fishing spot and was yearning to try it out."

Mister Cooper climbed down. "Oh, that's not good. I don't know what to say. I have to stay here and mind the store."

Phoebe turned away in desperation. "If I can't get someone to go with me, I'll have to go alone."

"Hold on there, young lady." He grabbed a rifle, some gun powder, and bullets from a shelf. "I'm not a hunter, but I can't let you go traipsing through the woods by yourself." He looked down the barrel. "I don't suppose you've ever shot one of these, have you?"

Phoebe was already out the door.

"Hey, wait up!" He quickly locked the door behind him and trotted after her.

Phoebe headed east toward the Reynolds' house. *Maybe I can find someone who knows how to use a gun.* Feona Reynolds was home alone but said that Roster Kittle might be home, because she had heard someone chopping wood this morning. Phoebe didn't wait to hear any more. She sped off toward the Kittles' house.

There she found Delly trying to comfort her mother. She told Phoebe, "Ross and Stafford have run off. Ma's mighty worried about them."

Missus Kittle got up and looked out the back window. "Those boys don't listen to me. I told them to stay put, but they was determined to go. Who knows where they might be?"

Phoebe said, "I think I know. Matthew's gone, too. I think I know where they are." She looked around the small house. "Where's your pa, Delly?"

"He's headed for the island, thinkin' the boys might be there."

Phoebe nodded.

Mister Cooper had barely caught up with her when she plunged into a path in the woods. "Hey! Slow down!"

Phoebe wasn't going to wait for him. Matthew was in trouble, and even though it wasn't her fault, she felt responsible. *He may be old enough to go fishing by himself, but sometimes, he just doesn't use common sense. I hope he doesn't learn it the hard way.*

She had left Mister Cooper behind, but she could still hear him hollering at her. "Wait for me!" *If Roster Kittle is heading to the island, he is in the wrong place. The fishing spot is farther upstream where the water runs deeper.*

A piercing scream tore through the trees!

Phoebe stopped.

She could hear Mister Cooper crashing through the underbrush behind her. The scream rang out again. Mister Cooper emerged from behind a branch near her and froze. "What was that?"

She whispered, "The cougar."

Then they could hear the boys yelling, "Help! Somebody, help!" Phoebe headed in their direction.

Jarvis called out to her in a loud whisper, "Are you crazy? The cougar's over that way!"

They pushed through pine trees and scrambled through prickly raspberry bushes until they came to the edge of the creek and stopped short at the sight in front of them. The boys were clinging to the dead branches of a tree that had fallen over the swift, dark waters. A large tawny cat crouched on the trunk, blocking their way back to land. It growled, the tip of its tail twitching back and forth.

Without moving, Phoebe whispered, "Shoot it, Mister Cooper. Shoot the cougar." Hearing no sound, she turned to look at him. His face was as pale as a tree swallow's egg. His mouth drooped open, and his arms hung stiffly at his sides. "Mister Jarvis, shoot the cougar!" It was as if he had turned to stone.

The cougar gave another scream, and Mister Cooper dropped the gun to cover his ears. Phoebe grabbed it, but she didn't have the faintest idea how to load it. Holding it above her head, she hollered as loud as she could. The cougar turned its focus away from the boys and to her. It turned, crouched, and looked straight at her. Phoebe held her breath. *Lord, help us!*

With an explosion of leaves and gun powder, a man burst from the bushes right upon the cougar. It was Roster Kittle! Missing the shot, he swung the stock of his musket like a sledge hammer at the huge cat. With a snarl, it rose up and spread its large paws around him. Its claws tore at his shoulders and back, and they tussled this way and that. Then they both fell into the stream and disappeared beneath the surface.

Phoebe ran to the fallen tree, but she couldn't see the cat or Mister Kittle. After what seemed like forever, they came up downstream. The cougar swam to the other shore and limped off into the gloom. Mister Kittle floated to the edge, his skin shredded and bleeding.

Phoebe called behind her, "Mister Cooper, help me!

He shook off his terror and hurried to Phoebe's side. The boys, trembling and crying, scrambled back over the dead tree to help drag Mister Kittle onto the shore. Phoebe leaned close to the man's bloody, wet face, but she couldn't feel his breath. *He isn't moving! He isn't breathing!*

They heard a call. "Halloo! Who goes there?"

Phoebe jumped to her feet. "Zeke! We're over here! Hurry!"

As Zeke and the other men took over, Phoebe waited with Matthew and the Kittle boys. It all seemed like a bad dream. Within an hour, the men of the town had carried the lifeless body of Roster Kittle out of the woods and escorted the children safely home.

That night, Phoebe couldn't sleep. Every time she closed her eyes, she saw Mister Kittle's body in the river. She doubted Matthew or the Kittle boys were sleeping either. She wondered if Mister Cooper was sleeping.

28
MIXED FEELINGS

Phoebe was walking through the woods, through the dark pine trees. She felt something watching her and looked back. Two yellow eyes peered through the darkness. She tried to run, but the bushes and roots tripped her. She was so tired, and her legs felt heavy. She could hear the animal growling. It was getting closer and closer. She turned and saw it leap at her with a loud –

"Meow."

Phoebe sat up in bed. Her skin was sweaty and her heart was pounding. Butterball rubbed against her and meowed again. "Silly cat, you about gave me heart failure!" She heard noises in the kitchen and went downstairs.

Things were pretty quiet at the breakfast table. Zeke sipped his coffee. "I need to ride over and talk to Liza about what happened yesterday. Would you two like to come with me?" Maseppa nodded. Phoebe stirred her porridge without saying anything. She wasn't ready to see or talk to anyone, especially the Kittles.

"Phoebe, you should come too. Delly will need a friend. I'll hitch up Ginger to the buggy while you two get ready. Maybe we could bring some food for the family."

Maseppa and Phoebe put some bread, cheese, and milk into a basket. Phoebe added some jars of jam and a sack of flour. They joined Zeke in the buggy. No one talked for a while.

"This ain't going to be easy," said Zeke. "But knowing a friend cares helps when someone is hurting. I know you must be dealing with a lot right now, too, Phoebe, but talking it over with a friend will help."

Phoebe's eyes filled with tears. Mister Kittle hadn't been the nicest man around. Yes, he changed when he got right with God, but it was hard to forget what he was like when he was drunk and made his family live in an old cold, leaky shack . . . but he was Delly's pa . . . and he died trying to save his boys!

As they drove past Mister Cooper's store, Phoebe looked toward it and wondered how he felt. She felt angry at him for not shooting the cougar. She blurted out, "It's Mister Cooper's fault that Mister Kittle died. It's his fault Delly doesn't have a pa anymore."

Zeke pulled on the reins. The buggy stopped short. He looked straight in her face. "No, Phoebe. It wasn't anyone's fault. Sometimes things just happen. It doesn't help to blame one person or another."

He flicked the reins, and they continued in silence.

When they got to the Kittles' house, Phoebe wasn't eager to get out of the buggy. Zeke said, "I'll go in first. No, it would probably be best if we all go in."

Phoebe didn't move. "May I wait here?"

He looked at her frightened face. "Yes, I'll tell Delly you're out here."

Phoebe sat alone on the buggy seat. The sun was shining through the trees and making the dew drops sparkle on the pine needles. The hound dog barked at her. The memory of Mister Kittle shooting Butch flashed through her mind. Soon the door opened and Delly came out.

"Phoebe?"

"Hello, Delly."

She climbed up next to Phoebe and just sat there. Phoebe thought she might cry, but she didn't.

"Pa's dead."

"I know."

"I don't know how to feel. I used to hate my pa. He used to be really mean to us. Sometimes, I wished he would die, so he wouldn't hurt us or Ma anymore. He was getting better this last year. Now he's gone."

Phoebe didn't know what to say. The wind blew in the tops of the pines trees.

"I didn't really want my pa to die. Do you think it's my fault?" She put her face in her hands and sobbed.

Phoebe put her arm around Delly. "No, Zeke said it was an accident. He said that your pa was a hero. He saved Matthew and Ross and Stafford. It wasn't your fault. It wasn't anybody's fault."

That day, Morris Reynolds and Parson Thomas helped Zeke take Mister Kittle's body to the church. Stanley built a casket for him. The funeral was planned for the next day.

The next day, at the funeral, Phoebe sat with Zeke and Maseppa. She looked at the long box at the front of the sanctuary. There were cedar branches on the top and someone had put a potted geranium among the greenery. The Kittle family sat in the front pew. Missus Kittle wore a black veil over her head and a black dress. The children sat next to her, wearing their school clothes. Delly sat on the end, looking down at her clenched hands. Phoebe wished she could sit with her. She knew Delly hated being there with everyone looking at her and her family.

Phoebe looked around at the people scattered here and there in the church pews. Most of them probably had never spoken to Mister Kittle. Most came out of duty for a fellow member of the community because it was expected of them.

Parson Thomas stood behind the pulpit. "Brothers and sisters, we are here to lay to rest a member of our community. Roster Kittle may have made some wrong choices in his life. I talked with his wife today. She told me of the many woes that have plagued them for years. They've lost their home to fire and then their farm because they couldn't pay the taxes. They lost a child soon after. Grief like that sent Roster Kittle to drink. We don't know but we would do the same if we were in the same situation.

"I say we are the ones who should be ashamed. How many of us tried to befriend Roster Kittle? How many of us gave him a hand to pull him out of the hole he had fallen in? I commend you, Zeke, for doing just that. You sought him out. You offered him friendship and a job when no one else even tried.

"Because of that kindness, Roster Kittle repented of his sins. He came to me and confessed the way he treated his family. He threw away his liquor and was determined to start afresh. Did any of you know that?"

The small congregation coughed and scuffed their feet. No one looked at the minister. No one looked at Liza Kittle and the children.

Parson Thomas opened his Bible. "The Bible tells us 'In as much as ye have done it unto the least of these, my brethren, ye have done it unto me.' It also says, 'show love to the fatherless and the widow.'" He took off his spectacles and looked around. "That is what we have right here today. Beloved, God has given us a perfect opportunity to show our love for Him by caring for Roster Kittle's fatherless children and his widow."

Phoebe saw Delly lift her face up in shock and defense, her lips clenched together. Phoebe knew that look.

Parson Thomas turned to the Kittle family. "I know you never asked for charity, and this must not be easy for you to hear these things, but this is how our church family can work as a body. Each of us will be at a low time sometime in our life. We need to learn to accept generosity as well as give it."

Turning to the rest of the congregation, he pointed to various ones. "Is there something you have extra of? Did you have a bountiful harvest? Maybe you have something you need sewn. I hear Missus Kittle is an excellent seamstress. Don't say anything now. Go home. Get on your knees tonight. Take a good look at yourself. Maybe you haven't acted in a Christ-like way before. Now is your chance to turn your life around. Being selfish is as bad as drinking too much. Sin is sin to God. It doesn't matter the degree of wickedness. Talk to the Lord about your sin and ask Him what He wants you to do about it."

He prayed the benediction, and the people filed past the Kittle family. Missus Kittle held little Sammy on her hip. Ross and Stafford stood in front of her. Delly stood next to her mother with her hands behind her back and her head down. Phoebe knew she didn't like all this talking about her papa – it was hard enough anyway. Missus Thomas stepped over next to Delly and put her arm around her shoulder. Delly pulled away from her touch. One by one, the people shook Missus Kittle's hand and said how sorry they were.

Zeke and Maseppa and Phoebe waited until everyone had gone except the parson and the Kittles. Zeke walked to the front of the room, his hat in his hand. "Ma'am?" He bowed slightly. "Beg your pardon, but you're welcome to stay at our place for a few days until you are ready to go back."

It was hard to see her face through the veil, but her voice was wavering. "Thank you, Zeke. You've been so kind to us, but we've often been on our own when Roster was off drinking. We'll be fine."

"Are you sure?"

She nodded. "Thank you much."

~ # ~

The next Sunday, Delly came to church with a new dress and shoes. The boys all had new clothes, too.

Phoebe met Delly with a smile. "I like your new dress."

"I don't." She plopped in her seat.

"Why not? It's beautiful!"

"It's charity," she whispered. "Ever since that preacher made everyone feel so guilty, we've had a steady stream of visitors come to the house bringing food and clothes and stuff."

"That's great!"

"They don't care about us! Where were they when Pa was alive? They looked down at us like we were pig manure. We were like pigs in a pig sty. They're only doing all this so they don't feel guilty!"

Phoebe closed her mouth tightly and swallowed. Delly was right. Even she had felt that way the first time she saw their house. She had hated their pa when he shot at Butch. If Delly hadn't become her friend, she might still feel that way. She looked down in shame. "I'm sorry, Delly. They just didn't know you."

"It doesn't matter. I'm glad he's gone. Mama doesn't have to hide her money from him anymore, and we don't have to hide in the woods when he comes home drunk."

"But he changed."

"Well, it wasn't soon enough for me. I'm glad he's gone."

"You don't mean that, Delly."

"What do you know about it? You don't understand."

Phoebe couldn't say anything. No, she didn't really understand.

29
ZEKE'S DUTY

After the cougar incident, tensions grew between Jarvis Cooper and the town. Fewer people shopped at his general store, and those who did complained that prices were higher than ever and that he was cheating them on their credit accounts. Zeke knew something had to be done. "Zeppa? I'm heading over to Albany. I'm hoping I can get help knowing how to deal with Jarvis. I don't know when I'll be back."

"This is not good."

"No, it's too bad. I hate to do this to our neighbor, but I'm thinking of all our friends and other neighbors. It's not right for him to be taking their money. I wish I could talk to someone I knew…" His face lit up with an idea. "Colstein!"

"Who is Colstein?"

"He's the solicitor in Albany that helped us secure the deed to this house. I know him. He'll know what to do. That means I may not be back until afternoon. You'll be praying for me, right?"

"I will miss you and pray."

He kissed her cheek. "Thanks, Zeppa."

He grabbed some bread and cheese and swung up to the saddle and was gone. Passing the parsonage, he decided to stop for some advice.

Parson Thomas shook his head. "Do you want me to come with you?"

"No, I don't think so. I think I'll go alone, but I may need you later to confront Jarvis with me."

"Well, I'll be praying for wisdom and guidance."

The sun was high in the sky when Zeke entered the solicitor's office. A memory from his previous visit made it seem as if he had gone back in time. Mister Colstein was hunched over his desk as before. The shelves of dusty books and the hissing tea kettle on the coal stove were all the same. Colstein lifted his finger in acknowledgement and finished calculating a row of figures. Finally he looked at Zeke and stood up. He was more hunched than three years ago and more near sighted, for he squinted at Zeke as he put out his hand.

"Good day, Sir."

"Good day, Colstein. I'm Zeke, Hezekiah Erstein."

"Do I know you?"

"You helped me settle Ben Johanson's affairs, getting the house and land for his daughter, Phoebe."

"Oh, yes! Yes! Sit down. What can I do for you?"

"Well, I married the Indian woman, Maseppa, and I've settled in Snyders Corner. We're doing quite well, but there's been something that's come up that requires some legal advice."

"And what might that be?"

Zeke stretched his legs and scratched his head. "There's a local store owner, Jarvis Cooper, who seems to be adjusting his prices unreasonably. I know a merchant has the right to make a profit, but he appears to be adjusting his prices differently for different customers. If he thinks they can pay more, he charges higher prices."

"Hmmm…" Colstein twirled his pencil. "not good business…it's going to come back to bite him."

"That's what I said, but he didn't listen. Is there something on the books to hold him to being fair?"

Colstein shuffled over to the shelf and pulled out a thick book. He dropped it on his desk and thumbed through it. Occasionally, he'd pause and "hmmm" or "ahh", then finally said, "No, I don't see anything that prohibits a merchant from setting the price as he deems right."

He sat down and looked up at Zeke "It means that he is not restricted from selling merchandise at a lower price in order to compete with another business, and there is no law on how high he wants to set the price. Of course, if it's too low, he'll never make a profit, and if it's too high, then customers will stop buying from him. I'm sorry, but there is nothing you can do."

"What about different prices for different customers?"

"There's no law against that either, but it's a risky policy."

"Well, I'll take this information back with me. I hope I can work this out because I don't like confrontations."

"I hope so, too. If you need any more help, let me know."

"You've already helped a bit. Thank you. What do you charge for this?"

"Oh, let it go."

Zeke chuckled. "Is that fair business?"

"There's nothing against giving your time away. Let me know

how it works out, if you're back this way."

~ # ~

Later that day, as Phoebe walked into town to get another book from Mister Phillips's store, she noticed an extraordinary number of people and buggies and wagons at the crossroads. She saw they were gathered at the general store. She had a feeling that Feona Reynolds's lips hadn't kept their silence long enough.

Phoebe heard a shout. "I want my money back!" Another voice yelled, "You're a cheater and a thief. We ought to hang you!" She squeezed through the crowd to a spot near a window, where she could see inside.

Mister Cooper was cowering behind the store counter, his back to the shelves. Zeke stood on top of it, waving his arms. "Quiet! Quiet everybody!"

Phoebe could see Stanley Gilmore, Morris Reynolds, Mister Phillips, and most of the men from the village. Parson Thomas slipped through the door, and Zeke motioned to him to come closer. A lone voice called out. "He's been cheating us!"

"Quiet! Will you listen to me?"

The mumbling hushed.

"I just came back from the solicitor's office in Albany. I found out that a merchant is free to set his prices at what he feels will bring the best business."

A growl rumbled through the crowd. "Do you mean he can charge me more than he charges the guy next door?"

"Yes, he can. I know that it's not always sensible, but it's legal."

The men moaned with disapproval. "It ain't fair!"

"Look at it this way. You, Henry, would you charge your son

the same price as everyone else?"

Henry shook his head.

"No," continued Zeke. "Sometimes, we even give our services away free to those we feel might need a helping hand. Phillips, I know you give the children a discount on certain books. So, as long as Jarvis is being honest, it's all legal."

"He's been hoisting up our credit debts, too. What about those?"

Zeke turned and looked at the proprietor, whose face began to lose its color. "Jarvis, just to clear this all up, would you mind letting me have your account books?"

Mister Cooper straightened up. "That's invasion of property!"

"Would you like me to fetch the law?"

"No."

Facing the crowd, Zeke asked, "If he's in the clear, would you all be willing to put this behind us? This is our neighbor and friend. Be longsuffering and forgiving."

"He's not my neighbor," hollered Peterson. "I'm taking my business elsewhere. I reckon I won't be gettin' my money back from this cheater."

The rest mumbled and coughed and let their tempers settle. They knew they had no choice as to how to get their supplies without driving all the way to the city. One by one they left until only Parson Thomas, Zeke, and Mister Cooper remained at the store.

The preacher stepped up close. "Jarvis, that crowd was on the verge of stringing you up. Now, I suggest you fetch your books."

Mister Cooper disappeared in the back room and dropped a

large binder on top of the display case.

Phoebe saw the blast of air send dust scooting away.

Zeke said, "Is that all?"

"How far back do you want?"

"I'd like to see at least two or three years, if you could."

He brought in three more books. "This will take you back to January of 1834."

Zeke lifted the heavy books. "Parson? Do you mind if I leave these with you? That way, there will be no case for dishonesty at all."

Parson Thomas nodded. "Yes, of course! I'll put them in my study."

"Jarvis, I warn you." Zeke poked a finger in his chest. "If I find any discrepancies, I'm taking this to the justice of the law. You better pray that I find a clean account of your records."

Mister Cooper didn't say anything, but his face blanched again. He gave a slight nod.

~ # ~

For days, Zeke and the parson poured over the columns of numbers. Zeke frowned and sighed. Jarvis had been adjusting the figures for a long time - not a lot at once, but a penny here and a penny there. All in all, it added up to quite a bit.

Zeke rubbed his head. "It's time to confront him."

Parson Thomas said, "Maybe he didn't know."

"Oh, I'm sure he knew." Zeke sighed. "He just hoped no one else knew. I suppose we've got to take these to the constable."

"Let's go talk to Jarvis one more time. I'll come with you."

The door jangled as they entered the store, but no one was there. Zeke checked the back room and knocked on the door of the living quarters above the shop. There was no answer. The preacher met him at the bottom of the stairs. "He's gone." The parson handed him a piece of paper. "He left this on the cash register."

Zeke,

By now, you have found my changes in the figures. I am leaving the store. There would be no future for me after this. Even if I had been in the clear, no one would have trusted me. I'll have to say, you are an honest man. I respect you for that. You gave me a chance to make good. Sorry, I disappointed you.

Zeke Erstein, I leave the store to you, to do as you wish. You'll find the deed and other legal papers in the safe (25, 10, 43). You will make a good proprietor, a much better one than I.

**Good luck,
Jarvis Cooper**

Zeke met the preacher's eyes. "I didn't expect that." He looked around the room. "You don't think the others will think I did it on purpose do you?"

"No, you handled it fairly. We'll call a town meeting, and I'll read this letter." He stuck out his hand. "Congratulations. You're the proud owner of a general store."

"I don't feel like celebrating."

"No, I don't blame you."

Zeke sighed. "Do we still need to take these books to the authorities?"

"Let's give them to that Colstein. Maybe Jarvis learned his lesson, but if he tries this again, then they have evidence against him."

"Yes, I'll take this letter and deed to him, too." Zeke rubbed his forehead. "It's been a long week."

The parson slapped him on the back. "Go on home. I'll take it from here."

~ # ~

Zeke had often thought of owning his own store, but he hadn't expected it to be dropped into his hands like this. It took a lot of work to transform it into how he imagined it should be. Maseppa and Phoebe helped him fix up the place. They spent many hours cleaning, making new shelves, and ordering new items. Business began growing. He hired Jeb Simmons as a delivery man, and took him to Albany and Troy to show him the best places to buy stock.

One day, Zeke wandered through the living area above the shop. It was roomy – big enough for a whole family. He didn't need it. Maybe he could rent it to someone. He smiled, knowing just the one to ask.

Zeke knocked on the dilapidated door that didn't quite hang straight.

Sammy Kittle opened it. "Good evening, Mister Zeke." Liza came to the door behind him.

Zeke removed his hat. "Good evenin', Liza." He picked up Sammy. "Guess what, little feller? I've found you a new home."

Liza put her hand to her throat. "A home? Where?"

"Maseppa and I don't need Jarvis's place above the store. I think it's big enough for you and the children. It will be plenty warm enough with the heat from the store. You can earn your keep by cleaning the store for me –sweeping and dusting and washing the front window. Is it a deal?"

Liza brought her thin hands to the sides of her face. "Oh, bless your soul!"

"I thought, perhaps, I could even find you one of those sewing contraptions so that you could take in some business of your own."

Zeke whistled as Ol' Sam clip-clopped back home. The stars seemed to twinkle and the moon seemed to shine a little bit brighter than ever. He could almost hear Granny saying, *The Good Lord has a way of working things out, doesn't He?* Zeke chuckled and said out loud to the night sky. "Yes, He certainly does."

30
THE PAW PRINT

It had been a long summer, with many changes. Now it was autumn again. Apples ripened, leaves turned yellow, and school classes resumed. It was Phoebe's last year in their little one-room schoolhouse. Next year, she'd be off to secondary school, that is, if she got high enough scores on her exams. Miss Edgecomb would be certain that Phoebe, Delly, and Scott studied hard this year.

"Phoebe Johanson and Adeline Kittle, please come up here!"

Phoebe felt her face turn warm and tears stung her eyes. This year was not beginning very well. She glanced at Delly, who held her chin up in brave defiance. She walked to Miss Edgecomb's desk like a proud queen. Phoebe followed, only after the teacher called her name again. "Phoebe, come here."

Phoebe could hear the snickers and whispers behind her back. She wished she could run out of the room. She caught a glimpse of little Jemmy, who looked as if she were about to cry too.

"Who wrote this?" Miss Edgecomb held up a tiny piece of paper.

"I did, Miss," said Delly boldly.

"Not only do I have rules about passing notes in class, but paper is too expensive to be used for foolish chatter when you should be doing your Latin exercises." She held the note closer and read, *"Can you stay the night with me?"* She turned it over and continued, *"I have to ask."* Miss Edgecomb looked at Phoebe. "I assume you wrote that."

"Yes, Ma'am."

"As punishment, I want you to write your Latin exercise ten times tonight."

Phoebe lifted her head in shock at the extreme discipline, but Delly just stared ahead without emotion.

"You may return to your seats, and I'll expect you two to obey my rules from now on. You are the eldest students in the school. You should be examples to the younger pupils."

So, that's why the punishment was so harsh, so no one else would dare write notes!

Toting stacks of books on their hips on their way home from school, Phoebe and Delly grumbled about all their homework and made plans of how to get together.

"It probably won't work until Friday or Saturday," said Delly. "That way we can whisper all night without having to go to school the next day."

"It wouldn't work on Saturday, either. Zeke makes me go to bed early, so I won't be tired in church on Sunday. Let's see if you can come over on Friday."

"I'll ask my ma," said Delly, and the Kittles separated at the crossroads. The Kittles went to their home above the store while Phoebe and Matthew continued home.

"Are you still my friend, Phoebe?"

"Of course!"

"Then why are you always talking with Delly now?"

"She's just another friend, a girl."

"You mean girls are better than boys?"

"No." She sighed. "Sometimes, a girl needs another girl to talk to. You are my buddy, and she is my friend."

Satisfied, he found a stick and dragged it behind him in a waggly line. Suddenly, he stopped and stared at the dirt. Phoebe caught up to him and looked. In a half-dried puddle, there was a print of an animal – a big animal.

"What is it, Phoebe? Is it a dog footprint?"

"I don't think so. You can see the claws on a dog print. This is more like a cat's print. They can pull their claws inside their paws."

"If it's a cat, it's a huge cat!" He put his palm above it. Suddenly, he stood up, his eyes wide with fear. "It's the cougar, isn't it?"

Phoebe glanced around and didn't answer. "Come, I'll race you the rest of the way home." For a little whippersnapper, Matthew was fast, and it took all her effort to keep up with him, besides she had her books and heavy shoes.

He jumped on his steps and turned around laughing. "I beat you, Phoebe! I'm faster than you now!"

Phoebe waved good-bye and trotted home. No one was in the house when she dropped her books on the table. She looked in the breadbox for something to eat. She found Zeke in the barn, sharpening an axe.

"Where's Maseppa?"

"She took a walk. You know how she is. She needs to get out in the trees and fields every so often."

Sometimes, it was hard for Phoebe to remember the times she and Maseppa lived in the woods. Maseppa knew all the plants and their uses for cuts and stings and broken bones and stomach aches. Being in the woods was part of her. She became restless if she couldn't get out where the wind and sun could calm her.

"Zeke, the cougar is back. Matthew and I saw its paw print on our way home."

He lifted the axe from the stone wheel. It coasted slower and slower without him pushing the foot pedal to keep it turning. "Where did you see it?"

"Not too far before Matthew's house."

"Hmmmm . . . could you show it to me before it gets dark?"

He put the axe back in the corner of the barn and followed her down the road. Bending over, he examined the print and measured it with his fingers. Walking back and forth along the road, he found a few more prints. Phoebe tagged behind him, watching his face get more and more worried.

At the Gilmores' house, he knocked. "Good day, Deborah. Is Stanley home?" Phoebe couldn't hear Deborah's reply, but she assumed Mister Gilmore was away when Zeke said, "Tell him that I'd like to speak to him when he does." He told her about the paw print and that Matthew should stay inside for a while. He put his hat on his head. "Good day, Ma'am."

"Zeke, are you going after the cougar again?" asked Phoebe. She had to take extra running steps to keep up with his long strides returning home.

"I'm going into town, Phoebe. When Maseppa returns, tell her that I'll be back soon. Can you fix your own supper tonight?"

"But . . . is Maseppa all right in the woods with the cougar?"

He stopped at the thought. "Don't worry about her, Phoebe. She knows how to take care of herself."

"Now, go inside and eat some supper and do your studies. Maseppa should be home 'fore nightfall."

Phoebe went one way, and Zeke headed toward town. He turned and said, "Keep Butch inside or tied up. I don't want him wanderin' around neither."

Phoebe was rarely home all by herself, and even then, only for a little while in the day when Maseppa might be out hanging out clothes and Zeke in the barn. The evening shadows crawled under the doors and filled the corners. Phoebe lit a lamp, but the light made the dark seem darker.

She fried an egg and sliced some bread for supper then sat down to finish her lessons. The empty house creaked and popped. She could hear the ticking of the clock on the mantel in the parlor. Butch was snoring on his blanket behind the stove. The kettle hissed softly.

A clunk and rumble came from the shed. Phoebe jumped. Butch lifted his head and growled. Her heart thumped. Butch walked over to the shed door. The hairs on his back made a ridge along his spine as he continued to growl and sniffed at the crack of the door. Phoebe could hear Ginger nicker in the barn.

What if the cougar is out in the barn? What if it gets Ginger?

She found a lantern in the pantry and a piece of string to tie around Butch's neck. Lifting the latch on the shed door, she slowly opened it. The light from the lantern flickered on the beams and rafters. As she made her way from room to room in the row of sheds, she trembled. The light shivered with her.

The first room off the kitchen was very much like a pantry, with sacks of flour and crates of apples. Strings of onions and garlic hung from the ceiling while bins of potatoes and corn lined the back wall.

The next shed held most of their tools: shovels, sickles, and hoes. Their winter wood for the kitchen filled half of it. There was an outhouse in one corner, but they used it only when it was too stormy to go all the way to the big one out back.

She wished the sheds went all the way to the barn. At the last shed, she saw the outline of the barn in the twilight. Zeke had left the barn door open when he left. She sprinted all the way across.

Ginger, still in her stall, greeted Phoebe with another nicker and an impatient stamp of her foot. "You must be hungry." She gave the horse some grain and a rub on her nose. Ginger seemed satisfied, but Butch was acting funny. The whole time, since they left the kitchen, he had been underfoot, keeping as close to her as he could and growling softly.

"Butch, stop it! You're scaring me." She almost tripped over him when he bumped against her and wrapped the string around her legs as he circled behind her.

She tugged and strained at the heavy barn door. Of course, Butch running around her feet didn't help. She finally got it closed and barred. Lifting the lantern, she looked about, but didn't see anything beyond the glow of the lantern. As they returned through the sheds, Butch, eager to get back, tugged at the string. Phoebe noticed that the stack of logs had shifted and a couple of pieces had fallen on the floor. "That must have been what I heard." Her voice sounded loud in the darkness.

Right when she entered the kitchen, the back door opened. It was Maseppa. Phoebe laughed at herself. "Oh, Maseppa, you gave me a fright!"

"I am sorry that I was gone so long. It got darker faster than I thought." She looked about. "Where is Zeke?"

"He's gone to town. We saw some cougar tracks on the road. Zeke told me to fix my own supper."

"Why is there a string on Butch?"

"I heard a noise in the shed and went to Ginger some grain."

Maseppa's face told Phoebe all was not right. "Did you see something?"

She didn't respond. Phoebe knew it did no good to ask Maseppa again. She would speak when she was ready. Maseppa refilled the kettle from the sink pump and added a few sticks to the fire. She stepped outside to the porch and stood there silently listening. Phoebe stood next to her, but they couldn't hear anything but a few geese honking overhead and something small, like a mouse, scurrying in the dry leaves.

When they came inside, Maseppa lit a lamp and put it in the window. Her hand shook as she set it down.

"What's wrong, Maseppa?"

"You do not walk to school tomorrow, you hear me?"

"Yes, Maseppa."

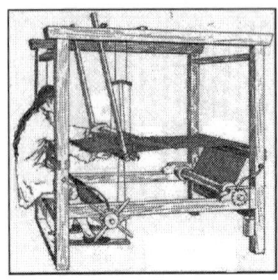

31
TESSA

No one went to school for two weeks. Every day, the men of the town hunted for the cougar. There was evidence of it around: paw prints, animals killed, and sharp screams in the night.

Phoebe was bored. She had done all her lessons, and had even worked ahead in her history and Latin. She was almost finished reading *Mary Woolstonecraft's Original Stories* and hoped she could go down to Mister Phillips's store for another book soon. She wandered into the sitting room to watch Maseppa weaving.

Phoebe gently fingered the strings of the warp, going up and down. She watched Maseppa shoot the shuttle through the tunnel of threads and pull on the beater board that pressed them tight. All the strings were a naturally creamy white. Deborah said it was good to learn to make an even weave before having to think of any colored design.

"Maseppa, can you show me how it works?"

She slid over on the bench. "It is not very hard. It is like making baskets, only softer. Do you remember we made the hanging beds in the woods?"

Phoebe smiled. "I loved my hammock." It had been so nice to sleep among the ferns and look up at the starry sky, to wake with the sweet dew of morning as her first breath of the day. It was the best part of living in the woods.

Maseppa gave a flick of her hand, and the shuttle scooted between the threads. She caught it on the other side and pulled the damper to hold the threads tight. Pushing the levers at her feet, the threads shifted direction, and she shot the shuttle back again . . . pull the damper . . . push the levers . . . toss the shuttle . . . pull the damper. It didn't look too hard, but it would take a long time to make enough cloth to make anything.

"What are you making?"

"I think this will be a cloth for the table. When I learn how to do it better, I will make some cloth to make a shirt for Zeke."

"May I try?"

During those two weeks, Maseppa taught Phoebe how to use the weaving loom. When Maseppa was done with the tablecloth, Phoebe thought she'd make a shawl for Madame Michelle, but winter would be all done at the rate she was going.

One morning, Stanley drove Deborah and the children up for a visit. Matthew and little Sally were glad to visit Phoebe instead of staying inside at home every day. Phoebe found her box of wooden blocks. She and Matthew built towers for Sally to knock down. Later, they played "Search and Find" while Sally napped.

"Phoebe, where are you?" Matthew called in a loud whisper, so as not to wake Sally. He looked under beds and tables. He looked in the woodshed, in the outhouse, and even in the potato bin. He walked back into the kitchen and wandered over to the pantry door, where he heard a slight scuffle behind the wall.

There was a wide crack along the edge of the door. He put his fingers in the crack and pulled. The door popped open.

"There you are, Phoebe Johanson!" He ducked down to peer into the little room around the big chimney. "Ooooo . . . where does this go?"

"Nowhere. It's just a space around the chimney . . . a good hiding place."

"Do you think we can go play in the barn? I'm tired of playing in the house."

"I'll ask," said Phoebe. "I'm sure it will be fine as long as we stay close."

Right when they had finished tying a rope to the rafters to be able to swing over the hayloft, Matthew's father trotted into the dooryard with the news of Seth Peterson shooting the cougar. It had been attacking his livestock. That meant school would resume and so would Sunday classes with Missus Thomas.

After the Gilmores went home, Phoebe wondered how many verses she had learned so far. She counted as she scribbled the numbers on a scrap of butcher paper. "Psalm 1 has six... Psalm 23 has six... Psalm 100 has only five. Psalm 96 has thirteen." She added up her figures. "That only makes thirty verses! I'll never be able to learn seventy more!"

She was working on Psalm 139. "If I take the wings of the morning, and dwell in the uttermost parts of the sea; even there Thy hand shall lead me, and Thy right hand shall hold me."

"Phoebe?"

"Yes, Maseppa?"

"Will you milk the cow now, before it gets dark? Give Doeskin and Ginger water and grain. Zeke will be late with his deliveries tonight."

"Yes, Maseppa."

She marked the page and put the Bible on the shelf. She grabbed the tin pail from the hook in the storage shed and she rinsed it at the outside pump. A cold wind blew down her neck as she shoved the door of the barn with her shoulder. The heavy door rumbled along its track, and the dim afternoon sun lit up the barn floor. Molly mooed at her from her stall. Phoebe smiled as Doeskin tried to lift her nose over the gate. She was almost as big as her mother now.

Phoebe tossed some pitchforks of hay in front of Molly. She set the three-legged stool nearby and put the tin pail beneath the swollen udder. Phoebe leaned her forehead on Molly's side and began squirting the white, creamy milk. At first, it made a kind of ringing sound like a bell, but after the bottom was covered, the streams of milk foamed into bubbles as they hit the surface. Butterball rubbed against her legs and the cow's legs. Molly tried to kick her away.

"Here, Kitty," She sprayed a stream at the cat's face and laughed as it got all over his fur.

When she finished milking, she set the pail near the door, filled Ginger's water bucket, and gave her a scoop of grain. She tossed a pitchfork of hay in the corner of her stall and gave her an extra scratch on the rump. She carelessly leaned the pitchfork in the corner, but it fell over. As she bent to pick it up, something dark moved away from her hand at the edge of the pile of dried grass.

Phoebe stared at the spot. It looked too big to be a mouse. Maybe it was a rat or a weasel. She grasped the pitchfork and dropped it deeper into the hay. Again something moved. She raised it again.

"No! Don' git me!" The hay scattered and a young woman crawled out. Her face was dark, and her eyes were like white moons in a midnight sky. "Don' tell no one I's here!"

Phoebe couldn't move. Her eyes told her that this was a Negro, one that she had heard about at school. She knew that their skin was black, but it really was! She subconsciously reached out her hand, as if to assure herself that this was real. The woman sat shivering as Phoebe touched her head of tiny braids and sweaty forehead. She pulled her hand back, ashamed of her childish rudeness. "I'm sorry. I never saw a black person before."

"Don' tell no one 'bout me. Please, Miss?"

"Are you a slave? Are you running away?"

"I's ain't stayin' long. I jes need t' rest fer a spell."

"Maseppa is good. She will give you some food."

"No! Don' tell no one! Dey's lookin' fer me!"

"Who's looking for you?"

"Da bad men. Dey want t' take me back, but I's ain't never goin' back!"

Phoebe sighed. She didn't want to leave this poor woman in the cold barn alone in the dark. "If you can get up in the loft, I can bring you a blanket and some food." She pointed to the ladder against the wall. "I'll be back in a while."

As the woman stood up, Phoebe noticed the woman's rounded belly, and Phoebe's eyes widened in recognition of her condition. "Maybe you shouldn't climb the ladder," said Phoebe.

"You don' worry 'bout me. I be fine in da loft." With that she climbed step by step until her black skin faded in with the dark space above the stalls.

"There are extra horse blankets and grain bags in the big box up there."

"I sees it. I 'preciate this, Miss."

Satisfied that the woman was settled, Phoebe turned to close the big door. She stopped with a thought and ran back to the base of the ladder. "Zeke isn't home yet. You'll have to be extra quiet when he puts Ol' Sam in his stall."

The woman peered over the edge and smiled. All Phoebe could

see were her eyes and white teeth. "I be fine. Jes' don' tell nobody!"

Phoebe grabbed the handle of the milk pail and returned to the house. Maseppa was still weaving. Phoebe poured the milk through the cheese cloth into the skimming pan and set it in the pantry. Tomorrow they would skim off the thick cream to make butter.

Phoebe looked over Maseppa's arm at the cloth. "You've gotten a lot done! It looks nice."

"It took you a long time to milk the cow tonight."

"I played with Butterball and rubbed Ginger and Doeskin a little bit."

"Did you strain the milk and put it in the pantry?"

"Yes. May I have some bread and cheese? I'm still hungry."

Maseppa looked at her and lowered her eyebrows. "You must have played hard with Matthew to make you hungry. Yes, you may have some more food."

Phoebe scooted back into the kitchen. She wrapped some bread and cheese in a towel. She set it on the back steps. *I'll have to go upstairs to get a blanket.* Walking as calmly as she could, she passed by Maseppa in the sitting room and up the stairs to the bedrooms.

Upstairs, she tiptoed across the spare room to the cedar chest and opened it slowly. Feeling with her hand, she grabbed a warm woolen blanket. As she was lowering the lid, it slipped the last bit and clunked. She froze and listened to see if Maseppa noticed. She could still hear the shuttle sliding back and forth and the damper banging against the fabric.

She grunted as she pushed up on the window sash. It hadn't been open since last spring, and it didn't want to move. She finally got it open about four inches, and she shoved the blanket through the crack. She heard the thud of it landing on the ground below.

Coming back downstairs, she said to Maseppa, "I forgot something in the barn. I'll be right back." She didn't notice the pause in the rhythm of the loom.

Slipping out the back door, she gathered the blanket and food and scampered to the barn. She wished she had left the door open. Now, she had to push it open again! Once inside, she ran over to the ladder. Holding the towel of food in her teeth and putting the blanket over her shoulder, she climbed up.

"Are you still up here?" she whispered. "I've got food and a blanket."

She heard movement in the darkness, and the woman crawled forward. "I thank ye, Miss." She stuffed the bread in her mouth.

"I didn't bring anything to drink."

"I's fine. I can get milk from da cow and water from da well."

Phoebe still couldn't stop staring at her white eyes and teeth. "My name is Phoebe. What's yours?"

The woman twisted her yellow kerchief between her hands. She stared deeply into Phoebe's eyes for a full minute before taking a deep breath. "I go by da name Tessa." She paused. The rest of her words came out in a half whisper, half cry. "But don' tell nobody. Dey's lookin' fer me."

"Good night, Tessa. I hope you can get to freedom soon."

"Do ya knows how t'git to Canada? I hears dat's where dey can't git me."

"Canada? That's a long ways! Maybe Zeke would know how to get there."

"No! Don' tell nobody 'bout me!"

"You can't get there by yourself . . . especially when . . . especially when you're going to have a baby."

It was quiet for a minute, and Tessa whispered so softly, "I's has to git t' Canada. Dat's where Toby was goin'. I's has to git there. I don' want ma baby to be borned a slave."

Phoebe swallowed and shrugged. "I don't know how to help." She glanced over the edge of the loft. "I've got to go. Maseppa will wonder what I'm doing. Are you sure you're fine?"

"Yes, I's be fine."

When she returned to the house, Maseppa was in the kitchen. "It is late. You need to go to bed, Phoebe. They will have school again."

Phoebe looked up quickly in surprise. She had forgotten all about the cougar and school and everything! She hoped she could bring some more food to Tessa before she went to school in the morning.

Phoebe lay in her bed thinking about Tessa in the barn. She wondered how far she had run from the South. She hoped it wouldn't be too cold tonight. At least Tessa wouldn't be sleeping outside. Phoebe gasped at a frightening thought, *Tessa had been out there with the cougar!* Phoebe heard Zeke come home from his deliveries and hoped he didn't hear Tessa up in the loft.

32
HIDING

"Good morning, Li'l Angel." Zeke's long legs stretched under the table, poking out the other side.

"Good morning. Did you have good travels last night?" asked Phoebe.

"It was fair. I was grateful for the bright moon – it made the riding easier. I'm glad that cougar was found. Now we can get back to our regular routines."

Maseppa finished stirring some oats in a pot and dished out the breakfast bowls . . . four of them. Phoebe looked from one face to the other.

"Is Uncle Pete back? Who's the other bowl for?"

Maseppa glanced at Zeke out of the corner of her eye. He returned her look and cleared his throat. "We figured you could take it to whatever you are hiding in the barn."

Phoebe stopped in her motion of pulling out a chair, her eyes widening. "You know?"

Maseppa calmly sat down opposite her. "You took too long milking the cow. You took more bread and cheese. You said that you forgot something in barn. I know something is in barn."

Phoebe turned to Zeke. "She told me not to tell anybody, and I didn't."

"Who told you?" he asked.

"Tessa"

He spooned some honey on his porridge. "I don't know anyone named Tessa."

"She's not from around here. She's a slave."

Zeke stopped his spoon mid-air. "A slave?"

"She's going to have a baby soon."

Now, it was Maseppa's turn to be stunned by Phoebe's words. "It is not good for her to be in a barn."

Zeke stood up. He paced back and forth. "We've got to do this carefully. There's a law that says we're supposed to report slaves to the authorities so they can take them back to the South."

"Take Tessa back? She's almost free!"

Zeke stopped short and shook his head. "I can't do it neither. There's a place in the Bible that says, "We ought to obey God, rather than men." This is one time I think we need to turn our backs to the law."

"Who's chasing her, Zeke? She's really scared."

"Slave hunters . . . There were a couple of them at the store, and I'm sure there are probably more around. They were a rough looking crew. I'm not giving anybody to them."

Phoebe grimaced at the memory of the man with crooked nose and missing fingers. "Could we hide her in Uncle Pete's cabin?"

"I don't think so," said Zeke. "They'd look there right away . . . the barn too."

Maseppa hadn't spoken yet. She silently stirred her cereal. "I know a good place," she said quietly.

Phoebe and Zeke looked at her.

"It is the same place we hid the keys and money."

"The chimney!" said Phoebe. "Of course!"

"What?" asked Zeke.

Phoebe laughed. It wasn't often that she knew something that Zeke didn't. Maseppa walked over to the pantry and Zeke followed her. She pulled open the crack to reveal the empty area.

He whistled. "That's perfect!" He poked his head inside. His voice muffled when he asked, "How big is Tessa? Will she fit in here?"

"I fit in there, if I need to be," said Maseppa.

Zeke crawled backwards out of the chimney space. He had cobwebs in his hair and dust on his nose. Phoebe smiled, and he made a silly face at her.

Becoming serious, he said, "No one could stay in there very long. I'll find a way to get her on her way." He sat on the floor staring at nothing and lost in his thoughts. "I think I know how we can do it."

"How?" asked Phoebe.

"I'll let you know when I've got it figured out. If I don't tell you, then you won't accidentally tell anyone."

"I can keep secrets, Zeke!" protested Phoebe. "I didn't tell Maseppa about Tessa last night."

"It's best I get some details lined up first."

While they were discussing escape plans, Maseppa busied herself with a broom and cleaned the chimney space as best she could. "I think it is time you talk to her, Phoebe, and bring her in the house."

In the barn, Phoebe climbed up the ladder. As she peered over the edge of the loft, she wondered if Tessa was already gone. Standing up, she could see where the woman had arranged the feed sacks into a more comfortable bed.

"Tessa? Are you still here?" she whispered.

At the familiar voice, Tessa emerged from a storage bin. "I done heered a man, las' night," she said.

"That was Zeke," said Phoebe. "I didn't tell, but they know."

Tessa's eyes widened, and she crumpled into a heap. She began to wail, a horrible cry that got louder and more mournful. When Tessa looked up at Phoebe, her face was wet with tears, and she sobbed with big shudders. "Noooo . . . I canno' go back! Help me! Please, help me, Miss!" She crawled over to Phoebe and wrapped her dark arms around Phoebe.

"It's all right, Tessa," said Phoebe. "Only Maseppa and Zeke know. They're going to help you. Come." She took Tessa's hand and gave a slight tug toward the ladder.

"No! Dey's goin' t' find me!" The wailing and sobbing continued.

"Come! It's all right."

Tessa refused to leave the loft, so Phoebe decided to go get Maseppa and Zeke. In a few minutes, they were with her in the barn. Maseppa climbed the ladder with Phoebe and gently cradled the frightened girl in her strong arms. Poor Tessa – she was so tired and lost that the touch of motherly arms felt like the softest bed. The short span from the barn to shed was the worst part. Soon they were safe in the kitchen, and Tessa was scooping porridge into her mouth as fast she could.

Zeke said, "Phoebe, you ought to get going to school."

School? School was the farthest thought from Phoebe's mind this morning. There were more important things than Latin verbs and geometry formulas. "Do I have to go?" she asked.

"Yes, we have to act as normal as possible so as not to attract attention."

Phoebe knew he was right, but it would be so hard not to say anything to Delly or Matthew today.

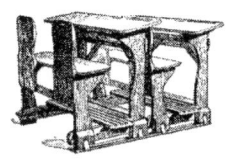

33
KEEPING QUIET

Stray snowflakes flitted past the school room window. It was only November. The snow probably wouldn't last long. Phoebe leaned her chin on her hand and counted the flakes that stuck to the glass. She had gotten to nine when Delly elbowed her.

"Phoebe Johanson!" Miss Edgecomb's voice made her jump. "Is your grammar lesson finished? Do you feel that you have learned your participles enough to be able to waste time staring out the window?"

Phoebe hung her head. "No, Ma'am. I'm sorry."

Delly had persuaded Miss Edgecomb to let her switch places with Priscilla so that they could sit together. She whispered very quietly after their teacher went back to helping the first class with their arithmetic. "What's going on with you, Phoebe? If you don't behave, she'll separate us for sure!"

Phoebe dipped her stylus in the ink and wrote:

THE YOUNG BOY READS THE BOOK TODAY.

THE YOUNG BOY IS READING THE BOOK NOW.

THE YOUNG BOY HAS READ THE BOOK ALREADY.

THE YOUNG BOY READ THE BOOK YESTERDAY.

THE YOUNG BOY DID READ THE BOOK BEFORE.

THE YOUNG BOY WILL READ THE BOOK TOMORROW.

THE YOUNG BOY WILL HAVE READ THE BOOK TWO TIMES.

All this talking about reading reminded Phoebe that she needed to return *Mary Wollstonecraft's Original Stories* so she could borrow another book. She hadn't even thought of it since she found Tessa. *I wonder how she and Maseppa are doing.* She looked out the window again. The snow was starting to cover the grass and road. She felt an elbow in her ribs again.

"Do your grammar," Delly whispered.

Miss Edgecomb looked at her watch and rapped her ruler on her desk. "Children, there's only an hour left, so I'll dismiss you early because of the snow. I know that some of you have a ways to walk."

The students emitted a loud whoop. Most of them scrambled to the windows to see how much snow had accumulated already.

Miss Edgecomb had to bang the ruler again to get their attention. "Everyone, sit back in your seats. We will still end our day with our normal closing song and prayer."

Knowing that the sooner they obeyed the sooner they'd be able to leave, the children scurried back to their desks and gave her their complete attention. They sang "God Bless Us for Another Day," and Miss Edgecomb prayed, asking for protection until they returned the following day. At the "Amen," there was a mad scramble for the back door.

Phoebe gasped at the beautiful change in the world with the crystalline snow. Each blade of grass, each pine needle on the trees, and each pebble on the road was coated in white. She hated to see the spots of black left by the footsteps of happy children released from school to enjoy this first snow.

Some were trying to have a snowball fight, but there wasn't enough snow to pack into balls yet. The flakes were falling faster, so it wouldn't be long until you wouldn't be able to see the grass or pebbles anymore . . . maybe even until next spring. *Good bye, autumn*, thought Phoebe.

"Phoebe!" shouted Matthew. "Do you think there's enough snow to go sledding?"

She gave him a half-smile. "I don't think so, but maybe by tomorrow if it snows all night."

Delly walked in step with Phoebe while her brothers and Matthew ran ahead to gather enough snow to make some snowballs and throw them at the trees. Whenever one of them hit a trunk dead on, the snowball would splatter and they would give a cheer.

Delly said, "I'm glad they got that cougar so we could go back to school, aren't you?"

"I guess so."

"What's wrong with you, Phoebe? You've been acting funny all day."

Phoebe walked about four or five steps before answering. "I don't feel like talking today. Anything wrong with that?"

"No, but it's not like you. Are you sick?"

"No, I just don't feel like talking."

"Are you mad at me about something?"

"No."

"Well, you sure don't act like you want to be my friend."

Phoebe sighed. This keeping quiet about Tessa was going to be a lot harder than she thought. She was glad when they reached the corner, and the Kittles headed off to their home.

"Delly's right, Phoebe." Matthew stopped throwing snowballs at the trees and walked beside her, trying to make his steps as big as hers. She made hers shorter so he could keep up. "You don't act right. Are you sure you're not sick?"

Deborah met them at the door, with little Sally on her hip. "I hoped you'd be dismissed early. It looks like it's fixing to be a blizzard. Would you like to come in for a minute, Phoebe?"

"No, thank you, Ma'am. I ought to be getting home."

She picked up the pace as soon as she left the Gilmores' house. She couldn't wait to get home and see how Tessa was doing.

She hopped up the porch steps in two steps, skipping every other one, and burst through the door. The warm air made her cold cheeks feel like they were melting and her toes began to sting as they thawed. She pulled off her wet boots.

She could hear Maseppa at the loom in the sitting room. She thudded in there, in her stocking feet, leaving damp footprints on the wood floor. "Miss Edgecomb dismissed us early because of the snow," she explained. "Where's Tessa?"

Without pausing the rhythm of the shuttle and damper, Maseppa answered, "She is asleep in pantry." As Phoebe turned to look, she added, "Leave her be. She is very tired."

"Why is she in the pantry? Couldn't she sleep in the spare room, upstairs?"

"It would not be good if the slave hunters or someone else came. The pantry does not have windows, and if she must hide, she can get in the chimney space."

"Did she try to get in all the way inside there? Is it big enough?"

"Yes, I put some blankets and water and food way back, if she needs to be there a long time."

Phoebe nodded at Maseppa's foresight. The shuttle scooted back and forth a few times, while Phoebe thought of Tessa being in that dark, dusty space. She hoped Tessa never had to hide in there.

"It is good that you are home early. You can do your chores right away while it is light."

Phoebe went upstairs to change her clothes. She noticed the book on her side table and hoped she'd have time to finish it tonight. She also had homework that should have been finished in class.

Thumping back downstairs, she put her boots back on and went out to the barn. As she grabbed the pitchfork, it seemed more like a week instead of a day since she last used it and found Tessa. The outdoor pump was frozen, so she had to return to the kitchen to get water for Ginger and Molly. It was too early to milk the cow. Zeke or Maseppa would do it later, after supper.

On the way back through the sheds, she stacked a few sticks on her left arm to take to Maseppa for the cook stove. She had noticed that the wood box was almost empty.

As she deposited the wood in the box, Maseppa called quietly from the other room. "Would you get a few potatoes for supper, too?"

Phoebe tried to be quiet as she went back and forth from the shed to the kitchen. As she dropped six potatoes in the sink, she heard rustling in the pantry. Tessa sat up quickly and cowered in the farthest corner until she realized that it was Phoebe and relaxed.

Phoebe ventured into the little room. "Hello, Tessa. Did you rest well?"

"Yes, miss. I's more tired than I's thought." She pulled herself up to a kneeling position. "Ach…oh! I's needin' to piss. Is it dark yet?"

"Oh, you don't have to go outside. We have an outhouse in the last shed. Come with me. I'll show you."

Tessa paused at the pantry door. She peered around the corner at the windows, both ways . . . toward the porch and above the sink.

"There's no one here but us," urged Phoebe. "Come."

When Tessa emerged from the little outhouse room, Phoebe noticed that she was holding her belly and leaning forward as she walked. "Are you alright?" she asked.

"I think da baby comin'."

Phoebe ran into the sitting room. "Maseppa, Tessa is having her baby!"

The thumping of the loom stopped. Maseppa quickly helped Tessa back to the pantry. They eased her down to the folded blankets in the corner. then, they heard stomping and thumping at the back door. All three faces turned to see the door open.

It was only Zeke! Phoebe laughed in relief. Zeke removed his hat and looked in the pantry. "How's things going?"

"Tessa's having her baby!" said Phoebe.

"WoooEee! That complicates things a bit."

Confident that the contraction had passed, Maseppa tugged Phoebe over to keep Tessa company. She pulled Zeke into the sitting room. Phoebe could hear them talking quietly but couldn't hear the words. As she got used to the dim light, she could see things in the pantry that she hadn't noticed before.

There were marks on the door frame and words and numbers. She fingered them, and a memory tugged in her mind. Looking closer, she could make out her name on the bottom line and the numbers 1837. There were five lines about an inch apart, with the next five years written next to them.

"What be dose lines?" asked Tessa.

"I'm not sure. My name is on this one," she said, pointing to the lowest one.

Soon Maseppa returned with some clean sheets and pillows to make Tessa more comfortable. Another contraction gripped Tessa, and they waited for it to pass.

"Maseppa, what are these lines on the wall?" asked Phoebe.

She leaned over Phoebe's shoulder and looked at them. Sitting back up, she stared at them. Phoebe could almost see her mind rolling back the years, trying to remember.

"Your papa made those lines. He showed how tall you grew on the day of your birth." She touched the bottom line. "This is when you lived one year. Your mama helped you to stand." She touched each line. "This is two year, three year, four year…" At the last line, she paused. Phoebe looked at Maseppa's face in expectation. "This one is the last one your papa made for you when you lived five years." She stood up, looking higher. "He drew a line for your mama and she drew a line for your papa. See? They are here."

Phoebe stood up and could see the lines in the wood. A wave of grief for the mother and father she could barely picture flooded over her. Her eyes blurred and she determined to look at the lines more closely later on. Tessa gave a moan, so Phoebe turned her attention to the girl.

"Phoebe," said Maseppa, "fill more kettles with water and keep them hot on the stove."

Phoebe hurried away, glad to be able to do something. Returning, she asked if there was anything else they needed. Not needed anymore, she found Zeke. He had finished milking Molly, dished out some stew that Maseppa had simmering on the stove, and was drawing lines on a paper.

"What are you doing, Zeke?" Phoebe asked, getting a bowl of supper too.

He didn't answer right away, but opened a map and compared it to his drawing. "It's our plan."

"Plan for what?"

"It's our plan to get Tessa to freedom."

"How are we going to do it?"

"Do you recall that I told you 'bout the Erie Canal? How a person could get all the way to Californie, if he went from boat and locomotive and all?"

"But Tessa doesn't need to go all the way to California. She only needs to get to Canada."

"Look at the map, Phoebe." He shoved it closer to her.

"See here? Canada is right here, on the other side of Buffalo . . . and the Erie Canal goes from Troy to Buffalo."

"But how can we get Tessa on a boat with nobody seeing her?"

"I know lots of people in the transporting business. There's this feller they call Bones that works for the Canal. He drives a mule that pulls the barges. He's part Negro, so I knew he'd be a sympathetic feller to help us."

Phoebe looked up from the map with a smile. "That's a great plan, Zeke!"

"I reckoned so, too. That's where I've been all day. I found Bones. He says that if we can be ready by Friday night, he can have a barge that'll take Tessa all the way to Buffalo."

"How will she know where to go then?"

"He says he knows some others that will meet him on the other end. We just need to get her to the Canal by six o'clock on Friday morning."

Right then, they heard Tessa moan again. Maseppa came into the kitchen to mix a cup of tea for her. Phoebe turned to Zeke. "What about the baby?"

He scratched his head and sighed. "I s'pose she'll just have to hold him close and try to keep him quiet. Tiny babies sleep lots. Hopefully, he won't cry much."

As if on cue, a loud squall came from the pantry, and Maseppa called out. "Phoebe, Ondàs!"

Phoebe jumped up obediently. Her eyes couldn't see anything at first. Maseppa handed her a bundle of towels and said, "Give the baby to Zeke and bring me pan of warm water."

Phoebe looked down at the small bundle of wet wiggly arms, legs, and wide open mouth. Zeke had stood up and was waiting nearby. He took the hollering baby, but didn't know what to do with it. Phoebe quickly poured some water in a pan and returned to the pantry.

Maseppa said, "Help Zeke rub the baby's skin and wrap it tightly in the towels."

Zeke heard Maseppa, and when Phoebe returned to the kitchen, he handed the crying child back to her. He spread some towels on the table and got some more water in a bowl.

"I reckon you can lay him on the towel," he told Phoebe.

When she put him down, the lamplight played over the child. His dark arms and legs waved in a panic. His eyes were clenched shut and its pink mouth wide open. Zeke quickly wiped his black, velvety smooth skin, from the thin feet to the top of his head, where tiny black curls lay flat on his throbbing skull. His palms and the bottoms of his feet were lighter colored, but the rest of his skin was dark and beautiful.

As Zeke wrapped the warm towel around him, the baby began to quiet down. Zeke put the tiny child on Phoebe's shoulder, and she took him back to his mother. Tessa, sitting up against the back wall, reached out her arms to take the baby. Phoebe knelt to watch as he suckled hungrily. Soon, everything was quiet. The baby had gone to sleep, and everyone else would soon be in bed too, wondering what adventures would await them tomorrow.

Phoebe sat up quickly in bed. "I didn't do my homework or finish my book!" Flopping back down on her pillow, she decided that adventures in books weren't half as exciting as real-life adventures.

33
THE PLAN

Phoebe was late for school the next day. Between not getting enough sleep and thinking about Tessa, she found herself reading the same paragraph over and over because her mind wouldn't focus on the words. She even failed her geometry test. Delly pried her with questions as to why she was so quiet. The day seemed to last forever.

After supper, Phoebe felt like her heart was all stirred up, like a muddy puddle. Life was getting so complicated. She couldn't sort it out in her mind. She needed to be alone to think. "Zeke, now that the cougar has been shot, is it safe for me to take a walk?"

He stood up and stretched his long arms and yawned. "I suppose, but don't go far . . . not into the woods at night. I prefer you stay within hollering distance of any house."

"I'm not afraid of the dark, Zeke."

"I know, but there are strangers around, and I don't trust them."

Phoebe knew he meant the slave hunters, and suddenly, she wasn't so sure she wanted to go for a walk. Yet, her mind was tangled with all that had been happening, and being outside seemed to blow away the confusions.

"I'll stay close," she promised as she pulled on a coat and

wrapped a muffler around her head.

The cold air took her breath away. The stars looked like crystals of salt sprinkled across the sky. She could see a sliver of the crescent moon through the leafless trees. The snow crunched beneath her feet. The frozen dirt felt like rock. It was strange how you could tell the temperature by the stiffness of the dirt. It would be months before she could squish in the mud again.

Phoebe wished she could talk with Missus Thomas. She wished she could tell her all about Tessa. She wandered down toward the road between the rows of empty maple trees, but she stopped at the end of the driveway and looked back at her home. The light in the kitchen window shone over the lawn. She could hear music. She smiled. It was Zeke playing his fiddle. He wasn't playing a dancing jig, but a mournful, lonely tune that sounded like the fiddle was crying too.

She decided to walk around the back side of the house to her swing in the apple tree. Rocking forward and backward, she listened to the sad music. Molly lowed softly in the barn. Smokey clouds drifted past the thin moon, and a little breeze picked up.

Without warning, her eyes filled with tears and sobs. She leaned her head against the rough rope of the swing and let the tears come. She cried and cried until she felt better. Sniffing and wiping her nose on her scarf, she looked up at the stars.

"God, I wish I knew why there are so many bad people in the world. When I was little, I didn't know things. I was only a child. As long as I had food and a place to sleep and had Maseppa nearby, I was happy. There must have been people who hated and got angry, and I remember some that didn't like Maseppa. I don't know why there are people who beat slaves, just because they have black skin. I don't know why there are men like Mister Cooper who steal other peoples' money and Mister Kittle who used get drunk and shoot dogs." Even though Mister Cooper had changed before he died, it still hurt to think about what he had done to Butch.

She felt a calm settle over her and knew that she couldn't do anything about the bad people, but she could still be kind to those they hurt. She was glad that she found Tessa. It was almost as if God wanted her to find her – and Delly, too, down by the stream. It was as if God had given her the job of finding lost and hurt animals - like Butterball and Peeper.

She felt better, like the cry had washed away the ache in her heart. She felt stronger now that she had talked to God about it. She had a job to do; she had to be a friend to those who need one. Her wet cheeks were cold, and she was ready to go back inside. She returned to the warm kitchen, her heart feeling more peaceful.

Zeke stopped as she entered.

"Keep playing," she said. "It sounds pretty."

He started another sad tune. Phoebe took off her wraps. She went in the pantry and sat on the floor next to Tessa.

"Do you's want t' hold 'im?" Tessa asked.

"Really?" Phoebe took the bundle from Tessa. The little boy was so tiny. His fist curled around her finger. Black curls fuzzed on top of his little head. Phoebe kissed his head. It smelled so sweet. She smiled at Tessa. "Have you named him yet?"

"No, I ain't thought of a good name yet. Maybe you's could think o' a good name fer 'im."

"Me?" Phoebe rubbed his curls. "I don't know what I'd choose. I'll have to think about it."

"You's a right good person, Phoebe," Tessa said.

Phoebe smiled. The baby squirmed and stretched his leg, and his foot became uncovered. Phoebe touched it and it must have tickled because he curled his toes and pulled his leg up. She giggled. He turned his head toward her dress and rubbed his face back and forth, looking for some milk. She handed him back to his mother.

"Good night, Tessa."

Zeke put his fiddle back in its box. "It's been a mighty busy day, hasn't it, Li'l Angel?" He gently pulled her onto his lap and wrapped his arms around her firmly. Phoebe melted into his embrace and let the comfort soak in.

She sat up and looked him in the eyes. "I talked to God, and I feel better now. I know that I can't do anything about all the bad people in the world, but I can help the ones that the bad people hurt."

Zeke gave her quick, tight squeeze. "You're growing up, girl. Most grown-ups haven't learned that yet."

The wind blew hard in the night. The bare trees rattled their branches against each other. Phoebe could hear a board banging near the barn. She was so tired. Tomorrow was Sunday. She hadn't memorized any verses in Psalms this week. There were too many other things to think about.

She dreamed that Ginger was being attacked by dogs. She could hear her neighing and hooves on the hard pebbles of the cold dirt in the road. She sat up. *It was a horse! But, it wasn't Ginger.* A loud banging on the door brought her to her feet. She got to the top of the stairs just as Zeke reached the front door, carrying a lamp. His bare feet and hairy legs showed below his night shirt. He put his finger to his lips and motioned for her to stay there at the top of the stairs.

Tessa! thought Phoebe. *Tessa ought to hide behind the chimney!*

Zeke was looking toward the kitchen, too. He didn't answer the door right away as if giving her as much time as he could. Another pounding on the door sounded like thunder above the roar of the wind outside. Zeke looked up at Phoebe and opened the door.

Two men burst into the house. Phoebe gasped and backed up into the shadows. One was the man with the crooked nose!

"We're lookin' for a darky!" he roared. "There's reason to think it's hidin' here." He pushed Zeke aside and strode into the sitting room.

The other man was in the parlor, moving the sofa and thumping on the walls. Then they looked in Maseppa and Zeke's room, pulling clothes out of the wardrobe and taking the lamp to look under the bed. They stomped up the stairs and looked in every chest, every closet, every corner.

The one with the lamp held it up to Phoebe's face. "You're the scrawny wimp in the store – acting like you didn't know nothin'."

She cowered against the wall, praying that Tessa made it into the chimney space and that the baby wouldn't cry. As the men tromped past her, one of their boots pinched her toe. Her mouth opened as pain shot up her foot and leg, but she didn't let a sound escape.

They went into the kitchen, Zeke and Maseppa and Phoebe following them. They opened the doors of the cupboards beneath the sink and the one with the lamp walked right into the pantry. Phoebe held her breath until he came back out. They stood in the middle of the room, turning this way and that, looking for hiding spots.

"You!" one pointed to Zeke. "You're comin' with us. Show us

the rest of the farm." They pushed him through the door to the sheds. As the light left the room, Maseppa closed the door against the draft and lit the other lamp on the table. Phoebe wanted to check on Tessa but thought better of it. She did look in the pantry. There were no blankets, nothing to show that someone had been camping there for the last two days.

Maseppa stoked the stove and sat in the rocking chair, her eyes closed and forehead puckered. A picture of Granny flashed through Phoebe's mind. Maseppa was praying just like Granny had. She was praying for Zeke and Tessa and the baby. Every breath of Phoebe was like a prayer. She whispered, "Please, Lord, protect them . . . Lord, don't let them hurt Zeke . . . Lord, don't let them see anything . . . " Sometimes, she only whispered the Lord's name.

It was a long time before Zeke returned. She and Maseppa looked up expectantly, but the men didn't come back in with him. He closed the shed door and leaned back against it. They could hear the horses' hooves galloping away.

"Are they gone?" asked Phoebe.

"Yes, they're gone," he answered. Phoebe ran to him and hugged him. He laughed and laughed. Puzzled, Phoebe backed up and stared at him standing there in his long underwear and bare feet.

"They were sure that slave was here. They looked everywhere. I'm glad I checked the loft this morning. She had dropped her kerchief." He pulled it out of his pocket and gave it to Maseppa. "Then those hunters poked the hay. They dug through the grain bin. They opened every stall and even the old pig pen. My feet were getting so cold. I thought my toes would freeze." He laughed again.

"Finally they got to the dung pit. They insisted that I open the trap door. I told them there was nothing down there but dung, but they didn't believe me. So I opened it." He laughed again. "I had spilled some water on the barn floor tonight when I watered the animals, and it had frozen."

Phoebe smiled in anticipation.

"One of those slave hunters slipped and fell half way into the hole. He grabbed his partner's pants, which sagged with the weight and the owner pulled away to keep his dignity. The first one tried to catch himself on the edge but it was too slippery. He fell in, cursing. I fetched a rope, and his partner and I pulled him up. Whew, he stunk! The last I saw of them, they were galloping back to town."

Phoebe giggled at the thought of the whole scene. Maseppa jumped up and opened the little door. She held the lamp inside the hole. "Tessa, Tessa, they are gone." Phoebe looked in beside her. There was nothing as far as they could see. Was Tessa in there?

Phoebe called, "Tessa, are you in there?"

Soon they saw the whites of her eyes reflecting the lamplight. She scooted toward them, with muffled whimpers. "I's so scared. I's heard the poundin' an' I knows, I knows dey was comin' t' git me! I takes the blankets and everything and goes way, way back. I hoped and prayed to the good Lord to cover me with His wings, so as dey can't see me."

She crawled all the way out, first passing the baby through the door to Maseppa. "Da baby starts his cryin' an' I don't knows what t' do . . . so I's feed 'im some milk an' whisper in 'is ears to hush, an' he stops his cryin'."

She took the child back from Maseppa and covers his face with kisses. "I's afeared that I mighta smothered him. Oh, Baby, is you fine?"

In answer, the little tyke started bawling. He flung his arms out wide and bellowed with all his might. For fear they might still be near, Tessa cuddled him close and tried to calm him down.

"Well, hopefully those men will keep goin' down the road and not come back, but in the meantime, we'll just have to be alert."

Phoebe sighed. "Do I have to go to school? It's so hard to concentrate on my studies or be quiet about Tessa around Delly."

"Yes, we've got to keep actin' normal until Friday, when I take her to Bones in Troy. That's only three more days. I think we can keep a secret that long. "

Maseppa settled the mother and child in the pantry again, Phoebe made a trip to the outhouse, and Zeke put some more wood on the fires. "I think I'll sit up for the rest o' the night," he announced. "You girls get some sleep. It will be morning 'fore long."

35
FOUND OUT

Phoebe made it through another day of school. *Wednesday – only two more days to go.*

She pondered over her arithmetic homework. "The square root of forty-nine is seven. The square root of thirty-six is six. The square root of ..."

"Knock, knock! Is anyone home?"

It was Feona Reynolds. She let herself right in without an 'if-you-please.'

"Good day, Phoebe. Is Maseppa around? We were coming into town, and I had some extra venison. I thought you might need some."

Phoebe got up from the table and politely took the meat. "Thank you, Ma'am. That's kindly of you. Maseppa is out taking a walk." She listened to see if she could hear Tessa moving in the pantry, but there was no noise. "I'll be sure to tell Maseppa that you stopped by."

Missus Reynolds walked over to the cook stove. "I've been wishing for one like this. Does the chimney draw well?" She walked around and looked at the back. Phoebe held her breath, but Missus Reynolds didn't look into the pantry.

"This kitchen is so cozy." She tried the kitchen pump and looked out the back window. "I do love a window to look at the scenery while I –"

The door to the shed opened, just long enough for Feona Reynolds to meet the eyes of Tessa returning from the outhouse. The door shut quickly, but it was too late. Missus Reynolds looked at Phoebe with her mouth still open, her last thought forgotten.

"Thank you for the venison," said Phoebe.

"Oh, yes . . . well, I'll be going. Tell Maseppa that I would like her to come over for tea sometime."

Phoebe showed her to the door and then went to find Tessa.

"Oh no, Miss Phoebe!" wailed Tessa. "Dey's goin' to find me!"

"Where's the baby?"

"I put 'im in da chimney hole, cause he was sleepin' . . . but now what we goin' to do?" She held her head in her hands and shook it back and forth. "Dey's comin'. I just knows it!"

Phoebe didn't know what to say. She wished Zeke or Maseppa was here.

"Tessa, just go back in the pantry. I'll keep a look out the window just in case." She put her arm around the frightened girl. "It will be fine."

Later that night, Zeke and Maseppa talked about the chances of Feona Reynolds saying anything about Tessa.

"I'm sure she'll tell her husband, but hopefully it will stop right there. He's a good man. He wouldn't report her," said Zeke. "It's just a matter of her keeping quiet just one more day. Let's just hope she doesn't visit anyone else."

Maseppa gazed steadily at Zeke. "That woman does not know how to stop talking. She will talk."

"Then we'll just have to be ready to hide Tessa, or to leave in a moment's notice." He took out his pipe and newspaper, and Maseppa cut a pumpkin into chunks for a soup.

Phoebe sat in the corner of the pantry with Tessa. It was cozy and comfortable there. She could smell the cinnamon and cloves. The cheese had a sharp sour scent, while the molasses smelled sweet. Phoebe watched Tessa cuddling her baby. "How long have you been running?"

Tessa cocked her head. "It be months. Toby was beat so that he couldn't hardly walk. We's hide in da days and walk in da nights. We get some help, but mostly we just foller the skies north. We heered that we can be free in Canada." She put the baby boy on her shoulder and patted his back. "When we gits near here, we seen da hunters around and I was gettin' so tired." She lifted her head and grinned – her teeth showing white in the dim room. "We seen you and da other chilluns makin' a little house."

"The tree fort on the island?"

Tessa nodded. "Toby swum over to see if it be a good place, but it be too hard for me to git there."

Phoebe smiled. "Maseppa saw a man's footprint. It was probably Toby's."

"He follered you home and tell me to wait here until da baby be borned. He had to go. If dose hunters find'm, dey would drag'm back to V'ginny. I know he'd get beat bad. Maybe even git killed."

"How will you know how to find Toby?"

"He say dat dere be dis place on de other side o' Buffalo, dat he be. He say to look for de marks on de fence posts . . . and look at da clotheslines. He say dey hangin' a quilt wid stars on it, for to show dat it be safe."

"I hope you find him, Tessa."

"I know'd I will." She handed the sleeping baby to Phoebe. "Did you's think up a name yet, Miss Phoebe?" asked Tessa.

Phoebe looked down at the bundle in her arms. He looked so tiny. She liked the way he puckered up his lips in his sleep and pretended to suck. She liked the way he curled his little fingers around her pinky. "I don't know. He shouldn't have an ordinary name, like Tom or Peter. He needs a special name."

When she stroked the top of his fuzzy head, he stretched his long arms. He was wrapped in Tessa's yellow and black striped kerchief. "I know the perfect name – Moses, just like the baby in the Bible that was hiding from the soldiers."

Tessa smiled, and Phoebe could see her white teeth in the semi-darkness. "Yeah, dat be a good name. Moses be a good man dat take his people to da free land."

"Moses, you sleep well tonight. Tomorrow night, you will be on your way to freedom." She handed him back to his mother and said "goodnight" to Tessa.

The horses' hooves were galloping closer and closer. She tried running, but it felt like she was running in thick mud. She fell down and her hands got stuck in the mud. Trying to get up, she felt it tugging her, pulling her.

She opened her eyes. It was Maseppa. "Phoebe, get up! Zeke says it is time to take Tessa now."

"Now? But it's dark!"

"Zeke says it is good to go when it is still dark."

Phoebe jumped up and pulled on her petticoat and dress. Maseppa was handing her more wool stockings and another petticoat. "It is very cold. You need to wear more clothes."

"Why do I need them?"

"Zeke say it is good for you to go with him. No one will ask many questions if you are with him."

"I'm going too?" She quickly put on the extra clothes and buttoned on her boots. She took the woolen hat and mittens and muffler that Maseppa put on the chair for her. "What about school?"

"You will not go to school today. You will go with Zeke."

Zeke had placed some crates in the bed of the wagon and covered them with a tarpaulin. From the outside, no one would know that there was a room in the center of the crates, just big enough for one person . . . and a baby.

"Phoebe, if we happen to meet anyone, we are just going to Troy to deliver this wood and these sacks of grain. You are coming with me to see the city and buy some new shoes . . . understand?"

She nodded. "May I bring some money?"

"Sure. We will do a little shopping before we come home."

"Are you coming, Maseppa?"

"No." Maseppa lifted the hood of Phoebe's cape over her head. "It is good for someone to stay here, to keep the fire burning and smoke coming from the chimney, so that no one will think something is different."

The stars sparkled across the sky, with no moon tonight to hide their light. It seemed extra cold too. Phoebe hunkered down under the wool blankets. She wrapped her muffler over her nose to keep it from tingling. Only her eyes peeked out. At the end of their drive, they turned to the left instead of right toward town.

"Wumf a mwe gwominf?"

Zeke chuckled. "What's that?"

Phoebe pulled her thick scarf down a bit so she could talk.

"Where are we going?"

"Shhhhh," he warned. "We can't be too loud. I don't know who could be watching."

She whispered this time. "Where are we going?"

"We're going to meet Bones."

"But it's too soon – it's only Thursday."

"Let's hope Bones can leave early."

Phoebe turned around to see if she could see Tessa in the back, but all she could see were the covered crates. The wheels left two dark lines in the thin layer of snow, and Ol' Sam's hooves kicked up clods of snow. Phoebe noticed that he wasn't wearing the jingle harness. Too bad there wasn't more snow. They could have used the cutter sled.

"What if the slave hunters come to the house? Will they hurt Maseppa when they can't find Tessa?"

A flicker of concern crossed Zeke's face, but then vanished. "Maseppa has her own plan. She's going to make tracks look like someone walking through the woods, heading north, hoping to send them off the trail."

"But what if they find her?"

"Don't worry. They won't."

36
THE ERIE CANAL

A bright star hung above the western horizon. Phoebe thought it looked like it was guiding them as they sliced through the dark roads.

"Zeke, how does the Erie Canal work? How is it different from a river?"

"Well, a river runs downhill, sometimes over steep cliffs making waterfalls. A boat can't go upriver very easily and has to portage around falls. The canal is like stairs, each section is blocked by gates or locks, making the water calm and level."

"Do they paddle the boats?"

"No. Although there are some paddle wheel boats, most of them are towed by mules. There's a path that runs alongside the canal for the mules and the hoggies."

"The what?"

"The hoggies—they're the ones who tend the mules and make sure the boat doesn't bump into another boat."

"How fast do they go?"

"Not very fast. In fact you could probably jump off a packet, run up the path to the next bridge and jump back on the same boat."

"Where is Tessa going to ride?"

"Don't rightly know, but I expect Bones will put her down with the cargo or where they stable the mules."

"Put her with the animals?"

"Well, it sounds bad, but it's safer there since no one really wants to poke around in manure to hunt for a runaway. Also, it's warmer there this time of year."

"I suppose there would be hay in there, too, for the mules."

"Probably. It's not a bad place to ride, but I'm worried about the baby. It's hard to keep a baby quiet."

As they neared the city of Troy, Phoebe could see lights, even though it was the middle of the night. The streets were lit with lamp posts, making it almost as bright as day. The snow beneath them was dirty and slushy. In fact, everything seemed dirtier and noisier. There were even people still moving about on foot or in wagons.

Zeke maneuvered down Canal Street and pulled behind an enormously long building with lots of dark windows. "This is the Steuben Warehouse." He pulled out his pocket watch. "It's almost midnight. Bones should be here soon." He turned around and lifted the edge of the tarp. "Are you fine, Tessa?" he whispered.

Phoebe didn't see her, but she heard a faint grunt. Zeke got down and checked the harnesses on Ol' Sam. Phoebe glanced around, wondering what Bones looked like. A wagon rolled past. Zeke saw it and nodded quickly but bent down to check Ol' Sam's hoof. A whistle blew. Zeke looked at his watch again. "Midnight," he said. He looked up and down the street and toward the warehouse.

"Zeke?" said a raspy voice behind Phoebe. She jumped. A very thin man with gray whiskers and a droopy mustache walked toward Zeke with his hand outstretched.

"Bones!" said Zeke. "I was hopin' I would find you tonight."

"Is everything fine for you?"

Zeke took off his hat and rubbed the hair on top of his head. "Well, there's a couple o' hitches that we need to deal with. First of all, we've got some hunters on our tail. They got wind she was at our house and raided us the other night. They didn't see nothing, but they knew something was going on." Zeke chuckled. "One got humiliated in my dung pit, and they took off, but they'll be back. I was hoping we could leave tonight."

"Hunters, huh? Did you get a look at them?"

Zeke's eyebrows lifted, "Why, yes, I did! I got a good look at them at the gen'ral store last week. One's got a couple fingers missing and a crooked nose."

"Fitch and Grabe," muttered Bones. "I've dealt with them before. They don't give up easy like." His eyes squinted in a full face grin. "You say one fell in a dung pit? I would've liked to seen that!"

Zeke chuckled again, then became serious. "There's one more little complication . . . and little is exactly right. Tessa, the slave, has just had herself a baby this week. He's a little feller and sleeps lots. She keeps him still, but you never know about babies."

Bones gave a moan and paced a few steps away and back again. "I don't like it. Babies are trouble. They're apt to cry for whatever reason just when you're needin' to be extra quiet. Then they're hard to carry, ifen she ever has t' run." He paced again. "I don't like it. Nope, don't like it at all."

Phoebe felt the wagon move ever so slightly. She knew Tessa had heard Bones.

Bones stopped pacing and looked at Zeke. "You think we can still do this?"

"We've got to try," Zeke replied. "I'll come with you. Two would be better odds against the hunters, and my daughter, Phoebe, could help with the girl, if she needs anything."

Bones noticed Phoebe for the first time and tipped his hat. "Howdy, Miss."

"Good day, sir." She wondered if it was appropriate to say "Good day" in the middle of the night.

He looked at Zeke and twisted his face as he thought. "I reckon having you along might help." He turned back toward Phoebe, but she could tell he was still talking to Zeke. "The girl will have to hide with the slave and the baby. I don't normally take passengers. It would 'pear unnatural-like." He paced back and forth again muttering under his breath.

Zeke stuck out his hand, "Good. It's settled then."

Bones shook his head and muttered something under his breath. "I don't like it. Babies make it more chance of being caught. I've already got the hunters watching me."

"It's just been born so it sleeps most of the time."

"I still don't like it."

"I thought we'd go as far as Schenectady. Is that fine with you?"

"Yes, yes! Another hand would be appreciated." He muttered to himself again. "I don't know about this baby. Being the last trip, they give the boats a good look-over at the weigh locks."

"Could they get off somehow and then get back on?"

"I don't know. The more movement, the more chance of discovery."

"I'll pay extra." Zeke counted off ten more bills into the gnarly hands of Bones.

"Meet me by the out lock, near the north side of the city." He drew a rough sketch in the dirt with a stick. "Do you know where I mean?"

Zeke nodded. "Is it near the Mohawk River Factory?"

"Yes! Yes! Meet me there." Bones scuffed away the map with his boots. "I can be ready in two hours. I'll tie a white kerchief on the bow if it's safe. If you don't see it, that means I'm being watched."

"What's the name of your boat, again? I forgot."

"It's the Sunny Belle. She's got a red stripe on her gunwale."

"All right, then. We'll see you later." He shook Bones's hand. "Thank you so much for this."

Phoebe turned this way and that, trying to see everything at once. It was noisy with whistles and people shouting. They rattled by the place where the canal boats were loaded. Ramps crossed from the canal's edge to the holds. A large wooden boom, with ropes and pulleys, lifted crates and bundles of produce. Phoebe's teeth chatter in her head as Zeke drove over the cobblestones.

"Phoebe, I need to leave Ol' Sam and the wagon at a livery stable. I'll drop you and Tessa off near the lock. You've got to keep hidden in the bushes until Bones comes along."

"But what if you're not back?"

"I'll be back. Just look for the white kerchief. If you don't see it, keep low."

"Zeke, don't be gone too long!"

Phoebe and Tessa hunkered down in the bushes away from any paths or open areas. Little Moses squirmed in his sling and started whimpering. Tessa put him to her breast and he quieted. Little by little the sky turned a pale pink.

A few barges and packets went by. Phoebe looked at the name plate on the front of each one. SALLYMAE, DORY, MARYLOU... She thought it strange that they all had girls' names. Phoebe kept looking back toward the road. *Come on, Zeke*, she thought. *I can't do this by myself. Please, come, Zeke.*

Another boat was coming up the canal. It was traveling slower, and it had a piece of white cloth floating in the breeze. *Oh no! Come on, Zeke!* As it got closer she could see the red color around the edges. The name was the SUNNY BELLE. *Zeke! Hurry!* The boat was almost to them.

She stood up. Bones was on the deck. He hollered at a boy on the towpath. "Hoggie!" The boy pulled on the halter of the nigh mule. "Tie them mules up on the snub post!"

"What's wrong, Sir?"

"I just want you to check something. I heard a noise in the back hold. I need you to check to see that it's not leaking or nothing is rolling around."

The boy hopped over the gap between the edge and the boat. He dropped down into the hold. As soon as he had disappeared, Bones motioned for them to come. Phoebe and Tessa ran to him. Bones helped them hop over the space between the edge of the lock and the boat. Phoebe's stomach lurched as the boat gave way under her feet.

Bones grabbed Tessa's wrist and hurried her to the front of the barge. He lifted a trap door into a small room. Tessa and Phoebe climbed down into it. There were some soft bags of some kind of grain and some blankets. He showed them a jug of water and a pail to use instead of an outhouse. Phoebe hoped she wouldn't need it.

"Make yourself comfortable in the straw in the corner. I'll be back soon."

Soon they heard Zeke return from getting his horse settled. He and Bones talked a little, but Phoebe couldn't hear what they were saying. Soon the ropes splashed in the water, and she could feel the boat sway sideways. Tessa put out her hand and Phoebe held it in hers, as much for her own comfort as for Tessa's.

As they were sitting there in the dark, Phoebe could feel and hear the water slapping the bottom of the boat. Sometimes it lifted and dropped as a swell pushed them. Neither of them spoke and it seemed like they just sat there for hours. They could not see outside at all, so it was impossible to see if the sun had risen yet, or not.

They could hear the mule's feet clink against a stone every once in a while and the low rumble of the men's conversation. The gentle motion of the boat and the darkness made Phoebe very tired, so she laid her head back against the grain bags.

"Hold up there!"

The loud call woke Phoebe. Another voice had joined the men outside. This voice was louder and brusquer than Zeke's or Bones's tones. It sounded familiar. Phoebe sat up and listened intently, holding her breath.

Bones spoke up. "Good day, sir."

"Where are you taking your freight?"

"I walk this path twice a week to Buffalo." Phoebe could hear a defensive tone to his voice.

"Did you go through the inspection station?"

Tessa gasped and Phoebe's heart took a jump just then too. It was the same man in Mister Cooper's store that was looking for a darky. Tessa clasped Phoebe's hand so tightly, that her fingers felt numb.

Bones bellowed, "Of course, I went through the inspection station. It's the law. I did it last night as soon as I was loaded."

Phoebe could hear restless horse hooves and clinks of spurs. There was more muttering and talking that she couldn't understand.

"Have you heard of any talk of someone transporting darkies up the canal?"

"If I do, I'll tell those who need to know."

The gruff voice swore and galloped away. Phoebe smiled in the dark. She sank back against the bags in relief and loosened Tessa's fingers on her hand. She heard Bones tell Zeke, "They can't touch me without any authority, but they're going to find a way. We pass another inspection at Schenectady. We'll have to stop before then and walk them past the weigh station."

"How far's that?" asked Zeke.

"Nigh to fifty miles. We won't get there til past noon."

Moses woke again. He whimpered a bit as Tessa adjusted her clothing to feed him. "Would you like some water and bread?" Phoebe asked Tessa.

Hearing a soft grunt, she put the water jug in Tessa's hand. When she handed it back, Phoebe put some of the bread Maseppa sent in her palm. Phoebe ate a little and drank some water, but she didn't want to take much because she didn't know how long this trip would take.

Even though she couldn't see the sun, she could feel its heat warming the tiny room. She could see tiny spots of light in the cracks between the wood, like the stars at night shining in the dark sky. It was amazing how her eyes adjusted to the little light. Phoebe could see Tessa's shape and her bright eyes, but Phoebe couldn't see her white teeth because Tessa had no reason to smile.

37
THE WEIGH LOCK

Phoebe woke up. The boat was rocking gently up and down, but they weren't moving anymore. She could hear Zeke and Bones talking on the deck. Soon the hatch opened, and Zeke looked down at them.

"What's going on?" asked Phoebe

"We've got to get Tessa off," Zeke whispered. "Bones says there's a weigh lock up ahead, and word's out that they're looking for a runaway. They'll be searchin' everywhere."

"How are we going to get her to Canada if she can't go on the canal?"

"She can get back on after they get through the lock. It just makes it trickier for her and Bones."

Phoebe could hear Bones muttering as he checked his tow lines. The canal was getting crowded as the boats piled up. "These inspections are making it take longer than usual! It will take us twice as long to get there at this rate!"

The boat ahead of them moved up, and the one behind them was shouting to them to fill in the space. "I'm movin'! I'm movin'!" Bones hollered. Lowering his voice, he said to Zeke. "If everyone gets off now, instead of at the weigh station then they won't see her. Cover her head with a shawl or something, so she blends in."

Zeke reached down to help them. "Shh . . . don't say anything." He lifted Tessa and Phoebe out. It was evening again. Phoebe could see lanterns from other canal boats around them.

Bones glanced around. "Don't be talkin'. Voices carry on the wind and over the water." He motioned for Phoebe to go first across the plank, which was slippery with a freezing rain and clumps of mule droppings, but there were cross boards that caught her from sliding down the ramp.

On the bank, Zeke hurried them across the towpath into the trees. The ice made everything crunchy, making it difficult to move around quietly.

Bones told the hoggie, "Move on, boy! I don't want to be an old man before we get to Buffalo!"

He said something to Zeke and pointed at something behind them, but Phoebe could only hear a few words. ". . . store . . . short walk . . . find a shed . . . rain." Then he got back on his boat and grabbed the tiller to steer the boat into the stream again.

Phoebe saw Zeke face the woods, his eyes darting back and forth. "Phoebe?"

She stood up. "I'm here, Zeke."

"Get down!" he whispered firmly. "Stay still. Bones said there's probably a shed nearby so we can get out of the rain. I'll find it and come back for you."

Again the fear of being left in charge swelled up in Phoebe. *What if something happens? What if Zeke doesn't come back?* The rain hit the dead leaves with a steady ticking. It was soaking through her wool cape and making her shiver. She could feel Tessa shivering beside her, hunched over so as to protect the baby.

Phoebe could see the lanterns on the boats going up and down the canal, mostly going up, because of the weigh lock. They watched three boats slowly drift by in their turn. The mules and hoggies, waiting in the rain for their turn, looked miserable.

Phoebe's leg was cramped, so she moved it a little. The leaves crackled, and a hoggie looked in their direction. She ducked her head to hide her face under her bonnet. Remembering how Tessa's eyes shone white in the darkness, she glanced her way. Tessa's shawl was pulled over her head so that even Phoebe couldn't see her face sitting next to her.

The hoggie threw a pebble in their direction, trying to scare off whatever creature made the noise. Phoebe held her breath and didn't move. Soon the boats moved up, and the hoggie led his mules beyond them.

Phoebe closed her eyes and wished she could go to sleep. A crackle in the leaves behind her made her jump. She waited. *There it was again*! She didn't dare move a muscle. It could be a squirrel or a cat, but it seemed to be something walking. Yes, the noise was coming closer and closer. She could feel Tessa hunker lower. The footsteps stopped a few feet away.

A low voice whispered, "Phoebe?"

"Zeke!"

"Shhh . . . "

"Zeke, you scared me!"

"Shhh . . . there's a place to get out of the rain, but these leaves are so noisy we'll have to be careful." He paused, and Phoebe could hear him breathing hard. "Stand up slowly. We'll need to move a step at a time." He reached out and caught Phoebe's arm. "Take hold of Tessa." Phoebe stretched out her hand and felt Tessa's shawl and clasped it. Zeke whispered, "We will move then stop, move then stop. Got it?"

"Got it. Ready, Tessa?" She felt her shrug. "We're ready, Zeke."

"Move," he whispered. They all took three steps. "Stop." Phoebe bumped into him, and Tessa bumped into her. "Move." Three steps. "Stop." This time they didn't bump. They moved three steps and stopped, three steps and stopped, until they came to the edge of the woods. Zeke squatted and the girls did, too. "The roof hangs out over a wood shed. There's room for us while we wait for the boats."

"How do we know where to get back on the boat?"

"The river takes a big curve, so we can cut across the land to the other side."

They dashed across the cleared land to the shed. Zeke shifted some split wood around to make a little alcove. They could hear the rain pattering on the roof. It felt good to be out of the rain, but they were still wet and shivering.

"I'll be right back-"

"No, Zeke!"

"I'm going to see if the store sells blankets. We need to get you girls warm."

He disappeared into the night. Phoebe leaned her head back against the stacked wood. *This isn't fun anymore. I want to go home, back to my own bed.* Tessa shifted her weight to make the baby more comfortable. Phoebe felt guilty. Tessa didn't have a home to go back to. She needed to keep going forward to be safe, to be free. Phoebe felt awful. Her throat felt tight and her eyes burned with tears. The rain seemed to be louder and heavier. Phoebe let herself drift into a sleep.

Zeke shook her shoulder. "Phoebe, wake up."

"Zeke!"

"I was able to get some blankets. Here—wrap this around you. Tessa, here's one for you, too."

"Did it stop raining? I don't hear it anymore."

"No, worse. It's snowing. They'll see our footprints."

The back door of the store opened. A man walked over to the wood pile and piled a few logs on his arm. He paused mid-motion and took a step toward them. "Hey! Who are you?"

Zeke stood up. "Sorry, sir. My girl and I are traveling. We are just trying to get out of the rain."

The man's eyebrows puckered. "Where's your wagon? You travelin' on foot? It's late in the year for that."

"We're going by canal boat, but we needed to get off while they weigh it. We'll be on our way come daylight."

"You can come inside, if you want. It's warmer in there."

"Thank you, but we're fine."

The man just stood there holding his wood, looking at them. "Are you sure? It seems silly sitting out here when you can get warm inside."

"We'll be fine."

"If you need anything, just come in that back door. The missus and I live upstairs, but I'll leave the back door open for you."

"Thank you kindly. We may just do that." Zeke stood up. "Come, Phoebe."

She looked at him questioningly, but obeyed. Tessa pulled back as far as she could into the stacks of wood. The man led Zeke and Phoebe into the back of the store.

"Warm yourselves near the stove. I'm sorry I don't have any vittles for you."

"That's fine, sir. We already have our own. We'll be leaving at the first light of morning."

The man left them alone amid the stock room shelves.

Phoebe turned to Zeke and whispered. "What are you doing?"

"It just didn't make sense to turn down his hospitality. He'd be more suspicious if I did."

"What about Tessa?"

"I'll go get her soon, so she can warm up."

Phoebe stood near the stove. Her clothes dripped and hissed on the hot metal. They could hear the man moving around above them. Soon it was quiet.

Zeke slipped out the door and returned with Tessa. She lifted Moses out of her sling, and he began to cry. She quickly tried to feed him, but he cried harder. They heard footsteps cross the floor above them and the shop keeper's voice. "Is all well down there?"

Zeke answered, "Yes, my daughter burned her hand on the stove." To Phoebe he whispered, "Cry."

"OWWWWW!" She tried to make it sound like Matthew when he got hurt.

"Should I fetch a doctor for the girl?"

"Thank you, but I put some snow on it. She'll be fine soon."

"Owwww . . ." Phoebe whimpered some more.

Moses was nursing happily, so Phoebe quieted down too. The man tromped overhead back to his bed.

Zeke whispered, "As soon as we're dried, we'll find Bones. He's probably through the locks by now and looking for us."

Moses snuggled back in his sling. Everyone felt grateful for the few hours of warmth. Just before sunrise, they gathered their things to leave, but when they opened the door, their hearts sank. The snow had accumulated to a few inches. There was no way to hide their footprints.

"It's good that the shop keeper knows about you and me, Phoebe. He will know our footprints. Tessa, do you think you can walk right in my steps?"

She nodded.

Zeke deliberately took smaller steps so Tessa could put her foot right in his tracks. Phoebe held his hand and walked beside them. Looking back, it looked like only two people walking in the snow.

"Zeke, do you know where to go?"

"Well, not exactly, but we'll figure it out as we get closer."

"Zeke, this is harder than I thought it would be."

"You're a brave girl. Keep thinking of Tessa. It's not easy, but we can't turn back now. We can't let the slave hunters find her."

While Zeke checked to see if Bones was past the weigh lock yet, he found another shelter for the girls. The wind was blowing hard between the boards, melting snow dripped from the roof. An hour or more passed, and Moses began crying. He wasn't just whimpering - he was bawling. All you could see of his face was a wide open toothless mouth. He was crying so hard that he wouldn't even nurse when Tessa tried to hush him.

Phoebe pulled her shawl closer around her shoulders. "What's wrong with him?"

"I don' know. I don' know what t' do!"

Zeke appeared around the corner of the shed. "I can hear him crying way down by the canal. You've got to stop him. The whole plan will be spoiled if he keeps crying."

Now Tessa was crying, too. She jiggled him up and down. Setting him down on her blanket, she unwrapped his blankets and swaddlings. Phoebe leaned over to provide more protection from the stinging rain.

"Phew!" Phoebe gagged. "That could be one reason!"

Tessa wiped his skin as best she could. His little arms and legs stretched out in shock against the cold. All the while, Moses was screaming. It had turned into hiccups and occasionally he'd choke and cough, which would make him scream even louder.

Wrapping him back up, Tessa held him close and jiggled him and hummed to him. Soon he calmed down enough to nurse, but it didn't last long.

"My milk is gone. I don' have no more!" Tessa wailed. "I don' know what t' do."

Zeke turned her shoulders so she would look straight in his face. "Tessa, you either have to go back or take the risk of the slave hunters hearing the baby and finding you."

"NOOO ... don' let 'em git me!"

"Then we'll have to go back." Zeke took off his hat and scratched his head. "You could hide at our house until he's older and able to be quiet."

She looked down at the squalling baby. Then she held him to her face, wrapping her arms around his little body. Both of their tears mingled together.

They all looked back when they heard a voice, "Yes, I've seen a man and a girl. They stayed in my storeroom last night to get out of the rain." They could see the storekeeper pointing to their tracks and then in their direction.

Zeke said, "Tessa, you've got to make up your mind now!"

Tessa sobbed as she kissed the forehead of her little baby. She turned and put him in Phoebe's arms. "I's hafta' go on alone. Phoebe, take care a ma baby. If I gets caught, he never be free."

Phoebe's eyes widened. "I can't take care of him!"

"I'll come back an' gets him soon." She slipped the sling off her shoulder and placed it over Phoebe's head. "I knows you take good care a him, like he be your own."

"But. . . .but"

Zeke tugged Tessa's sleeve. "They're coming. We've got to go!"

"What about me?" Phoebe looked up in panic.

"Go to the towpath and follow it back to Troy. If you get there before I catch up with you, ask someone to show you how to get to Montgomery's Mercantile. He's a good friend."

"Zeke, I can't -" But Zeke and Tessa had already fled toward the woods beyond the lock. They left footprints until they reached the trees. Phoebe looked down at the crying baby and then at the men walking her way. She scuffed her feet on the footprints as fast as she could before the men reached her. She decided the best disguise would be to be brave.

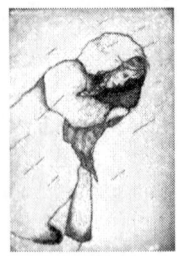

38
BABY MOSES

Tucking Moses into the sling and making sure his face was hidden, Phoebe walked with determination right toward the men as if on an errand. Her heart pounded harder the closer she got.

"Hey, girl!"

"Me, sir?"

"Yes. Have you seen a man and a little girl around here?"

"My little brother needs his mama, sir. He's mighty hungry!"

"Where's the boy's mama?"

"She's over there." Phoebe gestured with her chin toward the weigh lock as she jiggled the crying baby. "I've got to go. Good day, sir."

The men looked toward the lock, where dozens of people – men, women, and children – waited for the boats to be checked. She walked quickly toward the towpath. *Lord, thank you for protecting me and little Moses. Please help Tessa to get to freedom.* When she glanced back, they were investigating the prints in the snow around the shed.

She had walked for about a half hour when her legs began to hurt and the sling start to cut into her shoulder. Moses was heavier than she thought. When he stopped crying, she sat down gently on a rock to rest herself, but the cessation of movement awakened the baby. So she got up and walked. As she walked, she talked to him about the boats, about the mules, about Zeke, but she didn't talk about Tessa. There were too many people around.

"Noooo... Moses...shhhh..." He seemed to like the sound of her voice, so she kept walking and talking. "I don't know anything about taking care of babies, Moses. So, you're going to have to be patient with me." Her feet were moving, her eyes were open, but she walked without seeing where she was going, and she just walking and walking. Her steady footsteps began to make a rhythm in her ears.

"The Lord is my shepherd, I shall not want
He maketh me to lie down in green pastures."

On and on she walked. She saw the men searching the boats, but they weren't looking for her. They weren't looking for a white girl carrying a baby.

"Yea, though I walk through the valley of the shadow of death,
I will fear no evil; for thou art with me;
Thy rod and thy staff they comfort me."

Phoebe talked about the boats. "There's a steamer coming up the canal. It has smoke coming out of a big chimney. It moves faster than any boat I've ever seen. Look at those paddles going around and around."

Just then, the steamer gave a long TOOOOOOT! Phoebe jumped and so did Moses, and he started screaming again. She picked him up out of the sling and wrapped his blanket around him better. She held her cheek close to his face, and he turned his mouth and tried to suck her skin.

"Ohhh . . . you're so hungry. I can't feed you. I don't know what to do."

"Miss?"

Phoebe spun around. A woman motioned to her from a canal boat nearby.

"Miss? Do you need help?"

Phoebe didn't know what to say. She DID need help, but what if this lady told someone about Moses being a Negro?

"Well? Do you need help or not?"

"Yes, Ma'am. I don't have any food for this baby."

"Come here, Child." The woman laid a plank across to the edge, and Phoebe walked onto the deck of the boat and ducked through a small door. "Let me see your baby." The woman pulled back the blanket and gasped. "Lord o'Mercy! It's a black child."

Phoebe held him close and started to leave.

"Wait!" The woman put a hand on Phoebe's arm. "I don't know where you got this child – and it's probably best I don't know – but he's hungry, and he will die if he doesn't eat."

"I don't know how to feed him, Ma'am."

"He's so small; he needs mother's milk." She pointed to a cradle hanging from the rafters. It swung with the rocking of the ship. "That's my wee one. She was born just a week ago."

"Moses was born just last week, too."

"Moses?"

Phoebe ducked her head and clamped her lips shut.

"Never mind. It doesn't matter what his name is." She settled down and unfastened the front of her dress. "Now don't you go telling anyone I did this. My mister would have fits if he knew I was putting a Negro child to my breast, but I can't stand to let a little one starve to death."

Moses sputtered and squirmed, but soon he was sucking happily. The woman smiled and caressed his fuzzy head. "Ain't you a precious child?"

"Where's your mister?" asked Phoebe

"He's on shore – probably hunting for a pub while we're waiting for the lock."

Phoebe looked around the little cabin. There were curtains in the windows and a white cloth on the table. A clothesline hung across the rafters with some towels and clothes on it. There was a dress – too big for a newborn – and some knickers almost the size of Matthew.

"Ma'am, do you have other children?"

"Yes, little Audrey is napping in her bunk, and Cecil is off with his friends on another boat." She looked closely at Phoebe. "I've not seen you around the canal. Which boat do you ride?"

"I came up water on the – " She began, but glanced at the woman and shut her lips.

"You don't have to tell me, child. I'll respect your secrets."

The aromas from a bubbling pot on a coal stove were making her hungry. In fact, she was so hungry that she almost felt like she was sick. Phoebe's stomach growled. The room felt hot, and everything was fuzzy. Her ears buzzed.

She woke to hear Moses crying again and the woman looking down at her. "Child! Child! Wake up, Child!" She felt a cold cloth on her face.

Phoebe sat up and looked around trying to remember where she was. *Moses!* She jumped up but couldn't get her balance. She sunk to the floor again.

"You're sick, Child. Lay your body on the bench. When did you eat last?"

Phoebe couldn't remember what day it was. *Was it day or night?* She sat up and looked out the windows. The sun was still shining, but the afternoon shadows had lengthened. "I need to go. Zeke will be looking for me!"

"I don't know who this Zeke is, but you're not going anywhere until you get some food in your stomach. Now, here's some broth and a chunk of bread." Phoebe breathed in the rich aroma. The bread was soft. She bit off a huge piece. "Slow down, Child! You'll be chucking it up!"

The woman picked up Moses, who was crying again and nursed him on her other breast. Soon he was asleep, and Phoebe's stomach felt full and satisfied.

The woman helped her settle Moses into the sling. "Now if you can't find another nursing woman to help you, there is something you can do. Get a clean cloth and wrap it round your finger like so . . . " She demonstrated with her apron. "Then dip your finger in some milk and let him suck it off the cloth. It ain't as good as his mother's milk, but it will save his life."

She touched the top of his curly head again. "He's such a precious lad. Oh, if you can't find milk, just a piece of pork tied in the corner of a kerchief will do for a while."

"Thank you, Ma'am." She tied her bonnet under her chin. "Thank you for the broth and bread, too. I much appreciate your kindness."

"Twasn't nothing. Now get along to wherever you were going."

Phoebe scurried across the plank to the tow path. She turned back and waved. "Ma'am? What's your name?"

"Never mind that. I just saw you needed help."

With her belly full of food and her legs rested, and the baby sleeping quietly in the sling, Phoebe set off down the path to Troy. She hoped Zeke hadn't pass by while she was in the boat. She figured that if he got there first, he'd be waiting for her. With renewed strength, she adjusted the heavy sling on her shoulder and set off to find the Montgomery Mercantile.

> *"Thou preparest a table before me*
> *in the presence of mine enemies;*
> *thou anointest my head with oil,*
> *my cup runneth over."*

She remembered the Montgomery Mercantile from when Zeke had taken her and Maseppa there last year to buy some new shoes and things for the house. It was the biggest general store she had ever seen in her life – it even had stairs up to another floor. There might have even been more beyond that, but she had only seen the second floor, where there were fancy glass lamps and rugs from India. She liked the dolls with china heads and the music boxes. There were necklaces and watches and fancy brooches. Maseppa didn't look at those things. She was more interested in the new cooking pots and pans. Zeke was interested in the tools. There was even a soda fountain, where you could buy sweets and ice cream. Phoebe thought it would be a fun place to live. There was everything a person could want – all right inside the mercantile.

She had been thinking so much about Montgomery's Mercantile, she wasn't paying attention to the people and things around her. She knew it must be quite a ways yet to the city. Occasionally, she met a team of mules led by a man or boy. She stood to the side and let them pass. Some tipped their hats, others nodded, and some just ignored her.

All of a sudden the towpath stopped. Well, it didn't really stop; it came to a bridge over the canal. She walked to the middle of the bridge and looked over the edge. The water was a murky brown. You couldn't tell how deep it was. A barge was heading down the canal, and the hoggie hollered at her.

"Hey! Get off the bridge, if you don't want to be trampled."

She trotted to the side and let the hoggie and his mules pass over the bridge. The boat came so close to the underside of the bridge that the people on the top deck had to get off and duck their heads. *That could be dangerous if you weren't paying attention.*

The houses and buildings were more numerous now. There were some shops that opened right to a porch on the edge of the water. A house boat was tied up to a snub and some children were carrying sacks of flour and supplies from the shop to the boat. A man with a larger sack on his shoulder came out of the shop. He tipped his hat and said, "Good evening, Miss."

Phoebe nodded. "Good day, Sir."

Moses was stirring again, and Phoebe approached the shop. As she opened the door, a bell rang. A man behind the counter looked up. "May I help you, Miss?"

"Sir, do you have milk?"

"That I do. Would you like it by the quart or pint?"

Phoebe looked at the glass bottles. "I only need a pint, Sir."

"That will be three cents."

Phoebe had to put Moses down to fumble beneath her layers of clothes to reach her apron pocket. She pulled out her kerchief and untied the knot that held her pennies. She only had six cents. One by one, she laid three of them in the man's open palm. Her stomach growled at the aroma of some fresh baked bread.

"How much would a loaf cost?"

"They're two cents."

"I'll take one, please." *I might as well use the last penny too.* She looked around the shop. "Could I also have a penny's worth of cheese?"

She had hoped to buy something in the city with her money, but she knew there would be other days when she could spend money on frivolous things.

He wrapped them in a bundle and even tied a string on the neck of the bottle so Phoebe could carry it. She was feeling mighty fine as she strutted toward the city to find Zeke and the Montgomery Mercantile.

It wasn't long before the towpath ended at a livery stable, a warehouse, and a boat repair building. There were wagons and buggies and horses and people everywhere. She held Moses close to her and tried not to bump into anyone. It was hard to hold the package and milk and Moses all at the same time. She made her way to the side of the street and tried to think clearly.

What I really need is a place to sit down!

She ducked into an alley between two buildings. A cat meowed and skedaddled out of there. "It's not the homiest place, but I don't think anyone will bother us here." She leaned against the wall and closed her eyes. It felt good to rest.

Moses started whimpering. She untied the cardboard cover from the bottle of milk. Taking a long sip first, she wrapped her apron around her finger and stuck it in the end of the bottle. It dripped all over the place as she moved it to the little mouth. Moses stopped crying as he smacked at the liquid.

"You were hungry, little feller!"

Over and over she dipped her finger in the bottle and fed the baby, and soon he was back to sleep. Phoebe took a few bites of the bread and cheese and thought that probably Zeke would be hungry too. She put the cover back on the bottle and tied the string around it. Adjusting the sling to a comfortable position, she set off to find the Montgomery Mercantile.

The city was so big, and nothing looked familiar. She saw a man with a top hat and cane, leaning against a lamppost.

"Mister?"

"Hello, Miss. How may I help you?"

"I'm looking for a friend at the Montgomery Mercantile. Could you tell me which direction to go?"

"Of course! Everyone knows where that is." He tucked one thumb in the armhole of his vest and pointed with his cane. "Go four blocks down Canal Street – that's this one here – then turn left onto Main Street. Follow that for about six blocks. Montgomery's should be just a block on your right."

Phoebe repeated the directions. "Four blocks on Canal Street, turn left, six blocks on Main Street, and turn right"

"Perfect! You've got it." He pushed his spectacles on his nose and looked closer at her. "You're a wee bit of fluff to be out by yourself in the city. Where do you live?"

Phoebe didn't like the way he looked at her. "Thank you, Sir." She hurried off in the direction he had pointed.

She skittered across one street. "Four blocks down Canal Street and turn right on to Main Street...or was it left?" *Oh no! I forgot already!*

When she got to Main Street, she looked to the right. There was a hotel and restaurant. Across the way, she could see a theater and shoe store. None of it looked familiar. She looked to the left - the street seemed to stretch all the way to California. There were coaches and buggies and people walking everywhere. A woman with a pink parasol approached.

"Miss?" The woman stopped and wrinkled up her nose at her, and looked up and down Phoebe's attire. Phoebe looked down at herself and grimaced. She wasn't very presentable with mud and burrs all over her stockings and skirt. "Miss, which way to the Montgomery Mercantile?"

Without speaking the woman, pointed to Phoebe's left and proceeded on her way. Phoebe counted the blocks as she weaved her way in and out of the crowds of people. "Three...four...five...six!" If the first turn was left, then now she had to turn right. She looked for a gap in the traffic and sprinted across the muddy street. Her feet were caked in slime and horse manure, but it couldn't be helped. She stood there gasping for breath and looking around. *Now I know where I am!* She could see the tall building of the Montgomery Mercantile just ahead.

Holding Moses close, she trotted down the boardwalk. Waiting for a wagon to pass by, she ran across one more street. Just as she stepped up, her foot slipped in the mud and she fell. The bottle of milk shattered, and Moses screamed. She could hear the jingling of a harness and hoofbeats coming closer. Her foot hurt. She couldn't stand up. She could see a team of horses bearing down on her.

"NOOOO!"

A strong hand grabbed her arms and pulled her to safety.

Looking up, she saw Zeke.

"You did it, Li'l Angel. I knew you could."

Phoebe buried her head in his chest and cried. "Zeke, I didn't know what to do, and Moses cried, and the lady fed him, and I turned the wrong way, and I broke the bottle, and –"

"Shhh . . . no matter, now. You're here. Moses is safe. Tessa is on her way to freedom." Phoebe couldn't hold back the sobs anymore. Zeke held her close and let her cry. "Let's go home, Phoebe."

Home. Yes, it never sounded better.

39
GOING HOME

Seated in the wagon, Phoebe held little Moses close in her arms and wrapped a blanket around both of them. "Now what are we going to do?"

Zeke gave the reins a little flick and Ol' Sam picked up the pace. "Well, I suppose we'll do what's right. We'll take care of this little feller until his mama and papa come get him."

"What if something happens? What if they never come back?"

"Then we will teach him right from wrong, and to love God and his neighbor as himself."

"Tessa made me promise to take care of him, but I don't know very much about babies."

"You'll get help from Maseppa and Deborah and even me."

"You know how to take care of babies?"

"It can't be too hard. You feed them and change their clothes once in a while and make sure they don't wander off. That doesn't sound too difficult."

"Zeke, I think it's a little more than that!"

Ol' Sam clip-clopped along. The clouds blew away the rain and the moon shone over the land, highlighting each tree with miniature stars. Phoebe peeked down into the folds of the blankets. She could hear Moses making little coos in his sleep. He didn't smell so good, but soon they would be home and she could clean him up.

"Zeke, I was scared."

"Me, too."

"Really?" Her voice squeaked in surprise.

"Yup, but I knew that I had a job to do and didn't let my fear stop me."

"That's how I felt too. I just kept walking and going and didn't think of getting stopped by the slave hunters or getting lost or anything. I kept saying my verses and they made me feel better."

"Yes, God's Word will do that."

They rattled along for miles. Phoebe couldn't stop thinking of all that happened over the last day. It seemed like they had been gone for a week or a month. Flashes of the different faces appeared in her mind: Bones, the hoggie, the slave hunters, the store keeper, and the woman on the boat that fed Moses.

"Zeke, I think God put that woman right there at the right time. She wanted to help and she did help. What if someone bad had heard Moses? What if they took me to the police? What if – "

"Now, stop right there! We can't be thinking about all the 'what ifs' in this life. God directs our paths, and he directed that woman to be right there when you needed her most. You listened to God's voice and she did too."

"And all those other people that showed me the way to the Montgomery Mercantile?"

"All those others too. Now, just rest your mind and rest your head against me. We'll be home within the hour."

Phoebe leaned her head against Zeke's wool coat. Ol' Sam's hoof beat a tattoo while the rest of the Psalm went through in her mind.

*"Surely goodness and mercy shall follow me
all the days of my life,
and I shall dwell in the house of the Lord forever."*

She added a quiet "Amen" and closed her eyes.

Soon they turned up their lane. The lamplight in the kitchen window looked so warm. Maseppa must have been waiting for them, for she met them at the door. "You brought them back?" She looked from the bundle in Phoebe's arms to Zeke's face. "What happened? Where is Tessa?"

"She is on a boat heading north."

"Why do you have the baby?"

Zeke plopped down in a chair. "It cried. It was hungry and frightened. Tessa couldn't feed him all the time. Her milk was gone." He unlaced his boot. "Tessa knew that if the slave hunters heard the baby, they would take her back and punish her for running. She might not live, nor the baby." He pulled off his boot and began unlacing the other one. "The only solution was for her to go alone. She made Phoebe promise to take care of Moses until she and Toby came back for him." He kicked off the second boot.

Maseppa reached her arms for the tiny boy. His arms and legs stretched as she unwrapped the blankets. She touched his cheek. "A long time ago, Martha made me promise to take care of Phoebe." She looked into Phoebe's blue eyes. "Now, you have made a promise too."

"I don't know how to keep this promise."

"I did not know either, but you will do the best you know. Zeke and I will help you. You still need to go to school. I will help you keep the promise."

Phoebe stroked the soft black cheek. "Could he sleep in my room at night?"

"Yes, that would be good."

Phoebe pinched her nose. "The first thing we need to do is clean him up!"

While Maseppa poured some hot water into the sink and pumped some cold water to temper it, Phoebe laid the baby on the table and undressed him. Little Moses hollered.

Zeke laughed. "It's a good thing we don't have to keep him a secret anymore. He was born free. No one can take him away. We will act like he is our own little boy." He fixed himself a pipe and leaned back against the wall. "We're quite a hodge-podge of a family – a Jew and an Indian, with a blond haired girl and a negro baby." He shook his head. "What a home!"

Moses screeched and thrashed his hands and feet as Maseppa held him in the sink and Phoebe wiped warm water over his skin. Phoebe said, "I like our home." She wrapped a towel around the crying baby and laid him on the table again, then wiped him dry. His skin looked as soft as a summer night. She bundled him up again and held him close. "A lady on the canal fed Moses then she showed me how to feed him milk with a cloth."

Maseppa was already pouring a little milk in a pan and warming it on the stove. Phoebe wrapped a clean cloth around her finger and dipped it into the milk. Moses sucked until he fell asleep.

Zeke watched the whole thing with fascination. "I expect Deborah would be able to help you. She's had a baby not too long ago. She may have some baby clothes and such."

Maseppa nodded. "I will talk with her tomorrow."

Phoebe sat in the rocker, and Maseppa sang.

Wàseyà, kimàdjîgi,
Kimiwan, kinibàe,
Nôdin, kimashkawizi,
Pineshînjish, nigamo.

Phoebe said, "I remember that song. What does it mean again?"

"It is from my people. My mother sang it to me, and I sang it to you when you were little. The words say,

> The sun shines, you grow;
> The rain falls, you sleep.
> The wind blows, you strong;
> The little bird sings. "

Zeke jumped up. "There's a cradle in the shed. I reckon it was yours as a baby, Phoebe. I know right where it is!" He disappeared out the door. Within a few minutes they had it cleaned up and set up in Phoebe's room. Moses didn't even stir as Phoebe laid him in it.

"Good night, Phoebe" Maseppa kissed her forehead. "You are not a little girl any more. Today you have become a brave woman. I am pleased with you."

"Thank you, Maseppa. You taught me how."

40
CHRISTMAS BLESSINGS

It had been a month since that eventful day. Moses had become a part of their daily life and brought joy to their home. Now it was almost Christmas. Missus Thomas's class had been working hard on a program for the church. They practiced poems and songs and some of the verses they had been learning over the months.

Phoebe counted the verses again.
"Psalm 1 has 6,
Psalm 23 has 6,
Psalm 100 only has 5,
Psalm 139 has 24,
Psalm 96 has 13,
Psalm 34 has 22,
Psalm 19 has 14,
Psalm 27 has 14,
Psalm 150 has 6, making it 110!"

She added them all up. "Yes! One hundred and ten!" She only had one more week, but now that she had been doing this for months, it had become a habit. She noticed that she found it was easier to learn the words while she moved. She rocked Moses back and forth, as she recited, "For his mercy endureth forever!" She had milked the cow, punctuating each squirt with, "Bless... the... Lord... oh... my... soul..." Every step to school had become a word stamped into her mind.

Phoebe and Zeke had other Christmas plans, too. She watched for him to get back from his trip to the city. "Zeke's back!" Phoebe clattered down the porch steps.

She followed the jangling wagon into the barn. "Did you buy the leather moccasins for Maseppa?"

He reached in the back of wagon and pulled out a bundle. "It took a little while, but I found some."

"Oh, thank you, Zeke! I know she'll love them."

"I have another surprise. I saw Bones."

"Bones? How is he? Did Tessa get to Canada?"

"He gave me this." Zeke lifted a yellow scarf with black stripes.

"Tessa's kerchief!"

"Bones said she told him to give it you, so you'd know that she was safe."

Phoebe clutched the cloth close. *Thank you, Lord.*

"Bones said that the canal will be frozen and closed for the winter. Tessa and Toby will be back next year after the ice thaws."

As the time for the Christmas program grew near, Phoebe could hardly contain her excitement and joy. Finally, the night of the program arrived. Phoebe's stomach felt like it had a hundred Gimpys fluttering around in it. She hoped she didn't forget any words.

Phoebe scrubbed her elbows and neck. Maseppa helped her pin her hair up in a bun and tied it with a red ribbon. As she twirled around, her dress belled out around her. It was the prettiest dress she had ever worn. Missus Kittle said she made it just like the pictures of the dresses in Paris, France. Phoebe fingered the tiny, white rosettes embroidered on the smocked bodice and the ribbons at the top of each flounce.

She was glad that there was enough snow to use the sleigh. While she waited for Zeke to tighten the harnesses, she rocked Moses on her lap. He looked up into her face through the peephole of the blankets wrapped around him. She put her face close. "You look like a little cocoon. Yes you do!" He scrunched up his face and smiled wide.

The church windows glowed with lamplight. Ropes of evergreens draped over the doorway and around the railings of the front steps. People greeted each other as they arrived.

The class sang "Il Est Ne, le Divine Enfant." The little ones marched in on their cue as they performed the nativity story. Sammy was a shepherd and Ross was the innkeeper. They all sang "Angels We have Heard on High." It was almost Phoebe's turn.

Missus Thomas stood on the platform. "Ladies and Gentlemen, this year I challenged my Sunday school class to learn one hundred verses from the book of Psalms over the last six months. I am pleased that all of them have worked hard, some learning more than they thought they could. I would like each one to come and recite a portion of the Psalms tonight. Scott Peterson?"

One by one they went to the front and recited their verses. Some sped through the words so fast that no one could understand them. Some mumbled so low that you wondered when they were done. Delly said hers like someone singing a song, making her words go up and down in a regular beat. Phoebe was next. Her stomach lurched. *What is my first word? Oh yes –* "O sing..."

Missus Thomas waited for her to come to the front. "I want to tell all of you that Miss Phoebe Johanson is the only one of the class that has learned one hundred verses. In fact, when we added them up, we found she had learned one hundred and ten." Everyone clapped and Phoebe ducked her head. As she sat down, Missus Thomas whispered in her ear, "Bon Courage."

Everyone was quiet.

Phoebe swallowed. Her heart pounded. She saw Maseppa with

Moses on her lap. Zeke smiled. Phoebe rubbed her palms against her skirt.

"O sing unto the Lord, a new song…"

As she said the words, they came from her heart. She wasn't just reciting the words anymore. She was saying them with her heart, as if she had written them herself. She lifted her chin and spoke with confidence.

"O worship the Lord in the beauty of holiness.
Bow before Him all of the earth."

She didn't really see the audience anymore. She didn't see Missus Thomas mouthing the words with her. She didn't see Maseppa's eyes glisten with pride. She was saying the words to the Lord.

"For the Lord cometh! He cometh to judge the earth;
He shall judge the world with righteousness
and the people with his truth!"

Everyone clapped, and Missus Thomas clapped as she stood up next to Phoebe. "Ladies and Gentlemen…" She waited until things quieted again and wiped her finger across her eye. "Ladies and Gentlemen, I told my class that if they could learn one hundred verses, I would give them a Bible of their own. Phoebe, I am pleased to present to you this Bible. Read it often and follow its teachings." She leaned close. "You did a great job, Phoebe!"

Phoebe hugged her new Bible and quickly returned to her seat. She ran her hand over the Bible's leather cover. Her name was written on the bottom corner in gold lettering, PHOEBE JOHANSON. The edges were of smooth gold. She lifted the cover. To Phoebe Johanson, December 22, 1836.

Phoebe sat on the edge of the pew to watch as Delly tucked her fiddle under her chin. She gave a few tuning notes and glanced at her mother. Then with the first note of "Cantique de Noel," the whole room held its breath.

The spirit of Christmas filled every rafter, and the starry skies of that first Christmas descended to the room as she played. The last note lingered and slowly drifted to the ceiling. No one moved or breathed. With many teary eyes, they clapped and clapped. Delly curtsied and returned to her seat.

The preacher led the congregation in "Silent Night." Then he said, "I'd like each child to come up to the front as I call your name. Priscilla?"

One by one they went up, and Parson Thomas gave each one a gift. There were dolls and hobby horses and picture books. Delly giggled with glee as she opened her package. "Oh look, Phoebe, skates!"

Phoebe got a copy of *The Nutcracker and the Mouse King*. She could hardly wait to get home and start reading it. She was so happy that she felt like she would burst. It was the best Christmas ever.

That evening, when she gave Zeke a hug before going to bed, he held both of her shoulders and looked her in the eye. "Maseppa and I have something special to tell you."

She glanced over at Maseppa. There was a glimmer of a smile at the corner of her lips. Phoebe looked back at him. "What?"

He gave her braid a tug. "Do you know how you've been wishing for a little brother or sister?"

ALGONKIN GLOSSARY
(courtesy of Native American Languages)

Algonkin	Native Americans of southern Quebec
Ikwesins	little girl
Ondàs	"Come!"
Madji	bad luck

LULLABY

Wàseyà, kimàdjîgi,

Kimiwan, kinibàe,

Nôdin, kimashkawizi,

Pineshînjish, nigamo

"The sun shines, you grow;
The rain falls, you sleep.
The wind blows, you strong;
The little bird sing."

ABOUT THE AUTHOR

As Yvonne Blake travelled her pathway through life, she packed experiences and descriptions into the corners of her mind. The rugged hills of New York hold special memories. Her childhood years were a mixture of traipsing through the woods with her brothers, reading books, and making friends at school. Her home was often a refuge for those who needed to heal and rest along their way.

Phoebe's character was born in a creative writing class during Yvonne's senior year of high school. Over the years, the story developed and changed in her mind as she raised her family. Finally after teaching in a Christian school for twelve years and seeing the youngest of her eight children leave home, she was able to finish her novel.

Yvonne developed her writing skills by completing the Journeyman Course of the Christian Writers Guild and participated in Faithwriters for several years. She has continued to teach children how to write through workshops and her website, Polliwog Pages. Yvonne has published a variety of stories for all ages.

She and her husband live on the coast of Maine. They both enjoy their grandchildren and quieter times together. Yvonne is now unpacking the boxes of memories to put them into poems, short stories, and novels. She prays her writing will be used of the Lord to entertain, enlighten, and encourage others.

A HOME FOR PHOEBE

Maseppa and Phoebe wander the hills of the Hudson Valley during the mid-1800's. One flees prejudice, while the other yearns for a home. Through the friendship of a peddler, a blind granny, and a blacksmith's family, they learn of forgiveness and faith.

Find all her books at -
http://www.polliwogpage.com/publishing.html

Made in the USA
Middletown, DE
13 July 2015